PAPER CAGE

A Novel

TOM BARAGWANATH

ALFRED A. KNOPF

New York

2024

For Noah

THIS IS A BORZOI BOOK PUBLISHED BY
ALFRED A. KNOPF

Copyright © 2022 by Tom Baragwanath

www.aaknopf.com

Knopf, Borzoi Books, and the colophon are registered
trademarks of Penguin Random House LLC.

LIBRARY OF CONGRESS CATALOGING-IN-PUBLICATION DATA
Names: Baragwanath, Tom, author.
Title: Paper cage: a novel / Tom Baragwanath.
Description: New York: Alfred A. Knopf, a division of
Penguin Random House LLC, 2024.
Identifiers: LCCN 2023030432 (print) | LCCN 2023030433 (ebook) |
ISBN 9780593685105 (hardcover) | ISBN 9780593685129 (trade paperback) |
ISBN 9780593685112 (ebook)
Subjects: LCGFT: Thrillers (Fiction). | Novels.
Classification: LCC PR9639.4.B3957 P37 2024 (print) |
LCC PR9639.4.B3957 (ebook) | DDC 823/.92—dc23/eng/20230707
LC record available at https://lccn.loc.gov/2023030432
LC ebook record available at https://lccn.loc.gov/2023030433

Jacket photographs: landscape © sesameellis / RooM the Agency /
Alamy; torn paper © luckyraccoon / Shutterstock
Jacket design by Perry De La Vega

Manufactured in the United States of America
First American Edition
1st Printing

PAPER CAGE

IT'S MORE RAIN than I've ever seen, all the summer's hidden water coming down at once. The river's breached its banks down past the netball courts, and there are eels, slick black shapes lurking in the gutters. Thirty years in Masterton, and that's a first for me.

I'm almost at Sheena's, wading through the leafy mush covering the footpath, the warm wind grumbling at the edges of my poncho. It's only fifteen minutes from the station, but I'm soaked down to my littlest toe. The rent money is dry, though. Sheena's landlord will come by Thursday, and we can't have last month again.

I step over the deepest part of the gutter, half an eye out for stray river life, then through the space where Sheena's wooden gate used to be before someone destroyed it a few parties back. I'm going slow, mostly by memory; the path is uneven under the soup of grass cuttings and branches, and the last thing my bad hip needs is another fall. Her awning's still intact, thank Christ.

There's a light on inside. Beneath the steady thrum of water, the pulse of music. Sounds like UB40—enough to bring back the old shearing days and the oily feel of wool between my fingers. I always preferred Bob Marley but he was a bit much for some of the blokes, especially the locals we had to partner up with out on the coast. The mere thought of a sweating brown body was unsettling enough for some of those guys, let alone having to listen to brown tunes. UB40 was always a safer bet.

Before I can knock, the door swings open. A wall of body in a black singlet blocks the hallway.

"Lorraine." Keith's got his shades on as usual but I can tell he's taking me in; those scarab ovals moving slowly over me. "None of your lot at the station thought to give you a lift, eh?"

Your lot. These tiny demarcations, the daily lines drawn. Us and them, that and this. It's always there. In this place, anyway.

"I don't mind the walk." I look to the driveway but his truck isn't there. One of the other patched guys must have dropped him around. "Bit of rain won't kill me."

I try for the smallest smile but there's no point. His face is without expression, his mouth flat and waiting. I nod over his shoulder.

"My niece about?"

He shrugs.

There's a break in the music and a voice calls from the next room, hazy, but Keith keeps staring. I wonder how much of my last conversation with Sheena she passed on to him. For now, I keep my eyes on him. His fingers are dark with soil. An afternoon spent out back, probably, tending to the greens before the storm came in. There's a reason why Sheena's patch always yields more than mine.

"Aunty." A voice behind him, a hand coming up to rest against his shoulder. "Love, it's fine. Really."

It takes a few long moments, but eventually he turns away into the house. Sheena squeezes my arm as if to reassure herself it's really me. Behind her, Keith's footsteps rattle the hall.

"You're bloody well soaked through. Time for a drink? Cuppa tea or a quick gin?" She shifts her hair out of her eyes, her fingers quick and shaking.

"I'm okay, girl."

I go to reach inside my poncho for the money but think better of it. Keith might be Bradley's dad and all, but he doesn't need to know every little thing. I smell it, then: that musty waft between burnt sugar and vinegar. I get it whenever I walk past the evidence room at the station: all those shelves of scorched lightbulbs and tiny plastic bags stacked and numbered, waiting in the dark for court appearances. Sheena sees what my eyes are doing.

"It's not mine," she says.

I nod her outside, and she follows me with a quick look over her shoulder. The two of us stand close inside the awning's dripping halo.

"Is Bradley in there?"

"He's off running around." She looks down. "I'm careful."

"Careful? It's only three weeks since the Kīngi girl went missing. Don't tell me about careful." My arms come across my chest. "It's only a few towns over, Sheen. You don't think it could happen here?"

She looks past me into the silver static. "They're all together, Hēmi and them. They're just playing, Aunty. The cops said we had to . . ."

"I know what they bloody said."

I think of all those posters I printed downstairs in the station file room. Those stacks of pages, thin paper to keep costs down. The chief's always worried about that. It was tough going finding a decent photo of the missing girl, Precious Kīngi. Her mum didn't have much on hand. In the end we called Featherston Normal for last year's class shot, Precious right in the centre row with a wide smile, her ponytail nice and neat. Everyone looked happy to be there. Happier than I ever remember being, anyway. Even the teacher was beaming, tie flat against his chest, hands clasped at his front. And now think of her: disappeared on her way home one afternoon. Just gone, like someone snapped their fingers and carried the girl away into the sky.

Three weeks. Anything can happen in three weeks. Nobody's saying it but the knowledge is there, tucked between our other words—reports sent up the chain to Wellington, briefings to the papers. Nobody expects good news.

"You're coming on Saturday, right?" Sheena sets her fingers on my elbow. "I told Bradley you'd come."

6

"I'll be there, girl." I nod past her. "Just don't let Keith get too comfy, all right? Remember what we talked about."

Her eyes drop, scolded. Amazing how quickly we slip back into old patterns. "It's a visit, Aunty. That's all. He's mostly out Castlepoint ways now."

Mostly. I lean forward with a kiss. "Saturday, then. I'll bake a cake."

I move back into the rain, and the door shudders closed behind me. In the gutter, a grey fin twists between the wheels of Keith's junked Ford, curling through the water.

With each step, more of the tension leaves my shoulders. My mind is on home, on a dry room. Patty will have let herself in from next door to get a pie in the oven, some buttered peas and mint, and a couple of strong gins for the *Villa Wars* semi-final on One. Our favourite couple made it to the last round, and we fancy their chances. Someone might be out snatching kids, but there are still renovation shows.

"Look!" A childish squeal. Across the road, a clutch of thin bodies crouching behind a ute, some in T-shirts dark with rain, some bare-chested and shining. "There!"

A boy I recognise, Hēmi Larkin I think, points down into the gutter mush, his mouth taut in an expectant O. A flat-cheeked girl steps forward and shoves a garden fork hard into the water. When she brings it up, there's a black rope twisting itself around the tines, the eel's mouth open and tasting the air. The other kids all whoop and slap at each other as she holds the eel high, a long-limbed Neptune with her fishy mascot.

Despite all the commotion, they see me. Even now, my

hair greyer than I care to notice, body more like a marrow each year, children see me. I might be invisible everywhere else, but not to them. Kids notice everything.

"You've got him, love," I call across the street. "But what's the plan now, eh?"

There's a detonation of glee in the girl's eyes. "How's about we ram it up your hole, lady?"

The kids all fold into each other with delight, moving as a single animal. Maybe Sheena's right: in a group, they have each other.

The girl jiggles the eel in my direction. I see Bradley with them now, clutching a supermarket bag alive with thrashing shapes. He gives me the tiniest wave, undetectable to the others, and smiles just to me. Then, with quick hands, he grips the eel by the head and slides it off the fork, knocking it again and again into the bonnet of the parked ute as the others watch. A stock truck clatters past through the water, its steel belly tight with the last summer lambs on their way to the knife, wheels sending little waves out across the street. When it passes, the kids are gone, eel and all. Vanished into new mischief with a flash of a limb around the corner and a last shout before the rain replaces them.

Home, then. I shift myself forward, my hip giving me just the smallest twinge, but nothing unmanageable. Ducking between cars, I step across the road on the way to Rickett's Circle, my mind on the glow of bad television in easy company. There's a wet screeching behind me and I start to turn and my heart leaps as a vehicle roars and brakes and shudders in a wall of spray.

A station wagon, apple-red, its wipers working overtime.

Whoever it is, they've stopped just short of knocking me down. I raise a hand to see inside but I can't make anything out. I step across the lanes, and the car crawls forward past me, then turns down Sheena's street, headlights shining into the flood like buttery swords. It must be someone from around here; you'd need to know the shape of the road to be out in this mess.

The light starts to thin around me, early for February, the rows of houses damp and watchful as the low sky swallows the day.

JUST LIKE LAST time, the radio has it first, the bulletin clicking on as the morning light knifes the curtains.

I went to bed with brighter thoughts, the renovation semi-final and Patty's generous hand with the Gordon's helping to erase the bad taste of Keith and the near-miss with the station wagon. Now the old black cloud closes in again.

Hēmi Larkin. Eight years old. Missing.

I'm in the kitchen before I know what I'm doing, phone tight inside my palm, dialling for Sheena. Bradley was with Hēmi; if anything has happened to him, it'll be my whole world finished. The waiting tone fills my ear.

"Pick up the bloody phone, girl."

She's not answering. Part of me wonders whether it's more than just her usual nights on the bottle; whether she's back on that other shit again. Keith's horrid stuff surging through her blood, turning my niece into someone else. But there's no time to think. I fire off a text and pull on my gumboots, wading through the streets still submerged under the grey murk. It'll be useless stopping by if Keith's had a night on the bags. The best thing to do is get to work and see what's what.

The station carpark is empty, though a couple of guys from the local paper are already hanging around out front. They'll probably assume I'm the cleaner. Just in case, I buzz in through the back.

Straight downstairs to the file room. I check the case report in the system: it's the same Hēmi, all right; the Larkins down the end of Colombo Road, the place with the missing step and the gutters coming off in a long strip of rusted metal. The report only lists the one child missing, and I'm ashamed of the slackening in my chest. I close my eyes for a second and listen to the computer's faint hum.

The phone rings on my desk. I snatch it up.

"Sheena?"

"Did you hear?" Patty. She sounds out of breath. "It's ghastly, just ghastly."

"I'm reading the file now," I say. "Jesus, Patty. I only just saw the kid."

"The Larkin boy? You saw him?" I can hear her sit up straighter. "Where?"

"With Bradley and them, last night." I try to picture the boy's bright face, his arm outstretched and pointing. Everything is a wet blur. "They had a bag full of eels."

"The mother was on the news, the poor thing. How they get themselves into these situations, I just don't know."

They. Other times I'd be liable to pull her up on this talkback radio stuff, these creeping sanctimonies about poor life choices and level playing fields. This morning's no time for that.

"Listen," I say. "I need to keep the line free. My niece."

"Oh, sure, sure." There's the slam of a kitchen drawer in the background. "I'm on afternoons at the claims centre this week. I'll be around after."

It's my turn to get dinner. "Could be a late one, I think." There are footsteps upstairs now; Ambrose's heavy heels, and a lighter step I don't recognise. "I'll try to pick something up."

"Righto."

I check my phone: still nothing from Sheena. I run copies of the new report and bundle them with the most recent briefing packs on the Kīngi case. There's a new urgency in the footsteps upstairs, and rightly so. You can ignore one missing kid if you try hard enough. But two? Two's something else. Even with names like Precious and Hēmi, two gets attention.

Right on cue, Ambrose rattles down the last few stairs and into the file room. Full dress: buttons shining and ready for inspection. Those new footsteps upstairs must be Wellington feet.

"I assume you've heard?"

I hand him the box of papers. "It's all in there. The latest on the Kīngi girl, too."

"Did you fix the machine? The boys couldn't read the bloody things last time."

"It's single-sided," I say. "They'll be fine." He picks up a copy to check for himself. "Listen, chief. I was . . ." My phone vibrates in my pocket. Sheena.

Whats wrong aunty? U ok?

I let out a long breath, one hand on my desk.

"Don't let me keep you, Lorraine."

"Sorry," I say. "It's . . . look, the boy. I saw him. Hēmi Larkin."

"When?" His head is a furious egg. "Last night?"

"He was with my nephew on Church Street. Must've been six or just after." I picture the last flash of limbs around the corner, hearing again the screech of the station wagon on the road behind me, the wipers sliding in inscrutable motion. "They were playing in the rain."

His expression narrows. "That's Keith Mākara's boy, right? Your nephew?"

"That's right."

There's information turning in his eyes. I can guess what it'll be: Keith's full, and Sheena's half, so what does that make Bradley? It's the kind of calculation he makes automatically. Shit, it wasn't so long ago he was still writing "half-caste" in his reports.

"We'll talk after the briefing," he says. "For now, we're running low on trim. There's some change in my top drawer. Some gingernuts if you can manage it."

With a last scowl, he stomps off upstairs, leaving me to the hush of my stacks and boxes, my desk in the corner with its dim monitor waiting. His footsteps recede into the quiet guts of the building, and a door clicks closed. I wait until he's out of earshot and pick up the phone to try Sheena again.

I'm coming back from the petrol station, the sun burning away the moisture around me, the milk bottle nice and cold in my hand. The reporters are gone now; Ambrose probably gave them what little he has already. They'll be back, though. I buzz in past reception, and Tania stares blankly over her cross-word through the bulletproof glass. The same old spidery feeling comes through me as I step past the munitions room—even now, so many years later. I pour some coffee and head back downstairs, thinking ahead to the files I'll need to check.

"It's Lorraine, isn't it?"

"Jesus." I lift a hand to my chest, and some coffee slops across my fingers. There's a man at the end of the hall. Thin. Scruffy hair. Dressed like a stork that's fallen through a ward-robe. There's more fatigue in his face than the drive from Wellington would suggest; he looks like he hasn't slept in days.

"I'm Justin Hayes." He steps forward and lifts a hand. "From over the hill."

"I figured as much."

His eyes stay on mine. "You don't come to the briefings?"

"Me? Not usually, no. I sort out the papers and all that, but the chief prefers to keep things pretty contained in there."

"Two missing children, one for weeks now." A click of the tongue. "I wouldn't have thought this was the time for containment."

I give a shrug. "Did you need anything? Coffee?"

"One of the guys in there mentioned something about the Larkin boy's father." He scratches at his stubble. "An assault charge a couple of years back, something about a shovel."

"Jason Larkin?" I feel myself frowning.

"They're thinking there could be a connection somewhere," he says. "As in, this could be payback, maybe."

I have to shake my head. "I wouldn't say so." It's Dion, most likely; of all the constables, he's the one with the fanciful notions. "The other guy's doing time in Rimutaka. He picked up three years for armed robbery last summer. And it was a broom, not a shovel."

"A broom?" He gives me the ghost of a smirk.

"He and Jason Larkin were in the same roading crew, and they got into it one morning. Jason gave him a whack with a yard broom, and the supervisor was daft enough to call it in." I picture the stacks downstairs, all those lines of text, summing up this town. I'd written the report up myself; Dion was off helping Ambrose get his boat sealed. "I don't think we bothered with a charge in the end."

He nods to himself. "Anything else you can tell me? About the Larkins, or anything else, for that matter?"

I think of Hēmi under the rain, his mouth open in a wide circle, tucked in close with the rest of his mates. "They're not far from me, really. Just down the road from my niece." A moment passes. "I saw him, actually. Last night."

"The missing boy? You saw Hēmi Larkin?"

The door to the briefing room swings open, and a burst of brash laughter comes into the hall. The chief's eyes hold a laddish twinkle but they go hard when he sees the two of us. "I see you've met our file lady, detective."

Hayes turns to him. "Did you know she'd seen the boy last night?"

There's a blank expression on the chief's face. "We, uh . . ."

"I didn't get the chance to mention it yet." A pause. "I've been on the phone to Sheena all morning. She knows the Larkins, and she's a bit shaken up. Her boy was with Hēmi and the others."

Hayes glances between us. "How many children were there?"

"Five, I think. Maybe six. They were eeling."

"Eeling?"

"It's that part of town." Ambrose sets his hands to his hips. "They carry on a bit like that. The kids especially."

The detective narrows his eyes. "We'll need to see them, in any case."

"My niece already spoke to Bradley," I say. "He doesn't know anything. Said they split up right after they saw me, and Hēmi walked home by himself."

Ambrose huffs. "She would say that, wouldn't she?"

"What do you mean?" Hayes crosses his arms.

I sigh. "It's Bradley's dad. Keith. He's patched."

"Not just patched," says Ambrose. "This past year he's pretty much been running the local Mongrels chapter."

"Doesn't mean it's anything to do with Sheena." I keep my voice even. "Or Bradley."

Hayes turns to me again. "Any chance you could tell me the Kīngi address?"

"In Featherston?" I look between the two of them, feeling the chief's expectant gaze. "They're down Underhill Road. On the way to the camping spot, the swimming hole and all that."

"Detective." Ambrose lifts a hand between us. "It's all in the papers, there. My boys are across it. Why don't we just . . ."

"And the parents?" asks Hayes. "What about them?"

The chief pats Hayes's arm. "Bruce and Cass Kīngi are on file too, mate. We've got all the details we need."

I trace the swirls of linoleum under my feet, waiting just long enough to be heard. "*Cath* Kīngi. Bruce drives trucks for Grey's Haulage, out of Carterton. Mostly building supplies." There's a sting in the chief's eyes. "Cath's been seen around the tinny house on Waite Street from time to time, but she doesn't buy. The dealer's her cousin."

Hayes turns to the chief. "Your records clerk needs to be in on all briefings."

"Records clerk? You mean her?" Ambrose jabs a thumb at me. "There's really no need. The boys have the papers."

"I'll have to insist." The detective holds his eye. "She's given me more on the spot than your whole team managed in a half-hour briefing."

The colour drops out of the chief's face.

"It's fine," I say. "Really. I've got my hands full downstairs anyway."

Hayes squints. "You know we've got two kids missing, right?"

"Of course I bloody well know." I look towards the stairway, a low boil coming through my hands. I could tell him about all those nights walking past Sheena's at two, three in the morning, the cool air clothing me as I kept vigil in the empty street, looking for strange cars. "Look, all I do is keep my ears open and type what I'm given. The Larkins are just down the road from me. Our part of town, everyone knows each other."

"That's right," says the chief. "That's all it is, mate."

The detective keeps his arms folded, his hands poking out of rumpled sleeves. I haven't been onside with the chief in years; it's like I've put my shoes on back to front.

"You're in all briefings from now on." Hayes looks at his watch. "Starting with our two o'clock. Until then, try to pull together anything else that might be relevant. The Larkins, their neighbours, anything you can think of."

With a clacking of footsteps, they move away, Hayes's thin scraggly form next to the chief's rounding shape. I can see the tension in Ambrose's shoulders, the nerves all bunched and coiled. Next time he has the chance, he'll make sure I get some horrible job to do—defrosting the evidence freezer or laying rat traps behind the pipes again.

My phone buzzes in my pocket. Patty.

Everything all right there, Lo?

She always seems to know when I need a word. I don't have to respond; it'll be enough just to talk when I get home. I slump my way downstairs into my sanctuary, and my blood speeds inside me.

IT'S LIVELY AT Value Roast, like it is most nights. People need their dinners no matter what's happening with their kids, and they're hardly going to cook it themselves.

It's on Queen Street next to the old tea rooms. Not exactly my walk home but close enough. A bright red sign on the awning announces Mr. and Mrs. Leong's major draw, the nine-dollar meat-and-three special. You'd be hard-pressed these days to cook anything for that, even with home-kill. Inside, a row of serving windows displays tray after tray: steaming pumpkin slices falling out of their rinds, a mound of bread stuffing to choke a bullock team, and Mrs. Leong's Yorkshire puddings laid out in golden listening ears. The air is thick with the tang of mutton, a salty musk that lingers high in the nose.

I thought I'd swing by late enough to miss the rush, but I was wrong. All the regulars are here: the shiftless constellation of teenagers slumped against the bench staring into empty plates, the drinkers installed in the booths against the far wall. Those guys need the extra support, especially if it's dole day. There's no alcohol licence here, though the Leongs don't look too closely at what people bring in from outside. That leaves the middle tables for the patched guys. This is longstanding Mongrel Mob turf, though the local Black Power chapter has been known to step inside when everything else has shut for the night.

I'm in the back corner by the counter, waiting for my order and trying not to be seen. It's been one of the longer afternoons I can remember: the chief and his boys weren't all too happy to see me take a seat at the briefing table, and Tania from reception almost dropped her coffee walking past the doorway. Finding the other kids in Hēmi's eeling party took most of the day, and by the time Hayes and the chief were done talking to them it was getting near dark. Unsurprisingly, the kids weren't all that keen to say much to those two. I had a word with Bradley and made sure he got a nice bikkie from the staffroom, but he still kept his mouth shut. His father's son, I guess.

Behind me, the Leongs' noticeboard displays all the town's collected jetsam: job postings and cars for sale, a poster announcing the next burnouts at the aerodrome, and some optimistic soul hoping to teach Portuguese. My eyes scan across the cards. *Experinced babysitter, rates v. resonable. Garage to rent, $285/month, family of four max.* One of our Precious Kīngi flyers was up here last time I came in, her smiling face following me from the station. Someone must've taken it down.

With a low chime, the door swings open, and Keith steps inside with two of his heavies. He's in full gear: jacket across his shoulders, boots like a pair of leather rocks. He scuffs over to his usual table and leans down into a creaking metal chair. I can't tell if he's seen me; his sunglasses don't give much away.

"Here you go, Lorraine." Mrs. Leong gives me a tired smile across the counter and hands me a foil tray double-bagged for the trip home. I can see her attention is mostly on Keith; he's only just been allowed back in the place after tossing one of his own prospects through a window last year.

"Thanks." I return the smile. "See you."

Just as I get the last word out, a loud thud sends the place into silence. A pot-bellied guy in an old Farmlands beanie has fallen out of his booth to land next to Keith, emitting a meaty gurgle from what I can only pray is his upper half. Keith's eyes slide to the floor. An electric hush hangs over the tables.

"You." Keith thrusts his chin at a skinny teenager with a fringe. "Get here."

"Huh?" The kid looks to his girlfriend.

"She can't help you, my bro." Keith waits for the boy to shuffle over, then digs a ten-dollar note from his jacket pocket and slaps the money against the kid's chest. "Sort him out."

The kid is all eyes and elbows. "I dunno where he lives."

"Herbert Street. Behind the squash club." Keith stares back at him. "You've been paid, my man."

The big guy waits; he's good at that. Eventually, the kid and his girlfriend manage to get Farmlands upright, long ropes of drool hanging from his chin. I could pass a napkin but that would draw attention. Once they're all the way outside, the girl taking most of the guy's sagging weight, Mr. Leong appears with a bottle of ginger beer and a plate of end pieces, extra gravy, for Keith's table. The way is clear. I take my chance and head for the door, my head held low.

"Horrible thing, that Hēmi kid." Keith's voice freezes me in place; I nearly drop the bag.

"I told Sheena to keep Bradley inside," I say. "For the moment, anyway."

"Me and the fellas have been out and about," he says. "Looking all over." He holds me in his gaze. Two of his guys stare up at me from either side, instruments of his will. "I'll see you Saturday, eh, Aunty? Unless those pricks work you all weekend."

His mouth forms what passes for a grin. My eyes go to his hands, his knuckles split in a few places. It wasn't all that long ago, just before Christmas, I had Sheena in my kitchen, her hands shaking against the table while I poured some rum and tried to coax the story out of her.

"Sure." I stare into the black spheres in his head. "I'll be there."

With a flick of his thumb, he pops the cap from the bottle, drinking long and deep as his mates watch. It's up to me to decide when the exchange is over. He's in no rush to get to the plate; he knows what's waiting for him.

I can hear the television from the street. Rickett's Circle is dark around me, the houses all leaning into each other as if whispering. But at my place, there's a light inside, and the windows are open to let a little of the night breeze in. A pair of kererū cut fat arcs to the tree at the end of my garden, rustling as they settle for the night. I switch the roast bag to my good side and push through the gate.

"That you?" Patty calls from the lounge. "I was starting to wonder."

"Madhouse at the roast shop," I say. "How many spuds?"

"Two to start. Then we'll see." Her hand comes to my shoulder. Her eyes are wet, her cheeks puffy. It's her ex-husband, most likely. They've been scrabbling at each other ever since she moved next door, but it's really been on the boil lately. Sometimes I hear shouts at night when she's on the phone. She doesn't think it carries but it does.

"Everything all right, Pat?"

She wipes her nose with the back of her hand and smiles through whatever's on her mind. "I'll sort that out. The girls'll want to see you."

In the garage, Tilly is in her box with the kittens, their sleeping shapes like furred commas. I give her a scratch behind the ear and whisper low. The kittens start to stir, whining their tiny whines and climbing my arm. A dusty ginger girl with a white splotch around her eye bites my fingers with needle teeth. I've had her in mind as a present for Bradley; she's mischievous enough to keep up with him, and he's been asking Sheena for a kitten for months now. She'll do a lot to take his mind off everything with Hēmi, I'm sure.

"Go on, baby. Bite the shit out of me." I work my fingers through her fur, tracing the creamy spot around her eye. I've been calling her Patch. Two of the other kittens are wrestling, batting at each other with their paws and mewling. Tilly lets out an anxious trill. "It's all right, my love." My hand goes behind her ears again. "They'll work it out."

Patty calls from the lounge. "We're all set."

My plate is in its usual spot on the couch, a gin and tonic quietly fizzing on the bookshelf. I take a long sip, and everything starts to loosen.

"Jeez." Patty clicks the volume down a notch. "Rough one, was it?"

"Keith was at the roast shop with his mates," I say. "Talking about the Larkin boy and all."

"It's horrible, just horrible." Onscreen, two men are furiously plating meringues. "I can't even think about it. Your niece must be in such a state."

I bite into a mouthful of beef and cabbage. It's comforting, having company. The long day downstairs with just my papers, and now I have a hot meal and enough time to calm down before bed. It's more than can be said for Hēmi Larkin, and for Precious Kīngi. Probably.

"There's a detective over the hill from Wellington," I say.

"Oh?" Patty sets down her fork. "Does that mean they've got some leads, then?"

"Not really. He wants me in on the briefings though. A local touch, I guess."

She sets down her glass with a thud. "Lorraine, that's wonderful!"

"Jesus, steady on."

"No, it's just . . ." She swallows a mouthful of food. "How long have I been saying you should get involved? You know so many people around here, and that's what really breaks cases like these." Her eyes are bright. "Humpty Dumpty must be spewing."

I picture the chief's hard face in my doorway. "He's not exactly thrilled, no."

"I'd love to know what they've got to go on," she says. "The papers are calling them the 'Kīngi disappearances.' Did you read that?"

"Bloody hell, Pat." I can't help but shake my head. She's got shelves groaning with this stuff: all those true crime stories with their dark jackets and pointy lettering. David Bain damn near has a whole row of his own. It's never been my thing, really. I get enough gloom as it is; the last thing I want to do is wallow in it. "You might have to lower your expectations. It's not exactly *CSI Masterton* down there."

"Fair play." She smiles. "I'm just happy for you, that's all."

"We'll see. Any drama at the call centre today?"

"Oh, bugger that. That's not half as interesting."

She sweeps a hand through the air, and we both turn back to the cooking show. Later, with our plates cleared away and a second gin down the hatch, she steps into her sandals and slips across the lawn to the old Wikaira place. It's her place now, I guess, though it's hard not to think of old Mrs. Wikaira, even after three months. I push the door to the garage open and let a slice of golden light fall across the kittens in their box. I'll leave it open for the night in case they need me.

IN THE MORNING the reporters are back outside the station. I cut down the side to the back door where Dion's letting a stocky guy in freezing-works gumboots out into the carpark. His face is familiar despite the bruising—one cheek dark and swollen, the top lip split open. Our eyes meet for a moment, and something passes between us. There's sadness in there, mixed with something more pressing: fear. He stares down at the concrete and pulls out his keys, slipping inside a scuffed-up Nissan.

"That's Jason Larkin, isn't it?" I watch as he sparks the engine. "What's happened to him?"

Dion lets the door swing closed so I have to reach out and grab it. "You're late."

I look at my watch. It's ten to. "Didn't the chief say eight?"

"You don't think we've got enough on our plates without keeping you on time?"

He ducks into the briefing room, and I hear voices mixing. I pour myself a coffee and find a seat, feeling the chief's eyes on me from the other end of the room. Then the detective sweeps in wearing the same clothes as yesterday. There's the same hard glint in his eye: information to find, names to place in columns.

"All right," says Hayes. "What've we got?"

"The boys here finished up with the teachers yesterday," says Ambrose. "Hēmi arrived at school looking pretty shattered most days, they said. Too tired to do much. They even sent someone from child services, but it didn't come to anything."

"Our tax dollars hard at work." Dion shakes his head. "The neighbours mentioned a lot of parties lately, too. And not just weekends."

"Some rough customers there." Ambrose nods gravely. "I've seen Keith Mākara and his boys on that street more than once."

"That doesn't tell us much." I speak quietly but clearly. "Our part of town, everyone knows each other."

A long moment passes. "It's their part of town, Lorraine." Ambrose fixes his eyes on me. "You're just living in it."

Dion's grin spreads wide.

"Well, someone sure gave Jason Larkin a good knock around." Hayes stays standing at the end of the table, scratching at his beard. "Last night, probably right after they came in. He wouldn't get into it, but something's going on."

I think back to the roast shop, Keith's hands like scarred paddles against the table, the knuckles cracked and bloody.

For a moment I think about speaking, before I swallow my words. They wouldn't listen anyway.

"Did we get anywhere with the rugby-club angle?"

"I made a few calls," says Dion. "Nobody had too much to say about the kid. Enthusiastic in the scrum, someone said. That's about it."

The chief turns to me. "Get a list of names. Lorraine, you pull anything you can find. Anything at all, you understand?"

"Righto."

I climb to my feet and head into the hall, feeling their eyes follow me. Truth be told, it's a relief to get out of that room, even if it means a long morning scouring through the files. I'm almost at the stairs when a voice calls out behind me.

"Lorraine." It's Hayes. "Hang on a second."

I turn and wait. We're right outside the munitions room; the old scratchy feeling comes across my shoulders. The detective seems to understand, motioning me into the staff-room. I can hear the others talking through the wall: mumbling and bursts of laughter, the self-assured sound of men together.

"You up for taking a drive?"

"A drive?" I step from foot to foot, my bad hip sending aches through my side. "I need to collect those files."

"That can wait," he says. "There's something I need your help with."

We're in a car, the windows up, cool air blowing into my face from the dash. Outside, Masterton rolls by; in the distance, the Tararua Ranges stretch out in a thick shoulder of green, watching over everything.

"We're absolutely nowhere with Queenie Larkin," says Hayes. "She's beside herself, of course. But there's something else she's worried about besides the boy. Something bigger. And then Jason goes and gets a hiding." He breathes out through his teeth. "If I didn't know any better, I'd say they were mixed up in something."

He doesn't have to say it; it's right there between us. The trade. Chalk.

"I wouldn't know about that," I say. "The Larkins might be just down the road from my niece but it's not like they're close or anything. Queenie used to come around to Sheena's looking for Jason sometimes, but I haven't seen her in ages."

"Well, that's about to change. I thought she might respond to a familiar face."

"What? Me?" It's like something's knocked loose in my chest. "I've never done a thing like that, mate. That's for you and the chief to sort out. Dion, too."

"Sometimes a fresh start is all it takes, Lorraine. Especially these first days. Just pretend it's a neighbourly visit. You've heard what's going on, and you thought you'd drop by." The detective looks sideways, his hands thin and sinewy against the wheel. He seems to be weighing his words. "Look, is there something I'm missing here? With you and Ambrose?"

"You'd have to ask him."

"Right. Well, I'll add that to my list, then." There's a long pause, the road running out beneath us in a grey ribbon. "There's another thing, too. The Kīngi girl, and now Hēmi. You see it, right?"

"What? They're both Māori?"

He pauses again. "Well?"

We turn into Worksop Road, past the car dealers with their flags hanging straight in the heat, the windscreens dotted with bright hopeful signs. "This part of town, plenty of kids are. Featherston, too."

"And nothing about it strikes you as odd?"

My hands are fists in my lap. "Someone snatching up our kids, and nobody seeing anything? In a cheek-by-jowl place like Masterton?" I take a breath. "Yeah. It's odd. Watching driveways might as well be the national pastime here."

He nods to himself. My eyes stay on him, looking for something I can recognise. I need to know how a person can deal with this kind of information, this weight. The faces of Precious and Hēmi, their tiny details filling up stacks of paper downstairs. Friends, clothes, what they were wearing when last seen; every piece of it is another stone on my chest. It should never happen. And yet, it has. It's happened, and we've let it. And what are we doing about it?

"You've been on cases like this before, right?" My hands twist together. "With missing kids?"

He's quiet for a time. "It's always different." For a while, there's just the sound of our wheels on the road, and the quiet hum of the engine inside the dash. "I mentioned it to Ambrose. The Māori angle. Know what he said?"

I wait for him to speak. In truth, I don't need to guess.

"He told me it wasn't surprising. Only the hori kids walk home by themselves anyway, he said."

My blood quickens. "So what? You thought you'd ask the hori whisperer?"

"What?"

"You don't have to pretend." The street signs file past in a blur. "I know that's what everyone calls me. I'm sure you've heard it already."

"I haven't, actually." He sighs. "And anyway, that's not what I meant."

"Plenty of kids walk themselves home every day with no trouble at all. The bloody school's only ten minutes away." My head feels hot. "I've seen those mums up in Lansdowne driving to school in their fucking silver tanks, parking across the road and watching every second. You think everyone has time for that?"

"It's okay, Lorraine. I'm not having a go." He slows down for the turn onto Colombo. I can see what he's doing, pushing me into a state then apologising. There are things he needs to know, and I'm just the next source in a long list. "How long's the chief had you locked in the dungeon, anyway?"

"Nobody's locked me anywhere," I say. "I happen to like the file room."

"Out of the way, eh? Nobody to bug you." He gives me a knowing look. "Nobody to make use of you, either."

"Listen, mate. You've been in town ten minutes. If you think you can just . . ."

"Hang on."

He leans his head closer to the dash, peering down the road to the Larkin place. A tiny saucer of pink shows through the messy wires of his hair, the skin smooth and perfect. It feels too intimate, like something I shouldn't be seeing. We pull over, still a few houses down from the Larkins, but close enough to see their place: the weatherboards mottled with flaking paint, the gutter coming off in a ribbon of brown metal. It's strange, seeing things from this angle. My usual walk brings me past in the other direction.

"Car's still there," says Hayes. "We'll need to wait."

I stare through the windscreen at the house. Past the low fence with its sagging gate, there's a patch of grass baked to death with summer, and a BMX frame with the front wheel missing. Hēmi's, probably. I picture him walking home in the rain, his tiny feet scuffing through the water, the soles bare and feeling everything.

"Listen." I sigh. "About Jason. I might have an idea of who dealt to him."

Hayes squints through the windscreen, the sunlight still in his eyes. "It's okay, Lorraine. I get the feeling there's plenty of ideas you might have." He takes a long breath. "We'll get to Keith in good time, don't worry."

Before I can say anything, there's movement outside. I make myself small in the seat. Jason Larkin emerges from the house, hands jammed in his pockets. He's got sunnies on now, but they're not quite wide enough for the bruises. With a loud rattle, he reverses the Nissan back into the road and pulls away.

"All right," says Hayes. "Don't overthink it. Anything she can tell you will be better than what we've got so far."

"You're not coming?"

He draws his mouth into a thin line. "She's seen enough of me for now." He nods through the windscreen. "You heard about what happened, and you wanted to see how she was doing. That's all."

I stare into my hands. "I haven't brought anything."

"What do you mean?" He frowns.

"To visit." How many years has this man been alive? "I can't go in there without . . . ah, forget it."

I look into the back seat; there's only a jar of peanut butter and a half-loaf of Vogel's. With a long breath, I push the car door open, shaking my head. Every step towards the house leaves me feeling less like myself; it's like one of those dreams where I'm back at college, standing onstage, frozen for lines. Halfway to the house I turn to look back, but there's too much glare on the windscreen to see inside. My hands are trembling. I step into the cracked driveway; a dog barks from somewhere close. A big animal, sounds like. The curtains are drawn, the house hooded against the bright day outside. At the bottom of the steps, I stop. Part of me wants to turn away, before I see a pair of rugby boots tucked neatly beside the front door, their sprigs carefully swept of dried mud. I climb to the door, lifting my leg up and over the space where a step is missing. The wood sounds hollow under my knuckles.

"Queenie? It's Lorraine." A fat bead of sweat runs down my back. "Lorraine Henry, from Rickett's Circle. Sheena's aunt."

There's no sound; the house is shrouded and silent. Then, I catch the slightest movement from the corner of my eye, something flitting behind the curtains. After a long moment, there are footsteps. The door cracks open, and Queenie's face appears.

"Yeah?" Her skin is stretched at the top of her cheeks, her eyes shot through with red and yellow. There's a brief shard of recognition when she sees me, but it's replaced by hesitation. "What is it?"

"I'm just down the road," I say. "I wanted to come and see how you were. I know you haven't been by Sheena's in a while, but I . . ."

"You're with them, aren't ya?" Her eyes narrow. "I saw you there at the station. You were with those other ones."

"No, it's . . . I'm just in the file room." I clear my throat. "And anyway, that's not why I'm here. I thought I'd come and see if I could help out with anything."

"Help out."

A baby's cry comes from inside the house, cutting through the air. I think back to the file report: Manaia Larkin. He's not even a toddler yet. Queenie doesn't seem to have heard him; she just stares on at me through the dark gap, watching me. Soon, the cries become more urgent, the wails lifting until it's all I can hear.

"I could see to him, if you like?" I smile and nod over her shoulder. "Your boy."

There's a dark glimmer in her eyes. "You and Sheen might be whānau. But don't go thinking you can come around."

She lifts herself back on the balls of her feet, making herself tall as she shuts the door and seals the house against the sunshine. It's like someone's shoved ice down my throat. I turn back to the street, and my eye catches another glimpse of those tiny boots. My clothes are sticking to me.

WHEN SATURDAY COMES around, I'm still in no mood for people. It's been four days since the storm, and twenty-five since Precious Kīngi disappeared. Twenty-five days. You don't need to read too far into Patty's true-crime library to know what that means. Still, Bradley's only going to turn eight once. And anyway, there's nothing for me to do at the station but re-read the files and boil the jug for tea.

I pull on my best top and tie my hair back, rubbing a little cream under my eyes so the week doesn't look so long on me. Patty's baked a layer cake, chocolate and raspberry, right there on the bench in a carry container she bought special. She knew I didn't have time to do it myself, not with everything else.

"What about this?" She appears in the doorway with a toaster box from her kitchen cupboard.

"That'll do." I lay out a tea towel in the bottom and fold the edges of the flaps back to give the ginger kitten some room to see out. It's not such a long walk to Sheena's, but I want the little girl to know I'm there with her. I distract Tilly with some jellymeat in the lounge, then pick up Patch and get her settled. She's mewling and scratching at the sides but she'll be fine.

"You're sure you don't want to come? Not even for a bit?"

"Nah, it's okay." Patty smiles and nods out the window. "It's your thing. I need to get that garden under control, anyway."

Your thing. She's only been next door in the old Wikaira place a few months but already there's an agreed shorthand between us. It'll be a different circle of people at Sheena's, a little more local than she's used to, and she might get some unkind attention. At my feet, Tilly presses herself against my ankles, staring up at the box and trilling to twist my heart. I have to lock her in the garage so she won't follow.

"Righto." I sigh. "I'll see you in a few."

"You'll be all right, love. You're doing it for Bradley, remember."

Patty touches my shoulder, her fingers strong, and heads across the lawn. Outside, the sunlight hits me square in the face. I clutch the box under one arm, whispering down to the little creature, the cake in my other hand. At the end of the cul-de-sac, a stock truck bounces past with a crack like gunfire, puncturing the usual silence that hangs over the street. Some might call it peace, but that's not it. It's more like something lying in wait.

Sheena's is only five minutes away, but by the time Keith's junked Ford comes into view, I'm already damp across the shoulders. Up the uneven path, I climb the steps and peer through the house to the back. The usual guys are sitting in a ragged circle of deck chairs, bottles in hand, speaking mostly in nods. A slow bounce of bass from the speakers on the lawn. Keith's been hard at work: even from here I can see the new netting strung up around the greens, and the cherry tomatoes tied nicely to new stakes. Bradley's favourite. Nobody hears my knock, so I step inside.

In the kitchen, Sheena slides a tray from the oven. She's squeezed into a tight dress for the day, dark blue, the same shade as the earrings I bought her for Christmas. She's been losing weight. I didn't notice it earlier in the week, but it's there in her face.

"Look, sweetheart." She smiles and nods to Bradley, reaching for the bottle of Gordon's. "Look who it is."

The boy breaks off from his game, a big circle of pass the parcel, his eyes fixed on the box under my arm. The other kids pause for a second before resuming their tearing. The eel girl is there too, her bold eyes holding mine while the wheels of her brain clack and turn, trying to place me.

"Happy birthday, boyo."

"Thanks, Aunty!" Bradley stands still just long enough for me to kiss the side of his head. He's wearing a new Batman T-shirt, the cotton crisp and pungent.

"Here, give this to your mum, eh?" I hand him the cake, and he sets it on the bench without looking. Instead, he just stares at the toaster box with wide, waiting eyes. Back in the circle, there's one last tearing of paper and the eel girl thrusts her hands into the air, triumphant, clutching a block of Whittaker's fruit and nut. A smaller boy next to her reaches up and she palms him hard in the face, drawing a chorus of giggles from the mums. The boy looks up at them with a broken expression; he knows better than to complain.

"Here, you lot." Sheena passes around a bowl of sausage rolls. "There's sauce outside. You go have a run around, eh?"

"Don't go too far," I say. The women turn in my direction with blank stares.

This and that. Us and them.

"They'll be fine." Sheena passes the glass to me, the lemon wedges jostling against the ice. Her arms come to my shoulder, and she sets her head to my chest in the old way. "The others are watching."

It's like time travel. Without a word spoken, the last twenty years just fall away from the two of us. She's a girl again, waiting outside the school gates, backpack loose against her shoulder. She notices me looking into the hall.

"Keith's not here yet." She reaches to the counter for her rum and Coke, the ice clinking inside the black liquid. "Said he'd come by later. Few things to sort out at his place."

I feel some of the tension go out of me. "I saw him earlier in the week."

"The roast shop?"

I nod, trying to gauge the fatigue around her eyes. She's

smiling but it's still there. Bradley, Keith, Hēmi Larkin: it could be so many things. "You been doing all right, girl?"

"You know." She shrugs. "Heard you paid Queenie Larkin a visit."

"You did, did you?"

There's a complicated expression in her eyes. "Bet you didn't get too far." Then, a reluctant smile. "Bloody stroppy, that one. Had a go at me last year when she thought I'd been texting Jason, remember?" She shakes her head. "Still, what she's going through. It's too much to think about."

I set a hand on her arm and squeeze; she looks up into my face with wet eyes. Behind us, there's a low animal sound. Bradley is leaning into the open box.

"Not here, kiddo." I nod at the front door. "She's still young enough to bolt."

"The laundry's all ready for her." He takes off in a frantic run down the hall. "Come see, Aunty!"

I follow him with the box, and the hot-pastry smell of the kitchen gives way to the lingering must of damp sheets. The laundry is clean, at least: they've put down an old wicker basket with a nice thick blanket. Bradley will need to keep her inside for a few weeks yet. It'll be a good reason to keep him out of harm's way.

"Close the door, baby," Sheena murmurs. "We need to be nice and careful."

The kitten comes out mewling, her eyes wide with all these new people. I set her in Bradley's lap and show him how to pick her up, those eel-smashing hands so nice and sure under her belly, his usual fidgets calmed for once. He smiles in wonderment, his face lit up from inside.

"She's like a pirate!" He traces a finger around the edges of the cream-coloured fur over her eye. "Look!"

"Easy, now," I say. "Her ears are sensitive."

Sheena sits on the floor next to Bradley. "What's her name?"

"I've been calling her Patch." So far, the boy's a natural; he even lets her climb his shirt and explore his neck. "But you can choose something else if you want."

"Patch." He grimaces as her little claws dig into his collar-bone. "That's cool."

Seeing them there, all three together, something starts to well up inside. It's in Sheena's arms, the way she wraps Bradley inside the halo of her body, watching him with the kitten. One small animal caring for another. Images blend in my mind: Hēmi's arm pointing down into the water and Precious Kīngi's dark eyes trapped in the poster. There was an old evening countless days past, me and Frank talking in bed with the windows open, the streetlights shedding their thin lemon light across the lawn. There were so many ideas then, so many plans. As if the world cares.

"I'll just use the loo."

I stand up before Sheena notices anything. In the bath-room, I shut the door behind me, rubbing water across my cheeks and resting for a second. The air is full of a child growing: shampoo and dirt, soap and skin, the incalculable scent of years passing. When I open my eyes, I'm not ready to see myself. The mirror shows new grey at my temples, and my cheeks look like last week's bread forgotten in the bag.

"Jesus." I move my fingers over my skin, then flush the toilet and take a long breath. The glass comes to my lips and gin fills my mouth. For now, it's enough.

On the way back down the hall, I duck into Sheena's room and close the door, then slip the envelope from my back pocket. Enough for next month's rent, plus a little extra; even if the landlord's been by already, a few days shouldn't make a difference.

My niece's collected Ngaio Marsh is in its usual spot in the top drawer. I tuck the envelope inside the dust jacket. She's always been mad for Ngaio, even as a kid. Her eyes used to go wide on the pillow as I read to her. The puzzle stories: that's what she called them. The dead man stuck in the lift, and the other one smothered inside the bale of wool. Her mother would never have approved, but there was no way she'd find out. Debs used to spend weeks at a time out on the shearing gangs with Billy, and they were too tired and blissed-out when they got back to notice what little Sheena had been reading with her Aunty Lo.

As I'm setting the book back in the drawer, there's a rustle. I pull the handle out further, and the scratching in my heart turns into a cold fist. It's a plastic bag, almost empty, the powder inside like shards of dark sugar. The red lines at the edges of Sheena's eyes. That musty sweetness wafting through the hall on the night of the storm.

I'm careful. The way she'd looked to the floor. *It's not mine.*
"Christ, girl."

In the kitchen, she's fixing another drink. It's just us two now: Bradley's still in the laundry with Patch; the other mums have drifted outside into the deck chair circle. I set the glass down on the bench.

"You've made him so happy, Aunty. He's hardly talked about anything else." Sheena smiles. "Even with Hēmi and all." She looks up at me, and her expression changes. "What's the matter?"

"You told me it wasn't yours."

She frowns. "What wasn't mine?"

"It's that shit again, isn't it?" I cross the space to her, and my hand shoots out to grab her forearm. "Remember what we said? After last time?"

Her eyes slide to the ground. "Aunty."

"All those hoops I jumped through to make sure it stayed off your record, Sheen. Did you forget about that?"

"I fuckin' remember, all right." She pulls her mouth into a trembling line. "I'm not on it anymore. Not for ages."

"Whose is it, then?" I hold my arms tight across my chest. "Keith's?"

"Whose is what?" Her eyes go to the hall. "What are you doing, poking around?"

"Tell me straight, girl."

She fiddles with an earring, her fingers shaking. Outside, voices rise under the music. There's a sharp yell, then laughter.

"For fuck's sake. He's living here again, isn't he?"

"Please." She grips my arm. "You don't know what he's like. Not really."

I slap her hand away. "I told you at Christmas. If he's going to keep on . . ."

"He loves me," she says. "He takes care of us."

"He damn near killed a guy, Sheena!" I point through the window. "Right outside, remember?"

There's a flicker in her eyes. "That wasn't anything, Aunty. That was just . . ."

"Just what, hmm? Patched business?" I lower my voice. "You're putting Bradley right in the middle. You know you are."

Footsteps sound behind me. In the doorway there's a tall guy with a ponytail, someone I don't recognise. "Everything good?"

"You don't know a thing about it." Sheena's face fills with quick venom. "You've been on your own so long you've forgotten what it means to have someone. Twenty-odd years since Frank, and all you ever do is—"

"Watch yourself, now."

She leans back against the bench, breathing deep. No matter what's in her system, she seems to know she's crossed the line. Behind her shoulder, Patty's cake sits waiting, its layers of black and red ready to be cut open.

"That's the last envelope, you understand? You want him here, that's your call. I'm not paying his rent." Her eyes flash with hurt. "I'll be back for Patch tomorrow. Bradley can see her at my place whenever he wants, but I won't have her under the same roof."

"Go on, then." She's making fists at her sides, her knuckles pointing out through the skin. "Show Bradley what it's like when your family doesn't give a shit!"

I hold her gaze for a long moment. I want her to see me, really see me, but I know she can't. Not now. In the doorway, the ponytailed guy stands still, watching. My nose fills with the waft of tobacco from his skin.

"Leave it, Moko." Sheena sniffs.

He moves just enough for me to go; my hip knocks against the wall as I pass. At the bottom of the steps, I look back at the house. Bradley is still in there on the laundry floor, the kitten stepping uncertainly over his lap. I turn and walk away, my feet unsteady against the path, and my eyes turn everything to a wet smear.

The walk home doesn't do much for my nerves. I swing my feet under me, my bad hip feeling tender from the hallway. The storm drains are still clogged with trash and branches from the night of the flood; a few lawns hold shallow puddles of brown water not yet baked off. Cars fly past, but all I can hear is my heart in my ears. Everything I've done for Sheena, and she can still find it in her to cut at me like that. I pull out my phone, half-expecting an apology, but there's nothing. My fingers itch with unspent energy. Venting to Patty: that'll help.

A truck pulls to the kerb next to me. It's Keith, leaning through the driver's window. "Heading home already, eh?"

I hold my eyes tight to his. In his sunglasses, my reflection looks small. Over his shoulder, one of the other guys from the roast shop stares at me. There's a pair of blue chilly bins in the back of the truck, their lids taped tightly closed. I take a step closer and make myself tall.

"Listen, mate." My arms come to my hips. "You want to share a roof with Sheena, that's her call. But if I hear of any more patched stuff going on around Bradley, it won't be like last time."

At first, Keith doesn't react. Then, after an age, his mouth cracks open. "That's my boy you're talking about." He jerks a thumb into his chest. "Mine."

"You ever put another kid in hospital, he might not be."

My heart is even louder in my ears, the sound huge and watery.

"That's not like you. You don't want to be saying things like that." He lets his teeth show. "Everyone's been different since that boy went missing. That's all this is." He nods. "That's why me and Les here went and had a good long chat to Jase Larkin the other night. He needed calming down. Could do the same for you, you know."

Nobody moves; he lets the message sink in as the engine idles like something lying still in the hunt. Eventually, he turns his gaze to the road and pulls slowly away, and the truck recedes into the shimmering afternoon.

I'm left alone on the footpath, every nerve sparking through my limbs. I stand in place and watch them leave, my feet shaking under me, the sun hard across my shoulders.

PATTY WAS OUT when I got home. A good thing, probably; I'd have been terrible company, the state I was in. Too upset to even think about any leftovers, the beef or the pork, the stewed cabbage with the fennel and pepper. I barely had any mind to feed Tilly and the wee ones.

You've been on your own so long you've forgotten what it means to have someone.

Maybe Sheena is right. Maybe I have forgotten.

I let a hand slide out over the other half of the bed. Twenty-six years. Twenty-six years since that day. There have been others of course, both here in this bed and elsewhere. It would be ridiculous to claim otherwise. The occasional truck driver; a fruit picker back in the Bolger days. His boxes of apricots were a nice bonus before the talking got to be too much. But still, that's not exactly something you can tell a niece.

It's nearly three decades. And yet, how easily it comes back when I let it.

I'd been upstairs in the station that day, where the staffroom is now. I was typing up a report on crop damage from a loose mob of steers out past Alfredton, the typewriter clacking steadily through the morning until I could split my sandwiches with Frank. Egg and bacon, a pinch of chives chopped from the planter box on the windowsill; the yolk still runny the way he liked it. It was a hot day, I remember: the fan in the corner was straining to keep up. Then, mid-paragraph, with the words running out under my fingers and filling the pages, a flat crack sounded through the walls. The whole building fell silent, like someone flipped a switch, before a quick sound of footsteps started in the halls and voices rose in panic. Ambrose appeared in the doorway: just fright in a uniform. He was Sergeant Ambrose back then, still with his fading cape of ginger hair. His eyes found mine, and their wide white jellies told me everything.

It all came out over the next few days. One of the newer recruits had put down a rifle with a round chambered, the bolt only half-closed, and Frank had knocked it to the floor while they were packing down after a drill. As usual he'd been mid-yarn, reaching for a box up on the shelf while a story ran out between his lips, something about the farm, his temple lovely and waiting. Such a talker, Frank. Ambrose used to call him Mr. Kōrero. He'd never have known what happened. A snap of the fingers: lights out.

No more for you, my love. And no more of you for me.

Eventually, I give up my thrashing and switch on my bedside light. There's my book waiting for me, *Anna Karenina*, but I don't feel much like it. And anyway, I know where she ends up.

In the lounge, I stare at our two spots, once mine and Frank's, now mine and Patty's. This is what I have now. A sad empire and a niece I don't know what to do with. I sit and watch my reflection in the television's black surface, a single figure held in the slanted light from the hallway. It's warm here in the dark. Warm and still.

Precious Kīngi's smiling picture. A stock truck scraping through the flood, the lambs bulging through its slats like an overstuffed chair. Magpies darting and Hēmi Larkin's outstretched arm. If I listen hard enough, I can conjure all the sounds of the file room: the creaking of the floor upstairs and the printer's strange language of clicks and hums. They're there, somewhere. Two children, calling to me from inside those stacks of paper, waiting to be found.

With a low murmur, Tilly lands beside me.

"Jesus, girl." My heart slides into my mouth. "You trying to do me in?"

She steps across my lap, probing for a good spot until she settles herself down in a grey-smudged pile. I lean back against the cushions, my fingers playing through her fur, and everything in my head slows to a crawl.

I must have slept, because when the phone rings it takes me a few seconds to come back to myself. A wrong number most likely, only it doesn't stop. After a while I shuffle into the kitchen, all the night-time shapes fuzzy and unfamiliar.

"Hello?"

Someone is breathing down the line. In the background, voices cut against each other; I recognise someone yelling for her car keys. Somewhere, a door slams.

"Sheena?" Hot pitch fills my chest. "What did he do? I swear to Christ, if he so much as touched you, I'll—"

"*Aunty . . .*" A long sob tearing into my ear. "He's gone. Someone's got him."

My heart knows. And yet my mouth forms the words. "Who, girl? Who's gone?"

"Bradley."

I blink, staring at nothing. In my mind I'm on Queenie Larkin's porch again, empty-handed and feeling every atom of my otherness, watching shadows move inside the house. Hēmi Larkin, Precious Kīngi. Now Bradley, too. Lovely little Bradley Henry.

"He's not in his bed," she cries. "The front door was open, Aunty."

The moonlight turns the kitchen ghostly, a chalk sketch from the next world over. The familiar shapes are all laughing at me: the fridge and the toaster, the jug, the bottle of gin. Inside my body, pieces are breaking and twisting, swirling around a hole with no sides or bottom. I grip the phone tight until the plastic creaks.

"I'm coming, baby." Everything is so far away. "I'm coming now."

THE STREETLIGHTS FLARE above me in a streak of yellow, their bulbs dotted with moths. I feel my feet hit the footpath but I can't hear anything; there's a roar in my ears, a tall and looming wave blocking everything else.

It's just gone four in the morning. At the end of Rickett's Circle a car speeds past, its taillights red and sharp inside the dark. There: that's the spot where they stood with their bag of eels, that ragged gang. The girl with the garden fork, the skinny boys with laughing eyes. Bradley's face so bright with mischief, not wanting to let on to his mates that the shaggy Pākehā lady across the road was in fact family, his Aunty Lo, doting, always ready with a hug or a few coins for the dairy, whatever he needed, always thinking of him and only him. Whānau. Before the tall steel belly of the stock truck hid them from me, its tyres hissing through the floodwater, heavy with quarry.

Missing. Precious Kīngi. Hēmi Larkin. Gone.

Bradley Henry.

It could be a mistake. Wouldn't be the first time she'd made a mistake, my niece. All these parties, the rum and cokes and whatever else people brought, half the bloody street standing around the barbecue waiting for chops. It's like Patty says: it's a wonder they can keep track of their kids at all, that lot. He could've just snuck outside with the eel girl, the night warm with childhood larking, so many darkened lawns waiting for play. They could be hiding in that shrub right there, or behind that woodshed with the wind squeaking through the roof.

"Kiddo?"

I stand in the shadows of the oak tree cast out across the grass, night shadows, silvery blue. There: another rustle, child-sized. A tiny hopeful spark catches in my throat, but it's only the kererū settling in the tree with their fat wings.

Around the corner, I see the detective's car. Hayes made it across town from his hotel in good time; he must have heard the panic in my voice. A pair of guys watch me from Sheena's lawn, hands loose and ready. I recognise one of them from the party, the ponytailed guy in the hallway. Moko. He looks me over, staunch at first, before seeming to gauge my mood. He points behind him. "He's got her in the kitchen."

Inside, Hayes is talking to Sheena. She's still wearing the same dress, wrinkled now, the straps tight against her shoulders. They both look up, and Sheena's face folds like a tent in the wind.

"Aunty."

The detective slides his chair back. "Let me give you a second."

I move closer, and Sheena's head falls into me. Her voice is wet and thick, the syllables mixing.

"Hold on, girl." I can smell the party on her: bourbon and smoke, and sweat from the warm night. "Just tell me what happened. Tell me from the start."

"He was sleeping." She coughs and tries to clear her throat. "I went outside. The others were all there. The kids had finished the cake, and . . ."

Through the window, Hayes approaches the guys on the lawn. I'm listening but my eyes can't help but stay on them. Anything could happen.

". . . it was about one, I think. People were starting to leave. And then, he . . ."

A shiver rolls through her before the sobs take over. I rub my hands across her back. We've done this before, us two. Billy and Debs would leave for a month's shearing up north somewhere, and Sheena would come home to Aunty Lo after some new incident at school: an older girl stealing her bangles, or someone throwing a casual elbow to the eye between classes. The roles are the same as they've always been; the stakes that much higher.

Gradually, her breathing slows and I can make out her words again. "The laundry was open when I came in. I remembered what you said, about how the kitten might bolt, and I . . . he was . . ."

I look to the hall. "Where is she? Where's Patch?"

"I don't know, Aunty." She rubs at her eyes. "We checked all of Bradley's usual hiding places, but he's gone."

"They won't have gone far, Sheen." I picture the house from down low, seeing it as the kitten would. My eye snags on Keith's old Ford outside, its rusted nooks and shadowed corners. She's so small; the world would be so tall and strange. "Did you check under the cars?"

"It's just like the others." She drags a wrist across her nose. "Hēmi Larkin, and the girl, the Kīngi girl." Her hands are trembling. "They've got him. I know they have."

"What about Keith? Where was he?"

She sees the way I'm staring. "He took off with Les and the others. Why?"

There's a shout outside. We both turn to the window, and I see Hayes bend down to the lawn for his notebook, before the big guy, Sheena's mate, lifts a knee sharply into his chest. Hayes collapses into the grass, all knees and elbows.

"Christ's sake." Sheena moves to the doorway, then down the steps and across the lawn, setting herself between them. "Leave off, Moko!"

"You tell this cunt it's nothing to do with me." He looms tall through the dark, cricket-bat arms ready and waiting. "He doesn't need me in his fucking book."

I offer Hayes my hand. He pulls himself slowly up, coughing. "I'll notch that up as one bourbon too many."

"Eight years, arsehole. That was my last drink." Moko pulls a silver pennant from his singlet. "You should know who you're talking to."

Handing Hayes his notebook, I turn to Sheena, keeping Moko in the corner of my eye. The detective's face is whiter than usual; I wonder if he's going to throw up. There's so much space around us: the wide road under the yellow streetlamps, the scuffed grass covering the lawn, the long row of parked cars. Bradley was here, in this house, in his bed with the Star Wars cover we picked out at Farmers last Christmas, the Boxing Day sale. Now, the list of places he could be is growing, one concentric circle after another stretching out and away from this place, house into street, street into town, comfort into danger. Such a small boy, and such a big space.

"We need cars on the roads." I step closer to Hayes. "We should be looking for . . ."

The darkness fills with light and noise: the yelp of a siren; an engine's high-pitched whine. It's Ambrose, with Dion in tow. They pull up fast outside the gate, and Sheena's mates press their arms tight across their chests, ready.

"On the ground, now." Blue light bounces from Ambrose's head.

"There's no need." Hayes coughs. "They're cooperating."

"Cooperating?" The chief looks between us, then back to the pair. "That doesn't sound like the Moko Hepi I know. Does it, mate?"

The big guy doesn't react. Hayes leans into my ear. "We're coming up on an hour, here."

An hour. That could be sixty kilometres, or eighty. Bradley could be in the back of a car, a red station wagon, maybe, like the one I saw. Or a truck, higher off the road, watching the landscape slide past in the dark. Maybe he's seeing things he recognises: road signs and buildings, the branches of trees reaching out through the dark. My hands itch: it's as if I could just lean forward and pluck him out of that place, holding his smallness tight in my arms, safe.

"Come on, Sheen."

We leave the chief to his posturing, and Sheena takes us through the details one more time at her kitchen table, my hand on her arm, her cheeks pale and wet. Hayes pours her a glass of water; I have to point out the cupboard with the glasses.

"The kids all conked out on the couch," Sheena sniffs. "That was about ten, I think. I put a DVD on, *Ice Age*. They all love that one. Later on, I put Bradley to bed."

"What was he wearing, Ms. Henry?" Hayes speaks softly.

"His Batman T-shirt. It's new." The barest smile. "He wouldn't take it off for anything."

The detective looks to the hallway. "That his room?"

"On the left."

He stands. She waits until he's out of earshot. "I'm sorry, Aunty. Saying those things. I was upset."

"Hush, now." I take her hands in mine; it's something I can do.

"It'll be different, right?" Her eyes go wider. "You're here this time. You know about the others. You can help them. You can . . ."

"You need to tell Hayes about Keith." A nervous grimace flashes across her face. "About last year, with that prospect. I know you don't want to, girl. But he needs to know. He has to."

"It's not Keith." She shakes her head. "He'd never do anything like that. No matter how wild he gets, he'd never touch Bradley. Never."

That's my boy you're talking about. Keith's voice rolls through my head, his eyes hidden behind those flat black ovals, hands like boulders against the steering wheel. *Could do the same for you, you know.*

"Did you try calling him?"

She reaches for a cigarette. "Reception's no good where he is."

"The coast, right? Where, exactly? Riversdale, the usual spot?"

"Somewhere like that." Smoke wafts from her mouth; there's a shake in her hands, still. "Back in a few days, he said."

I nod to the hall. "We need to tell him, Sheen."

Panic turns her eyes bright. When I stand, she grips my hand harder. "I don't want anything happening, Aunty. It's nothing to do with Keith. Okay?"

I open my arms and wrap her tight. When she settles, I move into the hall. A finger of yellow light falls across the empty basket in the laundry. It's surreal: only hours ago I was showing Bradley how to hold the kitten, his fingers so steady and gentle, even when her pointy claws pricked him through his new shirt. Was it the same with Hēmi Larkin, I wonder? Is his bed still dimpled with his thin body? I blink, and I see Queenie's terrified expression in the open door, her eyes searching for better news in every new thing, then fading to disappointment, to resignation.

Outside the window, the lawn is a pool of silvery black. Past the leafy rows of Keith's silverbeet and over the fence, the neighbours watch from their porch, their faces lit by the flicker of cigarette tips, hard eyes telling me my place even as they drink in the details for later. My hands are clenched tight. The lawn full of wasted friends, Keith and his mates with their macho jackets, their patches and their crate bottles, their heavy boots. And my niece, wasted and lovely, spitting her sharp words across the kitchen, every one of them finding my heart. Part of me wants to tuck her into bed and lie with her until she sleeps. Another part of me, larger maybe, wants to slap her and not stop.

Patty. Patty would know exactly what to do.

I feel someone beside me. It's Hayes.

"These people," I say. "All these fucking people."

"There's a photo in there of Bradley with a patched guy. Short hair, built like a barrel." He takes a breath. "That's Keith, right?"

"That's him."

In the low light, the detective's eyes are shining marbles. "Anything else you can tell me?"

From the kitchen, I hear the flinty crackle of Sheena's lighter, and her shaky breath as she inhales. My hands are full of anger, like so much water collected underground. I look into this man's face, his bird's eyes watching me, waiting. The air is warm and sticky; everything is much too close.

THE MORNING BREAKS, and the sky reveals the rows of quiet houses. The streets are empty; nobody's ever up this early around here. Even if they were, they'd know to stay well away from police headlights.

We're in the back of Hayes's car, the detective's suit jacket draped over Sheena's shoulders, following the chief. He'll be on the phone as he drives, Ambrose—giving the particulars for Tania to type up and send off to the radio stations and the newspapers. Horrible, to think this is how it works. A brief statement, and Bradley becomes a list of dry details: height, clothing, last seen. Just the fundamentals, easy to summarise, told and retold until he becomes something else. A cautionary tale, a shiver down the back.

Three now. Lord help us. Two could be a coincidence but three is too much to ignore, even here. I close my eyes as fatigue slackens my body, the dimmer switch inside me moving in both directions at once: heart darker, brain brighter.

We arrive at the station, and I help Sheena out of the car. There's birdsong in the trees but it seems unfair to listen.

"We'll use room two," says Hayes.

"Wait, we're doing the whole thing?" I feel myself frowning. "Don't you have enough for a statement already?"

"We need to make sure we get everything down." He gives Sheena a look of encouragement, but I know it's mostly for me.

"Don't worry, girl," I tell her. "I'll be in there with you."

A flicker of hesitation shoots across the detective's face. We come in through the back, into the anonymous crackle of radio from the communications room. Hayes unlocks the interview room, and I do what I can to make Sheena comfortable. Truth is, it's a hideous box, even with the facts on your side. A chipped Formica table sits lonely and obdurate in the centre of the room, worn from generations of elbows. Through a narrow window, a slice of daylight taunts us with rising blue. There's still a summer morning out there: clear and uncomplicated for the lucky few.

"How about a coffee, eh love?"

Sheena leans into a seat, her face cratered with worry; I'm not sure she hears me. I go to the staffroom and click the jug on.

Hayes comes in behind me. "Listen," he says. "You'd do best to sit this out."

I set two mugs down. "I've seen too many of the chief's transcripts for that, mate. He'll push her to say anything."

The detective sets his hands to his hips, still wincing from the knock on the lawn. "It's not about her, Lorraine. You need to think about the boy. We need everything on record while it's still fresh, and she won't . . ."

"Think about the boy?" I lean closer. "Who else would I be fucking well thinking about?"

"See?" He watches me. "This is exactly what I mean. If you can't hear me out without losing it, then you shouldn't be in there."

There's a long silence. I can hear my heart.

"She needs me," I say. "I'm staying in that room."

In the hall, the chief is calling out. Hayes turns away with a shake of his head. My hands are clenched; it's too hot in this room. I open the freezer and push my face into the ice, breathing chill into my body.

We wait in the interview room while the chief mutters to Dion in the hall. When the door swings open, he's changed into his uniform. Buttons shining, all creases in place. He hasn't had time to shave, though; there's ginger stubble smeared like pollen across his jaw.

"Seeing as how we're *all* here"—he slides into the seat next to Hayes and casts an ugly glance in my direction—"how about you take us through the evening one more time, Ms. Henry?"

Sheena looks to me. "It's okay, baby." I set my hand against her back. "Go ahead."

She smokes as she talks, her voice cracked and weary. I've read plenty of transcripts where Ambrose makes a big fuss about letting people smoke in here, but he seems to be keeping his powder dry for now.

For a while, Sheena is the only one speaking. I watch Hayes, trying to hear what he's hearing. Party, sausage rolls, kitten, kids. She leaves out a few details here and there; I'm sure they can guess.

"This a regular thing then?" The chief squints. "Parties at yours?"

"Regular? I dunno." She fidgets with her rings. "The neighbours come over sometimes."

"And the drinking? That's regular, right?"

Sheena frowns and looks to me.

"I'm the one you're talking to here."

"Steady on," I say. "There's no need for that." Hayes gives me a calming look.

"Tell me where things stand with the boy's father," says Ambrose. "You and your aunt here had a bit of a disagreement, didn't you? About Keith?"

"What do you mean?"

A grin tugs at the chief's mouth. I look at Hayes but he doesn't react.

"He's on our books, Keith." Ambrose holds his voice steady. "Pops up in quite a few places. But you know that, don't you?"

"It's fuck-all to do with me." That's it, girl. "I don't know where he gets to."

"I'd say it's everything to do with you," says Ambrose. "Keith Mākara, Moko Hepi, and who bloody knows who else all in the one spot, right before your boy goes missing? Half the chapter was there."

"We're wasting time." I try to catch Hayes's eye, but he's watching Sheena.

"It can't be Keith." She shakes her head. "It's been hard enough getting him to spend any time with Bradley lately. Why the hell would he take off with him?"

"Hard because Keith's unwilling? Or hard because the boy's scared of him?"

"What?"

"Cards on the table, eh? We know about Keith having words with Lorraine last night. He as good as threatened to bust her up, just like he and his mate did with Jason Larkin."

Sheena crosses her arms. "He had nothing to do with that."

"Don't bugger us about now, Sheena." Ambrose leans into his elbows, one sausage finger pointing into her face. "Your boy's out there missing, along with two others. The Kīngis have been known to mix in with the rough crowds, you know. Larkins too. And we know damn well Keith and his lot have been setting up trade further north. Who's to say this isn't just some bloody turf war gotten out of hand, eh? And what if your man got spooked and took Bradley off somewhere just to keep him out of their reach?"

"Wait a second." I hold up my hand, ignoring a stern look from Hayes. "Are you being serious?"

"He would never do that," says Sheena. "Not without telling me. And he'd never let a child get hurt. Not the Kīngis, and not Queenie Larkin. Not for anything."

"Sure about that, are you?" Ambrose looks between us, his head pale in the lamplight. "We know about everything outside your place with the prospect last year, Sheena. The Mongrels might try to keep things in the ranks, but a story like that still gets around."

Sheena's eyes pan to mine, her face like a smashed plate.

"You prick!" I jump to my feet, leaning over Hayes. "I told you that in confidence!"

"Let's take a second." The detective nods for Ambrose to pause the tape. "Come with me, Lorraine."

He stands and holds the door open; I feel like a child being shown to the naughty corner. The chief leans back in his chair, quietly triumphant.

"I'll be back, Sheen."

She won't look at me. Instead, she sets her chin to her chest, a cigarette burning between her fingers. My eyes sweep across the room as I leave. The crisp clean uniform on one side, the dress creased with the night on the other. Hunter and quarry; how many times has the same situation played out in this room? Only now it's my blood.

Little Sheena. Little Bradley.

Hayes follows me to the staffroom and closes the door behind us. My legs feel heavy; the room seems to spin for a moment.

"Why the fuck would you tell him about that?"

"Tell him? Lorraine, he's the boss here. Whatever history you two have, there's no getting around that. Not with three kids missing."

I point to the room. "And what the hell was that shit about the gangs in there? You know as well as I do the Kīngis aren't involved in any of that rubbish. And Jason Larkin might think he's a player, but to them he's just a joke. They hardly pay him any attention, the Mongrels or anyone else. They'd never snatch up Hēmi just to make a point."

"Is that right? You're keeping tabs on every single thing the Kīngis get up to, are you?" Hayes narrows his eyes. "You know as well as I do it was Keith and his mates who tuned up Jason Larkin, Lorraine. You as good as said so yourself. What are they so worried he might've said to us, eh?" He motions us further into the staffroom, holding his voice low. "You're aware a good chunk of east coast territory is up for grabs right now, right? I know you've been out of the briefings, but surely you read the papers?"

"Course I bloody well do." I shake my head. Two Black Power prospects were found on the side of the road outside Woodville not a week before Precious Kīngi disappeared, both shot through the chest. The headlines were hard to miss. "But that doesn't mean Keith's behind any of this. And it doesn't mean you need to go rattling Sheena's cage." I feel a sob rising inside me. "She got no one on her side in there."

"She knows things, Lorraine. You know she does. And anyway, who's on her side isn't the priority." He takes a long breath. "Which is why you're staying out here."

"Excuse me?"

A look of distraction clouds over his face. "Look, you asked about my cases the other day. The other kids." There's tenderness in his expression. "People don't ever want to push too hard. Not with the mothers. But if we don't get it all on the table now, we're going to miss things. Details, possibilities.

They could mean everything later." He looks me in the eye. "It may be fuck-all to do with who runs chalk on the east coast. And you're right, we don't know for sure how exactly the Kīngis and the Larkins are involved. Jesus, they might not be involved at all. But we know Keith's been making a push further north, and chances are your niece has overheard some things. We'll never find out with you stomping around."

I picture Keith on his throne at the roast shop, his shoulders wide and relaxed, and the whole world at his bidding. Those big hands. Did they smash eels too?

"What if Ambrose pressures her," I say. "What if he . . ."

"I'll be there, Lorraine."

He sets a hand to my arm; his expression is like light through murky water. He's close enough for me to see my reflection in his eyes: a round grey woman held in miniature. It's comforting, somehow, to see myself inside that kind and bristly face. I might be coming apart in real life, but at least I'm whole somewhere.

"Okay." Behind his shoulders, the clock reads eight-thirty.

Five hours. We're coming up on five hours now.

I wipe my eyes. "I'll be downstairs."

He pats my sleeve and turns away, every angle of his body arranged for the task at hand. The interview room door clicks closed. Except for the soft crackle of radio, everything is quiet.

I'm downstairs in the stacks for hours, reading the files and listening for footsteps upstairs. There are the usual sounds: the creak of the building as the day heats up, the printer's paranoid clicks, and through the thin basement windows, cheers from the cricket oval. Three kids missing, yet the cricketers play, their white outfits drenched in the indifferent sun.

I wait, and my hands play idly through the Kīngi and Larkin files. Addresses and statements, names and phone numbers: a whole sorry constellation of facts—and yet we're nowhere. I keep half an eye on my phone; Patty will surely have heard the news by now. She listens to the bulletin after her psalms, when her knees are done communing with the bedside divots in her carpet. I'm surprised she's not here at the station, barrelling through the front door to get to me.

There: the floorboards creak. Muffled voices sound upstairs. It's nearly midday now: they've had Sheena in there long enough to tell her life story a few times over. I climb the stairs out of the basement, huffing. Near the top, the doorway shows a quick sweep of black hair.

"Sheen." I'm out of breath. "Sheena?"

She stands by the station entrance, tucked into Moko's broad shape. His hand is wrapped around her arm, her skin disappearing inside the cuff of his fingers.

"Are you all right, girl?"

Moko glares back at me. "She's fine."

"Where are you going?"

Turning around, Sheena fixes me with the kind of look I haven't seen since her teens, her eyes hard and dark. "Home."

"Hang on." I nod to the staffroom. "I'll get my stuff."

"No." She sniffs and coughs deep in her chest. "I don't need you."

She pulls her shoulders straight back and pushes through the door. With a long stare, Moko follows her. It's like I've seared a hand on the oven: the pain hasn't quite arrived yet, but the cheque's in the mail.

"You okay?" Hayes asks.

My mouth moves slowly. "What happened in there?"

"Few things for us to follow up." He flips his notepad closed, his eyes lingering on my face. "Might be worth getting some rest, Lorraine."

Outside, there's the quick yelp of tyres on asphalt. I rub a palm across my cheek, still not quite inhabiting my body.

"We about ready, here?" The chief calls to Hayes from the end of the hall.

"I'll get my jacket."

"What's going on?" I wipe at my eyes. "What did Sheena say?"

"It's fine, Lorraine," says Ambrose. "We're taking care of it."

I stand in place but it's no use: in his eyes I'm just an object to be navigated, some sad and forgotten thing. In the spare office, Hayes is tucking his gun into his belt.

"I need to know what she said, Justin." My hands are shaking. "Even if she hates me right now, she needs me to know."

He turns to face me. His features are lit up in a soft glow, all those craggy edges turned gentle. "She asked us to keep it close."

"Close?"

He places a hand on my shoulder, and I bat it away. A raw yellow feeling rolls through me.

Who could be closer than Aunty Lo?

"Keep your phone handy, all right? I'll call you when we're done."

"If it's Keith you're after, then you're wasting your time," I say. "There's no way he'd take Bradley. Even if they were in danger, it's not the kind of thing he'd do."

"That's not what your niece said."

I shake my head. "Not what she said? Or not what the chief got her to say?" The room around us seems much too small. "The guy's bad news, no arguments there. I'd be the first one to tell you that. But this whole turf war idea doesn't hang together. You know it doesn't. Who ever heard of gang kid-nappings?"

He takes a long breath; I can tell he's not listening. "Get some rest." He pauses at the door with an in-between expression. "And give your niece some time, okay? Just for tonight."

"You don't get to tell me that."

With a last look, he's gone. I set my hands to the desk, and the moisture in my eyes melts everything in the room. The briefcase and the spare shoes, the tie unspooled across the chair: everything looks flimsy, temporary. I could blink, and it'd all be swept away.

I grab my things and leave out the back door, avoiding Tania's probing eyes in the staffroom. There are a few report-ers out front now, clustered and waiting for information. One of them lifts his head to see me, then turns back to the group.

On the way home, I can't help but feel watched. The sun bores down like a searchlight; it isn't long before I'm sweating.

At least Bradley won't be cold, wherever he is. Hates the cold, that boy. Always asks for an extra hot water bottle in the winter months: one for his feet, too. As a toddler he was a big burrower. I used to fall asleep on the couch with him whenever Sheena was away, and I'd wake up with his head pressed hard into my neck for warmth, his hair plugging up my nose.

I wipe at my eyes, the footpath a grey smear under me.

At the end of Rickett's Circle, the gutter holds the last stubborn debris from the storm, branches and plastic trash all twisted together. It's the same spot Keith pulled over. I stand in place, and I see again the lack of interest in his eyes, the calm veneer as he stared through me. For a second I think about walking on to see Sheena, before her words at the station stab me again.

I don't need you.

I turn and head home. A gin with Patty in the lounge, the windows open to the breeze. Maybe some euchre if I can focus. That's what I need right now. She'll have questions, but I'll try not to let them get to me. She's probably inside right now, spare keys in the door, a glass poured and waiting for me. I can feel my head on her shoulder already, her voice low and calming in my ear, and her skin smelling of the apricot scrub she uses in the weekends. She'll know exactly what to say.

My door's locked; she's probably just playing it safe. You never know what might happen in this part of town, even on a Sunday.

"Pat." I step inside and call through the kitchen. "Patty?"

Tilly appears at my feet, scratching at the garage door. The kittens. I crack the door open and hear the mewling chorus from their box. Patch might be missing but the others still need their mum.

"This is some remarkable restraint, Pat." My voice echoes down the hall. "You must have your mouth bloody well taped shut in there."

In the lounge, her chair is empty. I check the spare room. She naps in there sometimes, even when I'm out; Mrs. Wikaira's place gives her the creeps, all on her own over there.

It's empty. The house is hushed and silent, the duvet pressed flat and smooth. My chest feels tight. She's never far away on a Sunday. Maybe something's happened. Something besides Bradley.

Outside, the lawn is hot under my feet, every blade of grass a tiny wire. I cross the space between our houses, past my cactus glasshouse and through the garden gate.

"Patty?"

I hold my hands to the glass while the cicadas scream. It's nearly three months she's been renting the place, and the kitchen still looks like a bad motel. There's nothing on the fridge door, and just her new toaster and jug combo on the bench, raspberry red. It's been a bad split with her husband; anyone can see that.

A low animal noise sounds behind me. Two of the kittens are halfway across the lawn, stepping on unsteady legs towards the road, their faces low and searching. Tilly appears on the porch, crying in alarm.

"It's all right, girl."

I step back through the gate and pick up the one closest, a little grey tom, his tail pointed straight up. He wriggles inside my palm, furious at his captivity. I lift him into my chest, the protector again. His claws are needles against my skin.

SOMEHOW, EVEN WITH the night sliding through my veins, I manage to close my eyes. A half-glass of gin on ice and my head lolls back into the couch. Tilly arranges herself beside me, whiskers twitching, not knowing a thing. Imagine what that must be like.

When I dream, it's all body parts. Not a mortuary type of dream, or anything from one of Patty's books with their toe tags and their freezers. These are happy appendages: hands, mostly. Strong, fleshy hands. Doing hands, like my dad's; hands ready for an afternoon of battening, or scraping the well down by the creek. Then there's a smaller set. I know they're Bradley's, those dear fingers of his like sticks of malted bread. They're calm, those hands, the usual mischief quieted for just this moment, set one over the other—in his lap, maybe— waiting patiently for whatever comes next.

Frank had lovely hands. That's where I begin when I think of him. Not the eyes, milky green like copper-stained porcelain, but the hands. He had those kūmara thumbs: graceful, but a large grace. The kind of thumbs to have a hard time with a woman's underthings, even on a Sunday, an afternoon as free and holy as they come. We're here, me and Frank, the very same spot but the old couch, corduroy, and he's brushing those lovely big fingers across the tops of my thighs the way he knows I like. There's a flare of mischief in his face. We're unrushed, nowhere else to be, nothing much on the mind. He leans over me, holding my body in his eyes. I want badly to tell him something.

Is it about Bradley? Or Sheena? Christ, there's a lot to explain. He doesn't know a thing about Bradley. Sheena's still just Debbie's wee one as far as he's concerned, her tiny arms reaching up from the bassinet we bought at the Boxing Day sales for forty per cent off. She's our tester, Frank had said: Debs and Billy were conducting a trial to see how the Henry stock might mix with the local elements. That's how he put it: "the local elements," his eyes jumping in suggestion, ready to get started. At least Billy had done him a favour, Frank said. By going first and getting old Mickey Henry used to the idea of a coffee grandchild. Though to be fair, Dad hadn't taken much of a push; not when the baby was as gorgeous as Sheena. It was everyone else who'd taken some adjustment.

Lordy, I've got some ground to cover if I'm going to get the situation across to the poor man. He doesn't even know what happened to him in the munitions room yet. The loaded rifle, the sausage-fingered cadet, the quick lights-out. That'll come as a surprise, I'm sure.

I'm opening my mouth to tell him; everything moves much too slow.

My eyes flicker open. Outside, the sun is lower in the sky. An engine slows in the street, a thin rattling sound like change in a can. Patty's Fiesta. I heave myself up, and my heart speeds, though my shoulders still feel wrapped in wire. Bradley might be gone, and I'm on ice with Sheena. But Patty's here. I can talk to somebody. I reach for a clean glass and move into the kitchen, hearing her knock against the door.

"Come in, Pat. Jesus, come in." There are already tears coming.

"Lorraine." I see her cheeks first, wide and pale. "I'm so sorry."

I expect her arms to open and circle me. Instead, she stands pinned in place, shoulder against my doorway, one arm clasping the other. It's too much, then: too many things are on me. I fall forward into her. She flinches like I'm a stranger again.

"He's gone." The laundry floor: kitten and boy. "Nobody knows where he is."

She swallows hard in her throat. "I . . . I don't even . . ."

"Sheena won't even bloody well talk to me. My own niece. Because I told Hayes about everything with Keith, last year and all." My wrist comes against my nose. "They think he's got Bradley, that it's some gang stuff. None of it makes any sense."

"Come on, now." Her voice is shaky. "You could use a sit down."

"I thought you'd be home," I say.

"The supermarket," she says. "The kind of week we're going to have, I thought I'd stock up. Plus, I needed to clear my head a little."

I nod. She doesn't have to say anything; I know how tough things have been with the divorce, and with Stuart being so late in settling. He's blaming the dry summer and the lamb prices but anyone listening can tell he's only drawing things out for her. I reach out to touch her, letting her know I understand, when I notice an angry raspberry blotch running up the inside of her arm. A burn. A bad one, and recent.

"Shit, Pat, what happened?"

She clasps her good hand over her wrist. "That bloody oven. I don't know how that lot ever managed a casserole without incinerating themselves."

"Here." I reach inside the freezer and crack some ice into a clean tea towel. "You'll need a bandage on that."

She takes the ice, wincing as it goes on. "Lorraine." A shake of the head. "I'm so sorry. I can't imagine what you must be feeling right now."

I let her put her good hand on my back; her fingers are strong and safe. The words come, then: the party and the fight with Sheena, Keith and his mate in the ute outside Rickett's Circle, and the call in the dark hours as I was dozing. I pour a couple of drinks while I'm talking, my hands moving automatically.

"The father, they're saying?" Patty stares across the kitchen. "That's the best idea? That he took the boy?"

"To keep him safe, maybe." I lift the gin to my mouth. "They think it could all be a turf thing, Precious and Hēmi too. Keith and his lot have been stepping into new territory, apparently. But it doesn't make any sense."

Patty gestures us into the lounge, and I find a clear spot on the couch.

"He was so excited," I say. "You should've seen him with Patch, and with his mates."

"Oh, Lorraine." She shakes her head as she tops up our glasses. "Everything you've done for your niece, and now this."

I wipe at my eyes, and the room blurs for a second. In the afternoon light, I get a better look at her arm. "That's going to need something on it, Pat."

"Hmm?"

"Your wrist. It must sting to buggery."

She pushes her mouth into a thin smile. "Don't worry about me, now."

"There's some salve in the bathroom, the cabinet under the sink." I drain my glass and lean back into the couch. Everything feels softer already. It's the company, and the gin.

"Where are they, then?"

"Who?"

"The chief," says Patty. "And that new detective you mentioned. What's his name?"

"Hayes." I clear my throat. "They wouldn't tell me. Keith's place, I think. Somewhere out near Riversdale."

She squints across the room. "You could always ask your niece, right?"

"She wouldn't even look at me," I say. "She'd never say."

"You could always try." Patty leans forward. "Why don't you rest up, then call her in a bit, eh? She needs you, Lorraine. You're her closest family. If there's anything we can do, we should at least try."

I blink, and I see the splotch of white fur on Patch's face, the cream peering through the orange. The room is slippery; I can feel my eyes closing again. "Think I'll rest my eyes a bit."

"That's it." Patty sets her glass on the table. "I'll be right here. I'll wake you."

THE LIGHT IS thinner when I wake; Patty must have closed the curtains. There's the sound of Tilly purring on the cushion next to me. Everything moves slowly.

"Patty?"

I hear the fridge door close. "You all right in there, love?"

"Yeah, fine." I shake my head and rub my fingers across my cheeks. A dull feeling hangs through my head, a heavy blanket pulled down over me. My eyes adjust. Through the open window, I catch the last of the daylight winking through my glasshouse. "What fucking time is it?"

Her head appears in the doorway. "You needed your rest."

I stand, and the room shoots past me like the contents of an uncorked bottle. The clock on the mantel reads a little after eight.

"Christ, Pat! Why didn't you wake me?"

"It was a long night for you." She turns a casserole tray over in her hands, mouth twitching as the tea towel touches her burn. "It's just a few hours, Lo."

I can hardly pull breath into my lungs fast enough. "I have to see about Hayes. And Sheena, she'll be . . ." I pat my pockets but my hands won't seem to do what I ask.

"It's by your bed," says Patty. "I put it on to charge."

"What about the landline?" I squint. "Nobody called?"

She looks to the floor. "It's been off the hook. Just since four."

There are rocks in my throat. "What the hell are you talking about?"

"Someone has to look out for you, Lorraine." Patty squares up, staring me in the face. "You're always doing everything for them. You needed to rest, and I made sure you could."

Her eyes hold me from the doorway. I smell it, then: pork and stuffing, salted potatoes and cabbage. Such kindness. "You went to the Leongs? On a Sunday?"

She smiles. "It was bloody heaving in there, I'll tell you that. Thought I might overhear something about Keith, but no such luck." Setting the dish on the table, she hangs the tea towel and grabs her keys. "I've had mine already. Yours is in the warmer."

Her hand goes out between us, holding mine. My thoughts rush together like mixing river currents. Bradley in his socks on the laundry floor, and Sheena staring back at me across the lobby as Moko held her in his big hands.

"I'll be next door if you need anything." Patty squeezes my

hand and shifts some hair from her eyes. Even with Stuart getting up to his tricks in court, and the rest of her worries, she still makes time to think of me. I'm lucky in that, anyway. "Go on, now. Better check your phone."

I turn to my room and hear the front door click shut behind me. Seven missed calls, all from Hayes. No voicemails. I push the screen to call back, pacing the hallway back to the kitchen.

"Where in shitting Christ have you been, Lorraine?" I can hear the chief in the background on his phone. There's a low murmur; they must be on gravel somewhere.

"At home," I say. "I had to—"

"Look, never mind that. We . . ."

The line garbles, then cuts out completely. Gravel roads; they must be a fair way out, then. Patchy signal. In the kitchen, I grab a roast potato from the tray in the oven and scoff it down. I drink a glass of water while I wait for Hayes to call back, then another.

His number comes up. "Hayes? Where are you?" My face feels hot.

"Near Martinborough, coming back from . . . where was it?" There's a crossing of voices inside the car. "Tora. Near Tora."

"Tora?" My spare hand goes to the edge of the counter. "But Keith's supposed to be further north, isn't he? Near Riversdale, Sheena said."

"She gave us shit, Lorraine. Sent us way out where the bloody gravel stops." He's spitting the words down the line. "She told us to take an old gravel track, and to look out for a cottage past some beehives. There's nothing out here."

81

My heart drops in my chest. "Where is she? Where's my niece?"

"We sent Dion around an hour ago. The place is locked tight." There's a new weight across me. "She took off, Lorraine. Probably with Keith."

Jesus, Sheena. I close my eyes, and my fingers go tight around the phone. The bedside drawer sliding open, the telltale bag. I'm going to slap the ever-living shit from that girl. I am.

"The interview."

"She had to wait until you were out of the room," says Hayes. "That's why she didn't want us to tell you where we were going."

"If she's gone off with Keith, then she must think he's got Bradley, right?"

"Hard to say. She could just be trying to wrap this all up without landing Keith in hot water." There's a bump in the background as the car goes from gravel to asphalt, and the rising thrum of the engine. "If he's got the boy, then we're not even dealing with an abduction. It could all just be one big jerk-around."

"Give me that phone." The chief's voice booms. "Listen, now. Dion's at your niece's place, but it's locked. We can't go kicking around there. You're family, though."

"Oh, so now I'm back in the loop, eh?"

"Shut up and listen." There's steel in his voice. I hate to say it but he's useful in a fast-moving spot. "Find me something on where that Mākara prick could be. Some mail, anything. And don't let Dion inside. This is just you."

"Okay." I reach down for my shoes. "I'll try Sheena too."

"Her phone's switched off. Either that or she's out of reception." The chief clears his throat. "Just get it done, Lorraine."

He hangs up before I can say anything. I grab my poncho and lace up my runners, reaching into the oven with a napkin for a slice of pork and another couple of potatoes for the walk. It could be a long night, after all. It's warm outside, still, though the last of the daylight is ebbing away. Across the lawn, there's the outline of Patty watching from her kitchen counter, her hands busy with something. I lift the food in her direction, and she nods to me.

I chew as I walk, my feet scraping the pavement, my thoughts a jumbled soup. There's Sheena's face full of brazen daring, her eyes boring into me as Moko stood at her side, and little Patch digging into Bradley's neck while the boy winced and laughed. Despite what the chief said, I try my niece's mobile; it goes straight to voicemail.

The signpost for Rickett's Circle floats past me in the twilight, the distance to Sheena's slipping past under my feet, and then I'm there. Behind Keith's junked Ford, Dion leans against the hood of his patrol car, arms folded tight across his uniform. He sees me coming, and his face forms the same mask of disdain the chief's been working on for years.

"Where've you been, then?"

"Pull your head in, boy." My mouth is faster than my brain. "There's no time for that."

"What?" His eyebrows slide up a notch.

"Any gloves in there? Bags?"

After a few blinking moments, he reaches into the back seat and hands over a pair of latex gloves and some evidence bags.

"I've already tried the doors," he says.

I head around the back without saying anything. The lights go on next door, curtains sliding across just so. I hear Dion behind me. Halfway across the lawn, I turn and lift a hand into his chest.

"The chief said to keep this as simple as possible."

"Yeah?" There's a seesawing between us. "Well." He coughs. "You should hurry up, then."

He steps back down the side of the house to his car. Across Sheena's fence, the same neighbours are huddled on the porch, eyes on me, letting me know exactly what they think.

Us and them. Aunty or no, it's still the same. Our kids might be missing, the answer just one locked door away, but these are lines that won't be redrawn. I reach down under the loose paving stone by the trellis and brush soil from the spare key, my eyes full of Keith's lush greenery, his thick leaves and his stems staked in their correct places. The lock's stiff but it opens. Inside the house, everything sounds empty and strange.

"Hello?"

I go through the motions; I can feel there's nobody home. In Sheena's room, the floor is patchy with clothes. The bag in the bedside table is gone, and so is my envelope. Except for an old stick of deodorant in the bathroom, there's no sign Keith was ever here. Sheena and Moko must've cleared everything out this afternoon, while I was asleep at home with the phone off the hook. The water's still running in the sink; I turn the tap off, avoiding my expression in the mirror. In the hallway, I muster the nerve to enter Bradley's room. Just the smell of him is enough to wet my eyes. It's like I have his head on my chest again, our dearest birthday boy held tight and safe inside these arms, these hands. Hēmi Larkin's rugby boots, and the poster of Precious with her staring eyes. I check everywhere. There's nothing to suggest an address.

In the lounge, I let myself sink down into Sheena's couch. Everything still smells of sausage rolls and cigarettes and bourbon. In the window, the dark lawn holds my reflection: hair a rough bundle out across my shoulders, my hands wrapped in these ridiculous gloves, like a kid playing dress-up. My thoughts drift then, and my eyes lose their focus. Outside, through my own image, there's the circle of deck chairs and the ashy gape of the barbecue open to the dark. An image flits through my mind like a skipped stone.

The bin. Keith and his mate had a blue chilly bin in the back of his truck, its edges taped closed. My feet race over the carpet to the back door; I flick the porch lights on, throwing the lawn into pale illumination. I'm at the barbecue before I know what I'm doing, the scuffed toes of my runners digging through the ashes piled up against the lawn. They don't take long to find. Crayfish shells. A dozen of them, and big suckers, too. I've never been so big on the crays, myself; Dad had a few too many years of gout for that, but Sheena and Bradley both love a split cray grilled in garlic butter, the legs snapped apart for the sweet strings of white meat.

I have to hand it to Keith. It's quite the birthday present.

I'm far from sure, but there's one spot everyone knows for crays, especially the big ones. I head down the side of the house, my body cutting open the space between the fence, oblivious to the eyes from next door. Dion sees me coming and cracks the car door open, his eyes holding a question.

"Mataikona." There's a wire strung tight inside my voice. Whatever nonsense Sheena has done, I can fix it. I can always fix it. "We need to try Mataikona."

THIS WAS ALWAYS one of Frank's favourite drives—we used to come for a week out at the Castlepoint campground every Christmas. Debs and Billy too, when they were done in the sheds. Year's end was always the busiest time for the shearers; by the time Christmas rolled around those two would be tired and lean, pockets stuffed, ready to take the drive with us out to the sand and the wind and the salt.

In my mind I still find Frank there behind the wheel of our old brown Morris, Billy in the passenger's seat to balance out the weight, me and Debs snug in the back, up to our ears in tent poles and diving gear. More than once we had guys come up to the car when Frank and Billy were inside paying for petrol, just to make sure we were okay, and to check we knew the two blokes we were with. You'd have thought we were driving around with Charlie Manson. They meant well, I'm sure. At least they thought they did.

There was a spot at the far end of the rise, not long before the Mataikona turnoff, where the Morris would boil over. You could set your watch: halfway up the climb the poor radiator would start to wheeze, and Frank would run his broad hand across the dash, as if all she needed was some encouragement. Bit by bit the temp gauge would lift, until tongues of steam licked out from under the hood and the car filled with the smell of hot metal. Frank would pull into a corner, and we'd break out the bacon and egg pie with the bonnet up. A bottle of beer too, if it'd been a long week. It'd be enough to have Debs jumping the fence for a place to squat; she always had a weak bladder, even before Sheena. And all while a parade of squinting potato faces came past, tutting to see these nice young girls with those two local boys.

They were always good, those drives, even with the glances. We'd pull out of Rickett's Circle and stop by their place—Sheena's place now—and the sweetest lull would come over us. It was the same for my sister: all the tiny things Debs had been picking over with Billy would drain away, and by the time we were past Henley Lake, we'd be nicely inside that stillness, that special holiday calm. She'd set an arm across the gear, fingers still smelling of lanolin from the sheds, and I'd hold on tight for my stomach.

That calm seems a world away now. By the time we reach the boil-over hill I'm feeling crook. Dion is leaning the patrol car sharply into every corner, and with the long shadows outside as the night takes hold, and thoughts of Sheena wrong-footing us, everything feels pushed together like too much washing in the machine. A shiny truck slips past in the other lane. Some townie kids in Daddy's ute. Our headlights catch the glint of a bottle inside the cab, and the driver's mouth forms a perfect O as we pass, his eyes like guilty saucers, waiting for the sirens.

"Little pricks." Dion lifts his eyes to the rear-view mirror. "If we weren't in a rush."

I stay quiet and breathe low through the corners, hoping he'll get the message. Outside, tree branches lean down like thin fingers from the road's edge, grasping at the last of the daylight.

"You'd better hope they're out here," says Dion. "The chief's really on the rag."

I let out a long breath. "It's a hunch, that's all."

"A hunch."

"I don't remember any bright ideas sliding out of your pie-hole, mate."

His eyes flicker. We come to the end of the rise, the patrol car fast against the incline, and the cleft in the hill gives way to the open air.

"Yeah, well." He coughs. "It's not my niece mixing in with that Mākara piece of shit, is it?"

I turn my head, watching him. *Are you okay in there, love?* They always seemed so genuinely concerned, those Pākehā faces approaching the Morris. *Do you know those two fellas?* Thirty years, and this is where we are. No one's learnt anything; not even Dion, with a Kahungunu connection of his own on his grandmother's side. I'm still deciding if it's worth saying something when his phone rings.

"Heya, love." Voice all honey. "I'm just . . . no, we had to . . . no . . . would you let me get a word in? It's the missing kid, the . . . Yeah. That one." He gives me the corner of his eye. "We're heading out the coast now. Mataikona. Might be a late night." There's a clench in his jaw as he swallows a yawn. "He get settled down okay? All right. Yep, I . . . listen, I will."

He slips the phone back into his pocket and leans harder on the accelerator, knifing the car against the centre line. There's a yellow twist in my guts, and it's moving higher.

"Would you mind?"

"Huh?"

I nod through the windscreen. "We're almost there. You don't need to thrash it."

A look of hesitation comes across him, before his jaw softens and he lifts his foot. We're still hugging the corners but there's less of the sloshing inside me. I take a long breath.

"You should do something nice," I say.

"Hmm?"

"For your wife."

A short laugh punches from his mouth. "We're not married."

"Doesn't matter. Just trust me."

"Yeah?" There's doubt in his voice. And what would you know about it, lady? His eyes are on me but I don't want to turn my head. It's easier if I focus on the white lines ticking beneath the dash. "Our boy's sleeping now," he says.

"That's something. Nurses said it might be colic, last time they came around." He yawns again, and his eyes crinkle into sleeves.

"How old?"

"Three months. No, four. Time's been getting away a bit." He rubs at his mouth. "Look, I was sorry to hear. About your nephew, I mean. Grand-nephew, right?"

I close my eyes. "Thanks."

"If they're out here, we'll find them." He points through the glass. "Even if it takes all night, we'll find them. There's only so many places, right?"

Under the hum of the engine, the radio crackles. It's the chief: he and Hayes are at the crest of the hill, a couple of minutes behind us. Hearing his voice, there's a sense of something puncturing, of our pocket of air and glass being shunted back into the world. My hands are shaking in my lap; I try to hold them steady.

"Some muesli bars in there." Dion nods to the glovebox. "These long days, y'know? Pays to stock up."

Wiping at my eyes, I open the latch. Banana and chocolate chip: Bradley's favourite. I unwrap a bar and take a bite, mushing the oat flakes into a sugary paste between my teeth.

"Might have one myself." I pass him a bar, and he pushes it out of the foil with his thumb, biting half off in one go. "You really think she would've come all the way out here, your niece? That other one too, what's his name? Moko?"

The sign for the Castlepoint golf course looms in our headlights, the fading paint showing a faceless man mid-swing.

"Honestly?" I take another bite. "I've no fucking idea. Not anymore."

In the distance is the lamplight outside the Whakataki Hotel. Except for a couple of trucks with boats hitched, the carpark is empty; it's probably just a few guys with chilly bins full of pāua and cod making the weekend last a bit longer.

We pull in, and Dion cuts the engine. Inside, the curtains slide open, framing curious faces. I can taste the salt in the air. Across the paddocks, the lazy shush of the ocean. Castlepoint is just a few minutes' drive from here: the bay and the store, the quiet waves for the families, the lighthouse pointing up above the dunes. To the north is Mataikona.

Hayes and Ambrose pull up not long after, causing a second flutter of the hotel curtains. The chief stomps through the gravel to the road's edge; I hear his piss hit the flax.

"Real prick of an afternoon we've had," says Hayes. His cheeks are slack, his hair sticking up from his head in fraying strings.

"You're sure you didn't bloody well know, Lorraine?" The chief strides back over and sets his hands to his hips. "What your niece was up to and all?"

"Me? How was I supposed to know she'd send you traipsing around?" I picture Sheena's expression in the lobby, and a fresh wave of nerves rolls through me. "If you'd only pulled your head out of your arse, we could've . . ."

"All right." Hayes lifts an arm between us. "It's done. Let's not dwell."

The chief stands with his feet wide in the gravel, red-eyed from the hours behind the wheel, and unfolds a map across the bonnet.

"Right," he says. "Where's this Mākara prick supposed to be, then?"

With a long breath, I tell him about the chilly bin and the charred cray shells. "Once at Sheena's I heard them talking in the next room. Keith was telling someone to meet them out at the pots. Take a left at the Whakataki Hotel, he said."

Dion nods down the road. "There's always pots out past the point, there. It's five minutes. Ten at the most."

"So, what? We're just supposed to drive up and down the coast looking for gang patches?" The chief squints.

"Your niece must have her phone, right?" Hayes asks.

I shake my head. "Switched off."

Tutting to himself, the chief jabs a thick finger against the map, tracing it along the coastline heading north. "There's thirty kilometres of track, here. Even if we take one end each, we'll be here all fucking night."

My eyes slide across the map looking for anything familiar. There's something in those green lines, a detail I'm snagging on. A number. *One-forty-seven.* One-forty-seven Mataikona Road. I've heard that somewhere. I close my eyes and let my thoughts drift to the basement shelves, the weight of the files so real inside my hands, a musty smell in my nose. There. Third row, up top where the frame meets the ceiling, by the spiderweb I never have the heart to clear away.

"Tommy Beetham." I point to a spot tucked on the shoreline, just past the edge of the pine plantation. "One-forty-seven Mataikona Road. You remember, last year? All those letters from that guy about reviewing the speed limit out here, the stuff about his goat getting knocked over? He wrote to the council and all."

"His goat?" The chief frowns and looks at Dion.

"He sent in a list of cars, handwritten." I can see it now: the blue ink etched deep into the page, the shaky columns suggesting a mind with too little to do. "Make and model, and the time of day they came past. The old guy was keeping a tally from his lounge window."

Hayes turns to the chief. "It's not far. Might as well take a look, see if he's seen anything."

Ambrose looks at his watch. "Quarter past ten." He sighs. "Could try, I suppose. Beetham, was it?"

"Tommy Beetham."

"All right." There's a begrudging glint in his eye. "Let's hope the poor old bastard doesn't mind being woken up."

"I'll drive your cruiser, Dion," says Hayes.

Dion looks to the chief, who shrugs.

"Come on, Lorraine." Hayes gestures to the car, his movements still ginger. Moko's knee to the chest, probably. "Few things you need to hear."

We crunch through the gravel. Hayes slides his jacket off before he gets in the car, his pistol hanging against his thin body. Pulling past us, the chief waits at the road's edge, the red dots of his taillights shining under the first dusty stars. I lower myself into the seat. There's something so ramshackle about Hayes behind the wheel. After Dion's front-row shoulders and giant mitts, the detective looks like a child playing at driving. He even has to scoot the seat all the way forward.

"Some bloody mood he's in." He nods ahead to the chief's car. "I've been on my share of pointless drives, but Christ, what a grump."

Outside, the sign at the intersection glints in the headlights: Mataikona Road. There's a minute's worth of seal before the car dips into the gravel, sliding sideways, and a low curtain of dust lifts behind the chief's car.

"She's on something, your niece." He sighs, leaving room for me to take in the information. "I wasn't sure if you knew."

"That's going to be the least of her bloody worries once we catch up to her, believe me." I take a long breath. "It's Keith. Not the first time he's had her using. Dion picked her up with a bag in her car last year, outside Fresh Price. Just the residue but enough to be charged. I had to plead with the chief to keep it off her sheet."

"Why didn't you tell me?"

There's more hurt in his voice than I expected. "You've heard enough about my family. Anyway, that party, most of her mates would've been on something."

He fixes his eyes on the road. For a while, it's quiet.

"She told us about staying at yours," he says. "Last Christmas, right?"

"Just before."

"It was an overreaction, she said. Just an aunty being protective."

"An overreaction?" A bolt of feeling moves through my head; I see her face at the door again, all the colour dropped out of it, and her hands hardly able to stop from shaking. "He almost killed that boy, you know. And Bradley saw everything."

"I'm just telling you what she said, Lorraine." His eyes shine in the light of the dashboard. "She mentioned you'd been spending a lot of time with your neighbour, too. Plenty of gin in the evenings, she said."

"So?"

He lifts his hands. "I'm not judging. We all need a little companionship."

Companionship. His voice nudges at a second meaning tucked inside the word.

"Jesus, mate." I shake my head. "Not you too."

"What?"

A hiss of frustration escapes my teeth. "Get to a certain age, and you can't make a friend without people nattering."

"I never . . ."

"Patty's a mate, okay? She's just over the fence, and she . . . Look, she's going through a divorce, for fuck's sake. Not that it's anyone's business."

"Lorraine, I'm only . . ."

"Telling me what Sheena said. Sure."

I know what people say. Rubberneck place like Masterton, the neighbours can't help but watch from their verandahs, tallying every Gordon's bottle as it goes in the recycling, rounding every short haircut up into k. d. lang. What was it Sheena said at the party? *I know you're on the gins now, you and that lady.* And all with that shit in her veins, that poxy dust speeding through her body. Christ. If we do find her out here, they'll need to put me in a separate car just for her sake.

"What else, then? You had her in that room long enough for a whole bag of stories. What other yarns did my niece spin?"

He pauses. "Directions, mostly. She was very specific. Told us Keith would be at one of two spots: out the back of Lake Ferry where the tide comes through the washout, or at Tora, at the end of the old station road."

All her panic about Bradley, and she still had the presence of mind to get them far out of the way. It's cunning enough to make me smile. Almost.

"She mentioned your history with Keith, too."

"I told you about that," I say. "We had a few words, that's all."

The detective gives me a long stare. "Sounded to me like more than that, Lorraine. Sheena mentioned you'd been trying to get her to petition for sole custody. Coaching her, she said."

"Coaching her?" My hands clench tighter. "She told you that?"

He nods. "Chances are she's told Keith, too."

Up ahead, the chief slows down. At the edge of the gravel, there's a water tank with a hole cut for a door; inside, a pair of green eyes float like jewels. A goat.

"One-forty-seven." Hayes nods to the mailbox and stops

at the road's edge, cutting the engine. The chief pulls in through the gate, heading up a driveway to a flaking cottage. A porch light comes on.

"He lied in the court proceedings," I say. "Told the judge he'd been paying Sheena's rent, buying Bradley's clothes, all that shit. She was too scared to say anything, so I held my tongue. Six months later she shows up at my door looking like she's seen a murder. And she nearly had, you know. She could've gone for sole custody but she wouldn't listen. And now, Jesus. Now look where we are."

Hayes nods. "She only told us so we'd keep you out of the loop." He lifts a hand to the dash. "It was my mistake, Lorraine. I should've seen it."

Outside, the cottage door cracks open, and a broad old guy in dungarees appears. Seeing the uniforms, his face splits into a wide smile; Dion and the chief are all but manhandled inside. The light goes out, and the road is thrown into shadow again. Hayes's stomach lets out a low churn.

"The glovebox," I say. "Might be a bar or two left."

As he's reaching in, there's a tiny glimmer of yellow at the next corner. I lean back into the seat.

"You all right, Lorraine?"

I rub a hand against my cheek. "Everything I've done for Sheena, and she picks him. Every time."

He takes a bite, chewing deliberately. "Most love is about fear, you know."

"What?"

"Fear," he says. The engine ticks as it cools. "Of being alone. Of other people, sometimes. Or both."

"I don't have time for any of that philosophical shit, mate. Bradley's still out there." I nod to the cottage. "What if this guy's got nothing for us? What if he's just some crank who wants an audience?"

"Then we'll drive until we find something."

The light reappears, brighter now. Someone's driving at a fair clip; no wonder this Beetham guy's been writing letters. The headlights come close enough to shine over us, before they waver, dipping like a toppled lamp.

"What's going on?" I stare out through the windscreen.

"They're turning."

Hayes clicks the headlights on, and I see the back of a boxy old Commodore raising a thick plume of gravel dust.

"That's an eighty-six," says Hayes. "Same as Moko's, right?"

Before I can say anything, he's gunning the engine. Up ahead, the Commodore rolls into the centre of the track, tearing off into the next corner.

"Get on the radio," says Hayes. "Tell the others."

We lurch ahead, hurtling down the dusty channel after the taillights, the ocean running alongside us in a thick dark shoulder. Over the engine I can hear the crash of the waves.

IT'S NOT A stretch of road I know that well. For a kilometre or so past the Beetham place the track is straight enough, before it turns into a tangled mess of corners. Hayes keeps the car in sight for a while but after a couple of tight turns we lose it. There's only the shroud of dust hanging through the air.

"These fucking roads."

Every corner sends us lurching sideways, the stones bulleting against the bottom of the car.

"You saw him, right? It was Moko?"

"The car was the same, for sure," I say. "No reason anyone else would take off like that, right?"

"I'd bloody well hope not," says Hayes. "I don't want to write this thing off chasing some other fucker."

We enter a long straight stretch. There's a quick blink of red in the distance, before it flares and disappears.

"There." My stomach is in my throat with all the slamming around; I can taste the sweet mush of the muesli bar. "Go!"

Hayes tries to stay at the centre, but with all the clefts carved into the road by the logging trucks it's tricky. At the end of the stretch he tucks into a tight left-hander and we come past a turnoff scarred with traffic. There's a rocky outcrop like a loaf of bread dropped into the ocean; our headlights pick up a row of white buoys bobbing in the dark, just past the waves. The cray pots. A brief glow of satisfaction moves through my stomach, the warmth of intuition borne out. It doesn't last. We've lost the Commodore.

"Fuck." Hayes knocks his hand against the wheel.

"Keep going," I say. "He could've just turned his headlights off."

"On this road?"

"Seems to know it, the way he was driving."

We drive on, and I lower the window, staring up into the tall screen of pines. There are a few turnoffs with mailboxes, and a makeshift bus shelter for the farmers' kids. There used to be a school out here but it closed a few years back; now they bus everyone into town.

On and on through the twisting corners, our headlights search ahead for any sign of the Commodore. The gravel dust settles in my nose; there's nothing but the silvery grey track heading north, the pines covering the hills on our left, the open air of the ocean on our right. If I squint in the rear-view mirror I can make out the buttery gleam of the lighthouse at Castlepoint spinning its sleepy arc. That was always one of

Frank's favourite things, whenever we stayed out here. Soon as the tent was up, we'd go for a walk along the beach in the dark, up to the lighthouse with a flask of something strong. The rocky perch overlooking the bay, the sturdy finger of the lighthouse behind us, and Frank's big hands moving over me.

Another time. Another place entirely.

There. It's gone, but I've seen it. High above the road, a shard of white light cutting through the trees.

"Stop." I grab Hayes by the arm. "Stop the car."

"What?"

"Stop!"

He pulls to the verge and looks where I'm looking. "What is it?"

"Shut off the engine. Lights too."

With the headlights off, there's only the moon's pale glow over the pines. They're so tall and thick, it's like staring into a wall. I get out of the car, my feet slipping on the gravel. It's quiet now; the waves whisper at our backs, and a timid wind calls through the branches.

"There!" Hayes points high. At the far end of the crest, another quick flare of headlights glimmers through the trunks.

"Jesus." I shake my head. "Where's he going?"

Hayes leans back into the car. "Must be an old forestry track."

He reverses up to a wide spot, his hands clumsy against the wheel. The radio crackles; it's Ambrose. I lift the handpiece.

"He's gone up into the trees," I say. "We're checking now."

"The forestry track?" Ambrose comes through in a crackle. "Fuck me dead."

Hayes turns the car around, and we scan each turnoff for any marks in the gravel. It's hard to make anything out. Then, on the third gateway, Hayes slams on the brakes.

"You see that?" He angles the car between the posts. The gradient is steeper here; my stomach twists just to look at it. Through the entranceway there's a scrape in the gravel, a tiny scar in the road's surface. Hayes reaches into the console between us and brings out Dion's flashlight. We get out and step through the gateposts, careful not to disturb anything. The mark is more distinct now, the dust pale and sandy inside the stones.

"How'd you see that from the road?"

The detective looks up at the track climbing the hill, his eyes wide and dark. I can tell what he's thinking. The snaking path, the steep ascent; it's not going to be a fun time.

"We could wait to switch with Dion?"

He gives me a stern look. "We don't know where these old tracks come out. We'll lose him if we wait too long."

Back in the car, Hayes spins the wheels in the gravel, leaving a clear mark for the chief.

"You'd better belt up." There's a tremble in his voice now.

He points us up the track and starts the climb, keeping to the centre. The car feels a lot larger all of a sudden, like some lumbering animal in a too-small enclosure. We move higher, sliding left then right, the track narrowing then opening again. There are more scratches in the gravel here: it's clear we're following him. At the crest of another steep stretch, the radio crackles.

"You mad bastard," says the chief. "You know that's an old bulldozer track, right?"

"Tell them there's no other way," says Hayes. "They need to wait at the road to make sure he doesn't shoot out again and take off."

I do as I'm told. Past the edge of the track, there's only a void, the dark space opening up beyond the cracked lip of earth. I breathe deep, watching as we climb. My eyes slide towards Hayes, his hands chalk-white against the wheel. "You're doing great, Justin."

We climb higher, and then, without warning, the road flattens out. "Shit." He nods ahead. "Look."

In twenty yards or so, the track broadens into a fork, one path heading to a higher ridge on the right, and the left running flat alongside a row of scaly trunks. Hayes stops the car and gets out to take a look, shaking his head.

"We'll have to put a car on each path." He swings the door closed and clicks the radio over. "You have any of these tracks on that map?"

"Not really," says the chief. "The marks stop about a hundred yards in."

Hayes curses to himself. "We're at a fork, heading right. If you can, come up and stick to the left. Stay on the channel, and if you find anything . . ."

"Got it," says Ambrose.

Hayes takes a long breath and shifts into gear. He's shaking now: the fork on the right is even steeper, a labyrinth stretching up and away.

"You're sure it's wide enough?"

"It'll do."

We cut to the right and climb higher. There are trunks on both sides, hemming us tighter and tighter. If I reached through the window I'd lose a finger.

"This can't be it," I say. "He must've gone left."

"Could you stay out of my fucking ear for a second?"

All I hear is the engine's steady hum, and the sound of my heart inside my skull. We push between a pair of wide trunks; my eye catches the brief flash of metal from a rusted fence. It runs alongside us for a second before we turn into a tight corner.

"Jesus!"

Hayes slams on the brakes midway through the turn and we slide to a stop on a steep angle. Our headlights shine up over the back of the Commodore, its windows caked with dust. It's parked between two posts, blocking an old gateway. Our wheels roll back, before the handbrake locks in tight, holding us to the edge of the track.

Hayes reaches for the pistol at his hip. Something is moving inside the car.

FOR A MOMENT, everything stops. I feel the weight and size of the forest around me: the narrow dirt track hard with summer, the pines watching like sentinels through the dark. It's as quiet as the surface of the moon, before a long horn blast from the Commodore splits the night. There's a second, then a third. When the sound stops, it leaves a hole torn in the air.

"What the hell's he doing?"

"It's a warning," says Hayes. "For the others."

I look past the car. The track bends around a corner thick with dried pine needles. Hayes steps out, pistol in hand.

"Out! Slowly!" His hands are still shaking but his voice holds firm. I check the handbrake, yanking the steering wheel to the side before I get out. On that slope it's hard enough just getting the door open.

"Stay inside, Lorraine."

He moves ahead to the driver's side of the Commodore and waits. It's hard to see his face from where I'm standing.

The door cracks open.

"Slowly," says Hayes.

A figure stands, illuminated by the headlights: Moko. I can see the low boil of malice in his eyes. The keys clink in his hand.

"A fella can't take a drive?"

"On your knees," says Hayes.

Moko turns and looks at me. Something in his expression tells me Sheena is close.

"Where is she?" I move forward. "Where's Sheena?"

He doesn't speak. Instead, he reaches an arm back and tosses his keys over Hayes's head, the tinkling silver tumbling down into the void at the edge of the track. It's enough of a drop that we don't hear them hit the ground.

"What did you . . . ?" Hayes looks to the Commodore jammed tight between the two gateposts. No getting past that. "Your knees! *Now!*"

He raises the pistol and moves closer. A shiver goes through Moko's jaw before he lowers himself to the ground.

"Get the flashlight."

I reach inside the car for the stubby metal shape and shine it over them.

"Where are they, Moko?" I'm out of breath just from walking. "Where's Bradley?"

He holds my gaze as Hayes clicks the handcuffs closed, his expression like the unbroken surface of a lake.

"Get the door," says Hayes.

"You arresting me, then?"

"Stand up." Hayes motions him forward. "Nice and slow."

Step by step, he moves the big guy to the patrol car and folds him down into the back seat. With the door locked, Hayes holsters his pistol.

"What do you think?" He's breathing hard.

"Me?"

He looks ahead to the Commodore. "We could try forcing the key column, maybe. These old cars, sometimes all you need is a screwdriver."

He glances down the side of the bank. The fence runs steeply down, the posts broken and leaning. "Did you see where he threw them?"

I look through the gateway. "She's up there, Justin."

"We don't know that." He sighs and steps to the edge of the track. "Pass me the light."

"There's no way," I say. "The keys could be right down the bottom of the bank."

He points to the gateway, his eyebrows furrowed. "We're not getting through there without moving that fucking car, are we? Jesus, we'll never be able to reverse down now anyway, even with Dion driving."

"All right, all right." I hand the flashlight over.

"Radio the others to let them know where we are, then sit tight." He nods to the Commodore. "I don't suppose you could drive that, could you?"

"You're joking, right?" My guts clench into a tight ball.

"I haven't driven in years. Maybe on the flats but not up here."

He sets his hands to his hips. "Just have to wait for the others, then."

"What if someone comes down?" I stare up into the dark. "What if they've heard us, and they're already on their way? If Sheena's up there, she could be . . ."

"Just wait in the bloody car, Lorraine. Lock the doors and don't talk to him."

He clambers down the bank with the flashlight, placing his heron footsteps between the tree roots. With my heart racing, I turn on my heels. There's a low murmur coming from somewhere; I realise the patrol car's still running. I slide in and cut the engine, feeling Moko's eyes on me through the partition. There's more static on the radio this far up. Eventually the chief seems to understand what I'm saying.

"All right," he says. "We'll park at the fork and walk up. No sense in getting both cars stuck."

"Hurry," I say. "Bradley could be up there."

"I heard you the first time, Lorraine."

The line clicks off. I turn around in the seat.

"You brought Sheena up here, didn't you?" My voice is shaking. "She's with Keith, right? You can tell me. You have to."

He doesn't react; just like before, his face is empty. There's a new weight inside my stomach, something dense and heavy.

"At least tell me if he's got our boy." My eyes are wet. "Is that it? Is Bradley up there, up in those trees?"

I stare back at him, the thick glass between us to keep us in our places. His jaw is clenched tight; I can see it's useless. I turn back and look ahead through the glare of the headlights, seeing the road curve away into the dark. When I close my eyes, Bradley's hands are there again, set one over the other, waiting patiently for someone to come. It's been a whole day now. He could be anywhere.

I take a long breath and push the door open.

"You wanna think this through, now." Moko's voice is quiet but strong. "Someone like you, a place like this. Safer to wait for your mates."

"Why?" The silence stretches out between us. "What's up there?" I stare back at him but he doesn't respond.

There's no time.

Outside, the night is warmer than before. I look to the boot of the patrol car. There's a rifle in there, in a gun safe I don't have the code for. And anyway, I haven't touched a rifle since Frank. It'd be a glorified walking stick in my hands.

At the road's edge, I look down and see the arc of Hayes's flashlight far below, moving methodically between the trees. Ahead, past the jammed gateway, the path. With a foot to the middle wire of the fencepost, I lift myself up and over, wheezing with the effort. The rusted steel crunches under my feet but it holds, and I'm on the other side. The path isn't quite so steep here but it's still enough to wind me. I walk on, gulping air. The headlights throw my shadow up against the trees, a trembling outline mixing against the larger dark.

~

I've worked in a basement long enough to know all the forms and shades of silence. There's the silence of an empty room, the kind that takes on the weight and colour of the objects in it: furniture, carpet, books. Then there's underwater silence. Bath or ocean, it's the same: the pressure in your ears, the blood's steady chatter, the muffled drumming of the heart.

This is a new silence for me. The silence of an earth track in the early morning hours, my feet carrying me higher through the pines and the thin silver light filtering through thick branches. It's like the forest is sucking the sound out of me; my breath barely wheezes from my lips before the furred green needles steal it away. I press ahead, one foot then the other, thinking only of Bradley, and of Sheena. Eventually the gateway and Hayes, Moko held captive inside the patrol car, even my own body: everything turns into a loose constellation of ideas. All I feel is my feet against the track, and the boxy shape of my phone in my pocket.

On and on. The corners take me left, then a second left, not so tight, and a long lazy right like a sickle. The track stays the same: narrow, with a dry cover of needles, and occasional dips and scars from the logging rigs. Then, around another corner, a shadow moves between the trunks. I stand in place, all breath locked inside me.

"I'd say that's far enough." A man's voice, not Keith's. With the flinty crackle of a lighter, he brings a flame to his mouth.

"It's Les, right?"

He stares back at me. "Take a second, catch your breath. Gonna have a little talking to do, up there."

"Up where?" I look past him. "Where are we going?"

He takes a long drag on the joint, sending an orange glow across his face. His eyes are hard.

"How many are there?"

"What?"

He nods past me, back down the track. It's only then I notice the stubby metal shape at his side. A sawn-off shotgun pointed at the ground.

"The cops, Aunty." It's strange, him calling me that. Except for the moment with Keith, we've never spoken. "How many?"

"It's just me," I say. "I came alone. I just . . . I need to find my niece."

The quick scrape of a foot and a white light bursts across the side of my face, the slap spinning me to the ground. He moves closer, and I lift my hands.

"Three." My voice is choked and small. "Three others."

He pauses, nodding for me to follow.

"Where's Bradley?" My ear is ringing. "Is he okay?"

He doesn't answer. I manage to stay just behind him, my nose full of his stale sweat. We come to the end of a long straight stretch, climbing higher, before the road evens out. Up ahead, there's a slope running steadily downhill, and a parked ute facing away. It's Keith's. Past the bonnet is the shape of a wooden shack; in the dark I can only just make out its edges. There's a new smell hanging through the air now: the oily smell of a lamp burning, and something else, acrid and heavy.

A thin slice of yellow shines through the dark, and there's the creak of a door opening. A voice sounds out. Keith.

"Three down below," says Les. "Not counting Aunty here."

"Fuck." Keith spits. "What are they driving?"

I look past them to the shack. "Sheena! Bradley!"

A large hand grips my neck, squeezing me silent. The chemical scent is stronger now, like old vinegar.

"I don't want to have to do anything to you, Aunty. But I will." Keith keeps his voice low. "Now, what are you lot driving? A truck?"

His fingers relax enough for me to speak. "Two cars," I say. "Patrol cars."

Keith turns to Les. He's jittery, and he's breathing hard. "Take the truck," he says. "Head out the back. The fellas'll be at the usual spot."

"Righto." Les drops the roach to the ground and stubs it out.

Keith gestures at the shotgun. "Leave that."

"What about later?"

"There's my twenty-two under the seat," says Keith. "Stuff's in the back."

Les clucks his tongue and steps to the truck. There's the descending click of the handbrake coming off, then the metal shape rolls silently away past the shack and down the incline. At the end of the stretch, the lights come on and there's the faint warble of the engine. I try to reckon the space between us and the gateway; we're too far up for Hayes to hear anything.

"Not your smartest move, coming up here." Keith sighs long and hard, nodding at my cheek. "Sorry Les had to do that. There's some water inside."

A sob escapes my mouth. "Where is she? Where's Sheena?" I try to look him in the face. "And Bradley, he's . . . if you've got him, you need to . . ."

He puts a finger to his lips, then nudges me through the dark, his fingertips guiding my shoulder. The door cracks open again, and we step inside. After so much time in pitch black, the lamplight is almost blinding. There's a long table at the far end of the room holding a bunch of streaky glassware, some scales, and a row of plastic bins with powders scattered about. They must've finished a cook not long ago; there's pepper in my eyes.

"Aunty?"

Behind me, in the corner, Sheena sits against the floor, back to the wall, wisps of hair stuck across her forehead. Her arms are drawn tight over her stomach. I look around her, checking the corners of the room, then stare down at her through the lamplight. Her eyes are wide, their pupils like tunnel mouths. She looks about as lost as I feel.

"He's not here." She chokes the words out. "I told you. He's gone."

HER HANDS MOVE unsteadily at her sides, clearing a spot on the floor for me. There's a chatter in her teeth.

"What the fuck are you playing at, girl?"

I cross the space to her, an arm raised and ready for her cheek. Then, closer, I stop. There's no focus when she looks at me; her eyes are rolling marbles. I hold her in my gaze, and the boil in my head recedes.

"Jesus, Sheena." I crouch closer to her, my bad hip yelling at me. Her hair is all across her face, a lank curtain of black, and when I put an arm around her, her skin is hot. Angry blotches at the backs of her hands—she's been pinching.

"What have you done?"

A vacant look, then something sparks in her. "You're bleeding, Aunty."

Keith stamps across the room and bends down to check me.

In the shack's single light, his shoulders are enough to cover both of us in shadow. "Looks okay to me. A scratch, that's all." He frowns. "Still. Les should've known better. That's on me."

The whole room seems to sway. These shifts are too much: one second, Keith's issuing veiled threats at the kerbside; the next, he's apologising for his mate overstepping.

"Never mind that." I feel Sheena trembling under my hand. "Do you have any idea of the state you two are in?" I point through the closed door. "You've got half the fucking station out there traipsing up and down the coast. They've wasted the whole day, and for what? Just so you could come up and finish a cook?"

Keith moves to the table, heavy-footed, his eyes fixed on the door. Breathing low, he reaches next to the shotgun, and his hands bring up a short stub of silver. There's the crinkle of a plastic bag and a lighter snap; a messy helmet of white smoke drifts around his head. No pretence of hiding the habit now—what would be the point? His eyes get the same glassy sheen as my niece's, and his features seem to tremble. His free hand rests next to the shotgun.

"He can help us, Aunty," Sheena whispers, clutching at my hand. "He knows things. He's got some ideas on how we can find Bradley. The others too, Hēmi and that girl." Her eyes dart to Keith, then back to me. "We could start tomorrow, he said. There's just a job they need to finish up first. A job in town."

"Help us?" My voice is rising; I can't help it. "Sheena, you convinced the station Keith was the one who took Bradley in the first place! They've got it in their heads that this is all wrapped up with whatever's been going on up the coast. The trade and all, the turf wars. It's . . ."

"Shush, now." Keith lifts a hand from the table. "Any louder and those mates of yours are going to hear." He stands up, blocking the lamplight again. "Maybe that's the idea, eh?"

"It's fine, love." Sheena beckons him closer, taking his hand between hers. "She's just come out to help, that's all. She's worried about our boy . . . the others too . . ." Some more of the niece I recognise comes into her. "You know how close she is with Bradley."

Keith's expression cracks and softens; his eyes are bright with feeling. He brushes a hand over Sheena's cheek, his knuckles resting against her temple. Those hands. Forcing a ten-dollar note on the kid in the roast shop; delivering a hiding to make sure Jason Larkin clammed up. And now here—affection. You can find it in the strangest places. I picture Sheena's face in my doorway at Christmas, so shaken up by what these hands had done. Maybe Hayes was right about love and fear.

"They think you've got Bradley." I lift my head to him, keeping my voice steady. "And maybe Precious and Hēmi too. If you can just tell them what you know, we can get it all straight." He doesn't even look at me. "The detective, Hayes. He's a good guy. He can help."

"It's too late for that." He stays where he is, his fingers brushing over Sheena. "They'll have this place soon enough. That'll be time inside."

"That's . . . it's not important right now. We have to find

Bradley. He's out there who knows bloody where." An eel in the rain. A plastic bag full of thrashing shapes. "He needs us."

"It's so easy for you." Keith shakes his head.

He reaches up to the lamp and twists it off, sending the contents of the room, the dirty glassware and the chemical bins, the rickety table and the dirt floor into black. There's the scrape of a heavy object against the table. The shotgun.

I bend my lips closer to Sheena's ear, smelling the day on her. "They're coming up the track," I whisper. "We have to go."

There's a rustle as the curtain parts; the moonlight holds Keith's face staring out.

"I'm staying." Sheena's words are running together. "We're going to find Bradley. The others too. Keith and Les, they have some ideas about where they could be. They've been . . ."

A sharp hiss cuts across the room. He means it now; the sound is warning enough. I lean as close to Sheena as I can, my lips up against her ear, and in the dark it's like she's a baby again. A tiny, mewling thing reaching out of her bassinet with grasping fingers, Debs and Billy looking on with that slack, tired expression of those first months with her, the faint smell of talc and milky shit in the room, and all the years stretched out and waiting ahead, unconsidered, taken for granted. I keep my hands steady against her, just like I did then.

"Listen to me now, girl." I grip her arm. "We have to go."

"Come on, Aunty." Keith is at my side, his hand covering my whole shoulder. I feel the shotgun brush against me. "I need you out there with me."

"Please," I say. "Just stop for a second. Think this through. For Bradley."

"It's okay." In the dark, Sheena's voice is strangely calm. "It's all going to be fine. You'll see."

Keith knocks the door open with his knee, his hand tight around my arm as I follow. Outside, there's enough light to see the outline of things. We move across the path to the cover of the pines, and Keith watches the track, waiting.

"Quiet, now." The shotgun knocks my leg, the stubby barrel tapping at my knee. His breath is hot against my face.

"It's not you, Keith." My heart is in my mouth. "They're only looking for Bradley. That's all."

"You brought them up here." His voice is low but firm. "You think they're just going to leave me be? With all this, eh?"

"I can talk to them."

"You can't do a fuckin' thing."

Far below us, there's a flickering shard of yellow where I think the edge of the track must be. Keith's seen it too; he pulls us tight against the nearest trunk, leaning around for a clearer view. I don't know where the gun is, or where it's pointing. Blood is rushing in my head, filling my ears with a watery tremble. High above, the branches shift in the breeze, playing through the stars.

The flashlight creeps higher, moving ever closer to us, sweeping the track from side to side. It looks like Hayes is on his own, still. He must have seen the scrapes in the pine needles by now; I was careful to drag my feet.

Keith watches, as still as hunted quarry, and I watch him.

Then, for just a moment, his grip relaxes. I feel around in my pocket, and my fingers find the edges of my phone, bringing it carefully into my palm. I slide my thumb over the side button, turning the screen on. Reaching up around the tree trunk's far side, I lift my hand for the glimmer to be seen, twisting it from side to side with my breath stoppered in my lungs. Keith's distracted; so far, he doesn't seem to have noticed what I'm doing.

There's a long moment, a silence between breaths. Then the flashlight holds still and the beam clicks off and on again. I'm seen.

The phone slides back into my pocket as a voice sounds out. "Lorraine?" It's Hayes.

Keith breathes in, his stout body filling with intention. He steps out from behind the trunk, his hand tighter against me now, pulling me with him. We move into a finger of moon-light; I see him point downhill, his long arm made longer by the shotgun.

"He's got a gun!"

My words send the flashlight scrambling to the edge of the track. Keith pivots beside me, and his hand slides to my face, squeezes my cheeks. "No more from you now, Aunty." His voice is cold. "No more."

I try to duck back out of his grip but his fingers are too strong. My teeth are being pushed together; I taste blood in my mouth. He's moving differently now, all his strength unmoored and waiting to be used. I try to look to the shack, to Sheena, but I can't move.

"Stay there!" Keith calls down the hill, full of roast-shop swagger. The flashlight wavers for a moment, then moves slowly to the centre of the track. "You fuckin' deaf or something?"

"It's okay, Keith." Hayes holds his voice nice and even. "I'm just standing here, all right? I'm not moving." He lifts the flashlight until the beam is on us.

"Get that light off," Keith barks. The detective shines it down towards our feet. I can see the outline of his face now, his eyes wide. In his outstretched hand is his pistol, a fistful of black metal cradled in the warm air.

"My name's Justin." He's practised in this. "I'm one of the guys out here trying to find that boy of yours. We've had quite the day, you know that?" He takes a step forward, his feet moving quietly over the carpet of needles.

"Don't come any bloody closer, mate." Keith grips the shot-gun tighter in his hand. "I don't want to have to do anything."

"All right," says Hayes. "We're all okay now. You're okay, and Lorraine's okay." I'd laugh if I could. Not for you to say, pal. "I'm just out here looking for Bradley. That's all. That's why we're here. Whatever else is going on, that's not my concern."

"It *is* your concern," Keith growls. "It always is. Your lot can't help yourselves."

Hayes pauses for a long moment. His eyes seem to be searching me out. "Look, I don't know what else has been going on with you and the chief, or any of the others. But it's not why I'm here. I can promise you that."

Keith stays where he is, still staring down the incline. A breeze shifts the branches, letting more of the moonlight through. There's something new in his expression. Hesitation, maybe.

"How about you put the gun down?" Hayes nods upwards. "Set it down just there, and we can have a chat."

"I don't know anything about it," says Keith. There's a tremble in his voice. "I only saw my boy at the party, that's all. We had a feed, a cake and that." He takes a breath, and the shotgun wavers in the air. "Now you're saying it's something to do with the Mongrels going after people's families for the trade?" He shakes his head, speaking through clenched teeth. "It's fucked."

"I know it is, Keith." Hayes takes another step forward. "It's not the idea I have in mind, anyway. I've spoken to the families, the Larkins and the Kīngis. I don't think it's bugger all to do with the gangs." Another step. "But I can't prove that to the others without some help from you."

He's close enough for me to see his eyes in the lamplight.

"I didn't even know he was gone until Sheen came up." There's a wavering in Keith's voice now, a door cracking open half an inch. Panic. You don't get to lead a chapter without keeping these kinds of emotions in control with the cops, but the mask's starting to slip now. It's Bradley, maybe. A missing child will rattle anyone's cage. "And now, it's all just . . ."

"It's okay." Hayes takes another step up the incline. He's close enough for me to know he can read my face. "We're all nice and relaxed."

The big man keeps the shotgun pointed at the earth. "Stay there."

"I'm not moving. I'm right here." The flashlight stays on us. "I reckon I'll put my gun away now. All right?"

Over my shoulder, there's a wooden creak. Hayes looks sideways; I feel Keith tense up, his fingers tightening around me.

"It's Sheena!" I try to yell through his clenched fingers. "It's just Sheena!"

The flashlight moves to the side, then back to us. Keith has the barrel higher again.

"How are you doing over there, Sheena?" Hayes calls out in a friendly shout. "We've had quite the afternoon out here, you know."

"You don't talk to her," says Keith.

"It's okay, love." Sheena's voice is cracked and torn, a length of wire sagging around the post. "They're just here to help. They . . ."

"Shut up! Everyone shut up!" Keith's fingers slide from my mouth to my neck. "You stay right where you are, Aunty. Sheen, start walking. Follow that track and don't stop. We'll come up behind you."

"I can't see anything, baby." Sheena sniffs, rubbing a hand across her nose. A whimper comes from her, something animal and confused. "It's too dark. I could fall, and . . . Bradley, he's still out there, somewhere. He's only got his Batman T-shirt. He loves that shirt, you know. But it might not be enough for him."

"Go!" Keith swings the shotgun across his body, the dark circle of the barrel staring up at me. "Go, for fuck's sake!"

In his distraction, he looks to Sheena, and the barrel wavers.

Past his shoulder, I catch Hayes's eye. In a single swift movement, the detective reaches forward into the yellow light of the beam and gestures downwards with a flattened palm, his eyes hard, the pistol still pointed forward. The meaning is clear. I close my eyes and drop my weight and Keith's fingers pinch tight in surprise before I slip from his grip. He makes a sound somewhere between confusion and disbelief. The shotgun barrel swings back to me and there's a blinding flash, a hundred sunrises flaring all at once. The world tears apart next to my ear.

As I'm falling, a single image flits through my vision. It's Patty, the afternoon sun slanted across her face in my lounge, Frank's old chair comfortable holding her, and her eyes keeping me in their warm bath. She's there with me, to talk, and to listen—and she'll have plenty to say about all this, I'm sure. We'll have a fair whack of talking to do.

Then I hit the ground. A second shot, a faint sibling to the first roar, then a third and a fourth and something heavy falls across my legs. Screaming. Is it me? No, Sheena. She's always had a good set of lungs, even in those first months in her bassinet. Debs used to worry about the neighbours but Billy only smiled and shrugged. A pēpi will cry, he said. I turn my neck to try and find her, my most darling niece, but I can't see her. I can't see anything.

LATER, THERE WERE things I remembered.

A spotlight moving through the trees as a bright white sword; the air being chopped apart. My head underwater, somehow. I couldn't tell if it was the noise from the shotgun or something else. The faces in the flickering light were mostly mute. Hayes, eyes wide and serious, rolling the heavy wet thing off me and roaming my body with his hands, and then later the chief, out of breath and sweating, looking down with the first creeping tendrils of sympathy I'd seen since everything with Frank in the munitions room, back when he had hair.

Is this what it takes? I wanted to ask. All this drama, just to get a little care and attention from station management?

Keith was sprawled on the ground by my knees, his eyes staring unblinking into the shifting canopy of branches. The lights showed dark patches on his chest, a wide wetness coming through his singlet and into his jacket. Every time I tried to move, different hands would hold me in place. I could hear Sheena crying, her breaths long and ragged. They wouldn't let me touch her.

Time moved strangely, then, one thing after another in a slow march, everything muffled and distant. It felt like something that was happening to someone else, something I'd read about in the paper and wanted to talk to Patty about. When they had me on the stretcher and up to the helicopter on the ridge, the feeling in my head started to come back. My hip was crying out, and I didn't know where Sheena had gone, but I could move my mouth again, at least. I heard Dion puffing hard above me, his big hands lifting my body. I wanted to remind him about what I'd said in the car, to do something nice for that girl of his, because it's always hard with the little ones in that first year when they're all just feeds and grizzles—I saw Billy and Debs go through it all with Sheena. Anyway, it was too noisy to talk.

At the edge of the helicopter, that angry metallic bee perched against the hillside, two men came out with jumpsuits and black microphones hovering in front of their mouths like subtitles. That gave me a fright, they looked so serious. I told them to leave me out, that we could all just walk down to the cars. Surely Hayes, the competent stork-man, the bird detective, had found those keys and moved Moko's Commodore by now.

They put a plastic mask across my face, and a clear sweetness came into my mouth and nose. It was easier after that. One of the helmeted guys slid me further inside the machine. I heard him trying to yell over the whoosh.

"Just her? I thought there was a second?"

"He's gone." Dion's voice, I think.

Gone. Keith Mākara. Disappeared. Bradley Henry.

The door slid closed, and everything lifted in a long, fluid motion, like horses running. The man with the helmet looked me over.

"Where's Sheena?" I tried to speak but the plastic was much too thick. "Where's my niece?"

The man moved his arm against me, letting his hand rest on my shoulder. A capable hand, with a steady set of trained fingers. A small thing for him to do, but a good thing. Maybe it was a gesture he'd used before with other people, other women rescued from other ridges with their own pine trees watching in knowing rows. Years ago they would've been natives, those trees: stocky tōtara and proud rimu. Now there's only row upon row of pine, fattening up for factories over the water.

Through the windows was open space. Whole acres of dark, the faint glimmer of the lighthouse far below, and in the west, pinpricks of light from Masterton. The dear dotted rows of the streets, some taking me to Value Roast or the police station with my files all waiting, and some flooded with eels and stalked by skinny Neptunes with makeshift tridents. My place, my red flaking roof and my cactus glasshouse, and a good friend in Frank's old chair inside with her makeup running and ice chiming in her glass. The Larkin place not far down the road, and the red station wagon turning through the flood with its wipers waving their hunt. That whole watchful kingdom, the lattice of footpaths all listening for feet, waiting to hear what people had in mind for each other, the rumours and the schemes, the plans. The corner dairies with three-for-two bread and Coke on dole day, and the car yards with hopeful colours pimpled across the windscreens. Branches and plastic all twisted and clumped in the Rickett's Circle gutters, and the fat kererū swooshing into high trees. And those precious little bodies so open to the rain, brown and white both, their shouts and shrieks a hosannah in the silver air, the absolute halo of joy holding them, their glee not yet checked by rules and preferences and us-and-them eyes.

Are you okay in there, love? Do you know those two fellas?

It was all still there for me, waiting. Or lying in wait. Home.

We tipped in the air, and my heart swelled up inside.

It rained the whole time we were in the car. My jersey had
wetted the floor so the man said put it in the back. There
were chip packets back there. Ready salted. Mum eats those.
The man saw where I was looking and said do you want
some. Because if you do want some it's no problem. We
pulled over at a dairy somewhere when the streetlights came
back. He left the heater on for me so I could dry out. He
came back holding a newspaper over his head for the rain.
He had two big packets of chips and a vanilla Coke cold
from the fridge and sour worms in a paper bag with a bit of
rain on it. They're for dessert he said. He laughed because
it was silly because that meant the chips were like the
dinner. I laughed a little bit too. He seemed all right. Kellen
and Jake get sour worms from Patel's sometimes but they
never give me any. Not even when I share my juice.

The man played music on the radio. It was something old with scratchy guitars and he tapped his fingers on the steering wheel like Dad does. He said I'm a friend of your dad's. I didn't remember him but Dad knows a lot of people. They're always coming around and staying at night. It makes Manaia cry sometimes because the music is too loud and he wakes up. The man said your dad's asked me to take you to a new place to stay for a bit. Everyone's going to come and meet you there soon. It's a nice place he said. Nice and quiet. You're going to like it there. Some things he said I didn't hear because of the chips crunching. I asked him about school. Mrs. Moore was still going with her list of homework stars and crosses and my project about the volcanoes and the lava. He told me she knew all about it too. He said he'd help me with the volcanoes because he was a volcano expert. He said did you know lava can eat up a whole car even the tyres. I didn't know anything about that but it sounded cool like something in a movie with Dwayne "The Rock" Johnson. After that I could choose my next project all on my own. Whatever you want he said as long as you write a short report.

Later the man said it's going to be a rest. For your mum because she's tired. I didn't know what he meant right away. But then I thought about it. Mum was yelling a bit more maybe and getting more cross with Dad than before. When I stood on some old glass in the milk alley she gave me a smack because my toe was bleeding and some of it got into my sock and my good shoes. It wasn't even my fault but I got a smack and then she got cross when some of Dad's friends came around and put boxes of their beer next to the couch. So I thought maybe that was what the man meant.

We must have drove real far because then the sound under the car changed. It was a rumble like when Dad drives us to the good swimming hole sometimes on hot weekends. The man lifted his hand from the steering wheel whenever another set of headlights came up through the rain. When that happened I could see red bits of skin around his fingernails. He kept putting them into his mouth and between the music I could hear a sort of sucking sound I didn't like. Other than that he was okay. I never had vanilla Coke before.

A girl was here already. It was still raining and I got a bit more wet walking from the garage after the man parked the car in there. She was by herself in the big house with the lights on in just one room but not normal lights. These round glass things. Lamps she said. I didn't see any light switches or nothing. There wasn't even a TV. The girl was reading from a big book. She seemed friendly but maybe it was because the man told her to be friendly. She was taller than me. She made room so I could sit next to her by the fire. The man said you'll dry off in no time at all. He gave the girl the second bag of chips and then she hugged him around the waist. They were both smiling and looking at me like maybe they knew me already. She told me her name was Precious.

By then I was feeling a little bit hungry even with the

chips and the worms. Me and Bradley and Kiri and the others were outside running around for ages after school and Jake took half my sandwich at break. The girl Precious got two bowls down from the counter and put something in them and said be careful cause it's hot. It was a yummy soup. She made it with Mr. P she told me from the vegetables growing outside the house. She said I'll show you in the morning if it's stopped raining.

Later when we were both upstairs in the room together I woke up. There was too much dark and I couldn't see the edges of anything and the blanket on my bed was scratchy just a little bit. She whispered to me and told me not to be scared. I was though. But she was there. She talked to me. After a while it was okay. She said I'll show you the horses in the morning. They love apples and it's good to feed them from your hands but you have to keep your fingers nice and flat or else they might bite you. The apples make their tails swish and then they make happy noises with their noses. She said I'll show you in the morning.

The rain kept falling real hard on the roof. It fell all night. It was loud.

IT'S ANOTHER BOILING day, the day they welcome Keith home, the sky laid out in a bright blue plate from ranges to coast. The marae is usually a quiet place, the wooden buildings serene and waiting, the grassy verge outside the carved gateposts calm under the staring sun. Today the road is a scrum of bikes and station wagons with the odd minivan peering above the fray. A tangi like Keith's, there'll be whānau from all over. Patty had to park the Fiesta way past the carpark.

Over the fence it's all bustle: every kid is being put to work carrying chairs and tables, buckets of potatoes and plastic bags full of cress and silverbeet. The Pāpāwai kitchen will be a madhouse for days yet.

"There's so many of them." Patty takes a sip of her flat white and lifts her eyes to the rear-view mirror, her mouth pulled tight. On the road behind us, the patched guys are gathering in a messy circle, everyone leaning in for hongi and big wrapping embraces. I can see Dion leaning against his patrol car, arms loose, chatting to one of the wardens. No wonder the chief tapped him for tangi duty; Dion has some whānau at Pāpāwai too. He's grinning nice and easy; the locals must be keeping things orderly.

"I don't know, Lorraine."

"What?" Everything is still muffled on one side; I twist in my seat to give her my good ear.

"How do you know they want you there?"

A shiver runs through me. "She's my niece, Patty."

I'm firm because I need to be. Inside, though, a thought sticks out like a burr in a plank of wood, something not yet planed off. Of course Sheena will want to see me; she's going to need me these coming weeks. And yet that night under the trees is still inside me, a quiet panic clouding over everything. I can't imagine how it will be for my niece.

A voice calls out, rising above the noise of the crowd. On the edges of the gathering, heads are turning towards the main road. Keith's hearse must be pulling close.

"Come on." I heave myself out of the car, my knee still shaky under me. Just a concussion, they said at the hospital. A little bruising to the knee and some aggravation in the hip from a month's worth of walking in one night. That's it, though. Nothing a couple of days in a hard bed couldn't fix, Patty at my side with a sneaky flask of gin.

Lucky.

Patty locks the doors, checking the handle and smoothing out her skirt in the window's reflection. Longer than she'd be comfortable in on a hot day, but I told her it'd be ex-pected. "You'll have to leave that."

"Hmm?" She stares down at the coffee cup in her hand. "Why?"

Too tired to explain, I give a quick shake of the head. Eventually she drains the cup and sets it on the bonnet. I take a long breath to calm myself, and we start the walk to the grassy verge outside the gate. There are still more cars pulling up behind us, slamming doors and hushed voices, everyone wanting to be seen before the pōhiri gets properly underway. When Patty takes my arm, I can feel the tension in her, every finger like wire stretched between posts.

There's so many of them.

"It's okay, Pat." My free hand goes to her arm, careful with the pink splotch running up the inside of her wrist. I told her to ask the nurses at the hospital to take a look but she wouldn't hear of it. "Just follow what everyone else is doing, you'll be fine."

We get close enough to merge into the crowd, and the sounds all drop to a whisper. There's only the scraping of boots against the road, and in the background, the burble of tūī in the trees. Far past the crowd, a stock truck bounces through the intersection in a tall blue rectangle of steel, clang-ing like a gun gone off. My hand comes to my chest without me willing it. The pine needles under my back, the moon through the trees, and Keith's weight across my legs. It should never have gone that way. He didn't mean it, any of it. I see his expression under the swaying lamplight in the shack, his hand on Sheena's cheek. The love, and the tiredness, the hunted panic. And something else. Something I couldn't place and still can't.

"You all right, love?" Patty whispers. "Why don't we move to the back?"

"I'm okay here." I ignore the stares from the faces around us.

Inside the courtyard, a kuia in black starts wailing, her long undulating vowels full of breath and sorrow. There are spiders across my back; it was the same at Billy's, I remember. We were here too, at Pāpāwai. Boiling hot weather for a tangi, though nobody thought to complain. The sun shone hard in my face, and I held Sheena's hand in mine. She spent the whole three days being cooed over by endless aunties, the little girl, and discovering a whole new trove of cousins. I wonder if she remembers; she wasn't much older than Bradley at the time. Things were different with Debbie's. We had her in the earth before Billy had even arrived home, our prayers already whispered, a short column in the back of the *Times-Age*. A much smaller affair, her funeral: just close family and a few mates from her year at school. I don't think Dad even told our cousins up north when the service would be; he was still a bit funny about Debs going with Billy, even then. An easier bill for the caterer's too, Debbie's funeral, not that Dad would ever have admitted it. Nothing like those three days for Billy, the songs and the words, the bustle in the kitchens, hands and faces, rows of bright eyes smiling as they cried.

People everywhere. People.

A channel parts inside the crowd, letting us see the open hearse with a double row of guys lifting the coffin, their faces stoic, strong despite the hurt. And inside that wooden vessel, Keith.

A long shake moves through me, as if the road is sliding beneath my feet.

"Lorraine?" Patty grabs me by the arm.

My feet stay under me. Behind the coffin I can make out Sheena, her face covered in wide shades, hair loose at her shoulders. Moko's there with her, his arm on hers, holding her upright as she walks. Seeing her here in the hard light after everything in the trees, everything so open and bright, so unshielded; I want to gather her to me, to take her away somewhere. I recognise the selfishness of the impulse. Then, the local kuia's karanga fades, and a new wailing comes in response from the front of the crowd.

Moko moves forward, exchanging looks with some of the patched guys. I wonder where Les might be. The papers already had the story about one of the chief's other boys picking him up in Keith's ute near Mount Bruce. Just over a kilo wrapped in a tea towel between the back seats and a sawn-off twenty-two calibre under the driver's seat. He's in something of a tight spot, Les. Most likely still being held. Then I see Queenie Larkin, head bowed low, moving forward inside the crowd, her hands hanging empty.

Hēmi. Precious. Where will they be, a boiling day like today?

"What are they doing now?" Patty lifts a hand to her eyes, staring ahead. "They should have someone to explain all this."

The men move with the coffin, carrying Keith from road to gateway, then passing through into the courtyard. There's a yell from inside the crowd, and the men, patched and unpatched, start into a haka, the quiet of the day split with living sound. It's the same every time; I wonder what it would be like to understand what's being said—for this song to breathe with meaning. From the side, Dion sees us, then looks to Moko and back to us. His eyes hold a shard of worry.

"It's so loud," mouths Patty.

There are people staring. The men finish their haka, and the locals take up a new song. Footsteps against the road, tūī in the trees. And in the distance, the low murmur of traffic from the main road like a voice in another room. Through the crowd, I see Moko staring at us. My niece is still tucked into his side; I can't tell if she's seen me or not. He nods to Queenie behind him, and she takes his place propping Sheena up. Then he's walking.

"That's her," someone whispers. "She was there. The forestry."

Voices are rising around us. Patty's fingers grip me tighter. More heads are turning, the crowd around us moving like a single being addressing some found presence. A thorn in a paw, a seed in an eye.

"Lorraine."

I stare ahead, looking for my niece. Then Moko is in front of us, materialised from the rows and rows of shoulders and arms. His eyes are unshielded, and do not blink.

"*Stay in that car*, I said. *Wait for your mates.*" He leans closer, making us crouch. "And now look."

I try to peer past him to see Sheena; he lifts an arm to block me.

Patty moves between us, making herself tall. "Don't you touch her."

Moko's eyes dart to her, then back to me. "This isn't a place for you."

For a moment nobody moves. Moko looms over us, the fact of his body keeping us in place. Keith is nearly home now, his people around him, protecting him, preparing him for what is to come, and readying themselves for what will come without him. It makes me think of Debbie, of the miserly preparations we gave her. An hour next to a pine box, then straight into the ground.

"Who says?" Patty points into his chest. "Who put you in charge, eh?"

"Hey, now." Dion shoves his way to us, hands placating. "We're all fine here."

Moko is close enough that my nose is full of him. It's the smell from the hallway, the night of the party: sweat and tobacco, the faint salt of a close body. There's a sting in my eyes; when I blink, I see Bradley on the floor of the laundry, his face jumping with delight at the kitten in his lap.

"Here." My free hand goes to the envelope in my back pocket. I hold it out between us, the paper bisecting the empty space. "Koha. For today."

He takes the envelope. Then, without shifting his gaze from mine, he lets it fall to the road. Turning back into the crowd, he slips through the watchful faces. The heads around us turn away with him, and the people walk on.

"Are you all right?" asks Dion.

"What the hell are you here for, eh?" Patty points a finger

into his chest. "That thug threatens us to our faces, and you just stand there?"

I watch the people move past us, disinterested, like water around a stone. Sheena. She'll be with the others now. Held.

"It's okay." I hold myself steady. "We're leaving."

"What?" Patty is all fire now, the early hesitation gone. "Lorraine, you wanted to be here. You said you had to be." She turns and points through the archway. "We're going. We're going in there. We have every right."

Dion sets his hands to his hips. He's strangely boyish when he's sympathetic.

"Come on." I turn away, stepping into my own shadow, my feet scuffing against the road.

"What about the envelope?" Patty bends down. "There's fifties in there. One of them is going to . . ."

"Leave it."

She looks to Dion, who gives a tiny shake of his head before turning back to his patrol car. The envelope stays on the road, a tiny finger of white against the tarred surface.

Voices lift through the air, the song carrying out through the heat to our two figures alone on the road.

LOOSE PIECES OF gravel crunch under the Fiesta's wheels as Patty pulls us into the station carpark. It's early enough that it's mostly empty. Around us, the low sun covers the buildings in a shimmering border of glare.

"You sure you're all right, love?" She shoots me a concerned look. "We could wait for someone to help you inside."

"I'll be fine, Pat." I push the door open and heave myself up and out. I'm steadier than yesterday, yet I still need the crutch on one side. "I just need to get back to it, that's all."

She stares out at me while the engine rattles like an old freezer. "I'll swing by the roast shop after my shift." A long pause. "Don't wear yourself out, now."

I wave her away; she'll be late if she's not careful, and the supervisor's on her back already. She reverses into the road then hovers, watching until I reach the door.

It's cooler inside the building. There's that comfortable institutional smell: old paper, and a faint waft of chemical lemon from the night cleaners. They polish the floors every Wednesday. Just knowing that is enough to quiet my heart. Routines. Whatever else is happening, there are still routines. I scan my ID and push through the doors, past the munitions room a few steps quicker, then into the staffroom for coffee. A return to normal is what I need. By now there will be reports to read, and hopefully something new on the kids. It'll help to slow my thoughts to something manageable.

Five days. Five days since Bradley.

"Lorraine?"

"Shit." My hands come to my chest. Dion. "Since when are you here so early?"

"What are you . . ." He looks around him, moving closer and speaking low. "You're, uh, you're back already, eh?"

"Not a lot to do at home, mate." I muster a smile. His eyes linger on the walking stick; the bruise under my eye. "That boy of yours sleeping any better?"

A small grin. "He's okay. I took your advice, actually. About doing something nice, I mean. Asked Mum and Dad to come and stay for a bit. Just a couple of weeks, so Jacqui can get some rest."

"A visit from the in-laws, eh?" I pat him on the arm. "Room for improvement."

"Hmm?"

"Here, would you mind?" I nod behind him. "These bloody stairs."

I hand him my mug, and we hobble down the stairway to the file room. Each step sends a jolt up my side; by the time we make it to my desk I'm out of breath. It's cleaner than I remember; the files have all been tidied away. The Kīngi and Larkin interviews, the photographs of houses and streets, the cars, the faces: it's all gone, leaving the scratched surface with its familiar wooden eddies and whorls.

"Who's been down here?"

"I, uh . . ." Dion looks to the doorway. "I'm not sure if anyone . . ."

"Speak up, now." I lean my good ear to him.

"The shooting and all." He rubs one hand inside the other. "I don't think anyone expected you back so soon."

"It wasn't all that serious, mate. The way everyone's talking you'd think I was the one shot." I sink down into my chair. "Listen. About everything at Pāpāwai."

"It's fine, Lorraine. Couldn't be helped."

"How was Sheena doing?"

"She had people with her the whole time." A soft look comes into his face. "They'll stay with her all the way through, I think. Right up until they bring her home tomorrow."

"All right." I wipe at my eyes. "Ta for that."

"I'll let the chief know you're here." He stands in place, tall under the low basement lights. "He'll want to have a chat, I'd say."

"Righto."

I slide the drawers open, looking for my good pens. Nothing is in its usual spot, and the only working hole punch has been moved. There's a plastic takeaway cup in the bin beside the desk, from the café where the farmers' wives go for biscotti after their haircuts. Tania's been down here; it's no wonder things are all askew. My notepad is still in the bottom drawer, with my early scribbles from when they had Sheena in the room upstairs. That's something.

I boot up the computer and pick up the only folder waiting in the in-tray. It's Dion's write-up of everything on Sunday, with handwritten amendments from Hayes. His tiny compact script takes up the whole margin in places, adding and correcting.

Moko Hepi detained in patrol car while Detective Hayes searched for means to move vehicle blocking passage. Upon return, Lorraine Henry assessed to be absent, likely having ascended the forestry track. Hepi offered no further information. Hayes progressed on foot with pistol drawn.

It stops my breath.

The next page is even harder to read. There's the confrontation with Keith, the shotgun lolling in one hand, his other around my arm.

Hayes attempted to negotiate the release of Lorraine and Sheena Henry. Mākara became hostile and belligerent. After repeated and escalating threats, Mākara discharged shotgun. Hayes discharged three shots, striking the shoulder, chest, and abdomen. Lorraine Henry found unconscious, seemingly from a blow to the head. Sheena Henry in a state of distress. Hayes secured all firearms and tended to Mākara. Some movement before loss of consciousness. Arrival of Chief Ambrose and Sergeant Jones shortly thereafter.

Mākara no longer responsive. Decision made to airlift Lorraine Henry to Masterton Hospital.

Shoulder, chest, and abdomen. A state of distress. No longer responsive.

I see Sheena at the tangi, her eyes downcast, following the coffin. Such an incredible distance between us; the space filled with other people—people closer to her. A shudder rolls through me, filling my eyes with new moisture.

I wipe my fingers across my cheeks and type in my username but it won't log me on. My password. Maybe I changed it before everything with Bradley. Things have been a little scrambled lately. I'm reaching for the phone and trying to remember the number for head office IT when a broad shape fills the doorway.

"Lorraine?" Ambrose squints across the room, framed by the brighter light of the stairs. "What are you doing?"

"Forgot my bloody login."

He moves closer, hand out for the phone. "Here." He sets it in its cradle. "You should have called first."

"It's only been a few days, mate." I gesture to the desk. "Where did Tania put everything? The Larkin files, and everything on the Kīngi girl?"

He leans against the desk and crosses his arms, his body like a sealed envelope.

"Upstairs," he says. "Upstairs would be best."

"What do you mean, administrative leave?" I lean back in my seat; everything seems to be coming at me from the end of a long tunnel, all sounds muffled and strange. "What does that even mean?"

"Call it what you want." Ambrose sets his elbows against the desk, turning himself into a shiny-headed pyramid. "You'll be paid. And when we're done with the restructure, we can see where we stand."

"Restructure?"

He sighs. "It's been on the cards a while now, Lorraine. You know that. Most stations don't even have clerks anymore. The fellas just take care of it themselves." He waves a hand dismissively through the air. "Head office can always send someone over if they need to."

"Hang on." I grip the sides of the chair. "Is this about me recovering, or about migrating to the new system? Because I can always . . ."

"Does it have to be one or the other?" He opens his hands as if appealing to some audience beyond the room. "And anyway, wouldn't some time at home be a good thing, right now? With your niece and all?"

"Don't fucking patronise me." I feel my eyes narrow.

"Listen." He stands and moves around to the chair next to mine, sitting and leaning in close. It's all I can do not to scream. "There's no need for any nastiness. We don't know what the recommendations will be. There's a consultant coming down from Auckland. We'll have their report next month, I'd say. Until then, rest up at home, and we'll let you know."

I look him in the face. "Tania's been down there, hasn't she?"

"She took care of a few things, sure."

"You know she locked herself in the evidence room last year, don't you?" I'm shaking my head. "She had to piss in the bloody wastebasket! And now she's on the files?"

"It's been working out, actually." Ambrose looks to the door; we're probably out of earshot of the front desk. Probably. "She's made some real progress scanning the old files to PDFs."

"You miserable prick." I grip the arms of the chair. "Everything we've been through, and you're just going to toss me out? With my nephew still missing, and Sheena in a state?"

"We don't know what'll happen, Lorraine. There's a chance you'll be back at your desk soon enough. You could always think about taking the early pension, you know." He stands. "Better to hold off playing the Frank card for now, eh?"

"The *what*?"

The edges of everything in the room seem unstable, a loose constellation of shapes that could fly apart at any second. I reach out for my crutch and stand, leaning as close to him as I can bear. His shirt is stretched over his stomach, the buttons working hard to stay anchored, the cotton less crumpled than usual. Ever since Hayes arrived, the chief has been paying a lot more attention to how he comes across.

"You're an empty man." The words spit from my mouth, weighted with the years. Surprising how easy they come. "Why don't you just admit it? Three missing kids and nothing but some half-arsed gang theory to show for yourself. Now

Keith Mākara gets shot, and suddenly it's high time you reviewed the station's administrative situation?"

There's colour rising in his cheeks; his eyes are wide with disbelief. "You put us all at risk!" He points a finger in my face. "Waddling up into the bloody dark, leaving Hayes fumbling around on his own. What did you think was going to happen?"

"Sheena was up there. I had to . . ."

"I've heard enough about your meth-head niece." He hisses through clenched teeth. "If she hadn't sent us on that detour, then that Mākara prick wouldn't have gotten himself shot, and we wouldn't be . . ."

"Wouldn't be what?" I step closer until I'm right beneath his chin, staring into the twin caves of his nostrils. "Completely lost? Be honest for once. You've fucked it."

He takes a deep breath and turns away. "Dion will see you out."

On cue, the door opens, and Dion nods into the hall; I wonder how long he's been out there, and what he's heard. Ambrose leans back down into his desk and pulls open the nearest folder. He's fighting a smirk but the smirk is winning. "You'll get a letter," he says. "About making a submission."

Dion lets the door close, following me down the hall. At the reception desk, Tania watches through the glass, her expression telling me exactly how far our voices carried.

"He, uh . . ." Dion holds the front door open, nervously eyeing my swipe card. "The chief wanted me to ask you to hand that in."

My heart is pulling itself apart. I unclip the card and set it in his palm, squinting out into the sunlight. As I'm turning, I catch a brief twitch of curtains in Hayes's office. I wait for him to call out to me but there's nothing. Even if he's here, I doubt he'll want to see me now. Not after the forestry. My feet carry me slowly down the stairs to the footpath, slower on one side while I place the crutch.

"Wait," says Dion. "Let me give you a ride home at least."

I walk on without looking back. A dusty hatchback swerves around me, beeping. A man's voice calls from the driver's window, ugly and strained. It's all I can do to put one foot ahead of the other. Soon, my feet crunch over the loose gravel marking the edge of the park. A pair of young mums are perched across a nearby bench, thin-rolled smokes burning in their hands, their strollers parked in the shade. I pass right in front of them, face wet and nose running, but they don't even see me. This town's full of limping casualties. At the cricket oval, the groundskeeper is out mowing, carving clean, even lines into the careful green. He sees me watching and gives me a wave, then returns to his work.

I sink onto a bench and slip my shoes off, savouring the scratch of the concrete against my heels. What am I now? If someone stopped to ask me my opinion on the disappearances, some local flavour for the national coverage, how would I be credited? Resident woman? Great-aunt to a missing boy? Ratepayer? When I close my eyes, I see Bradley there again, eyes alight with mischief, his thin body wrapped in that red T-shirt, the Batman logo in a golden splotch on his chest.

I rub at my eyes until everything turns to a white smudge.

Five days. We're nowhere. Especially me.

A magpie skirts from the pavilion into the trees behind the rose bushes. It's nesting, probably. They're mean as anything, those birds, but they're only protecting the most important thing. Can't fault them for that. I take a long breath, held in the hard sunlight, and I let my ears fill with the mower's steady din.

I'VE MADE A basket. Orange and date muffins, a banana loaf, and a big bag of greens cut from the garden. All of Sheena's favourites, set in a nice wicker basket Patty found in a closet at the old Wikaira place. I tried to convince her to come with me but that same strange look came over her. Everything at the marae must still have her feeling spooked, I guess.

There's a breeze coming through the street today, a welcome change. The radio said we might even get some rain. No doubt the farmers will all be watching the sky and waiting. It's been a dry summer besides the eel storm, and the pastures could do with a little life. The knee is easier with this cooler weather. Maybe I'm on the mend. I swing the crutch forward over the cracked pavement, basket balanced against my hip, halfway to Sheena's place. At my side, the wind sets the trees talking.

I don't know where I'd be without Patty. All it took was a call, and she left her shift early to come to the park and pick me up. We were early enough to the roast shop that there was hardly any line. A nice early dinner with Tilly snoozing in my lap, a few gins, and a friendly ear. Nothing better to get things straight in the mind.

Around the corner, there's a figure out front of Sheena's. Shorts and jandals, a green Aertex shirt, leaning against the fence. Queenie Larkin. She looks thinner than I remember; even from where I stand, I can see a new slope in her cheeks, a sharper angle in her jaw. She stares at me, watching me come closer.

Whatever I am, I'm still Aunty Lo.

"Hello."

She says nothing. Each step I take is measured in her gaze. It's the same glare she gave me on her doorstep while Hayes waited in the car. A lifetime ago, before Keith. Before Bradley. Her eyes flicker to the basket.

"A few things for Sheena," I say. "Some greens, mostly."

"That's a laundry basket."

"Hmm?" I stare down at the frayed handle. "What do you mean?"

"It's not . . ." She shakes her head, impatient. "She's got her own patch, you know. Keith sent Hēmi over to ours with a bag just last month." Her eyes bore into mine. "She'll be tending it herself now, I s'pose."

A wave of heat slides down my back, strong despite the day. I set the basket on the fence and find a spot to sit, leaning the crutch where I can get to it. "I don't know what you've heard, or what's been in the papers. But we didn't mean for anything to happen. Not like that."

"They came around, you know." Queenie leans forward and spits onto the footpath. "Your lot, from the station. They waited until Jase was out. Wanted to know if Keith ever had anything to do with our boy. If he'd ever threatened him." Her mouth curls at the edges. "He told me it was safe, the bald guy. He said I could talk now and not have to worry."

"I'm sorry." I shake my head. Even for Ambrose, this is tactless. "I . . . Actually I'm not going to the station at the minute." A pause while the words come. "They put me on leave while everything gets sorted."

At the corner of the street, a grey minivan appears, moving slowly towards us. I recognise it from the tangi.

"Yeah, well." Queenie scratches at the side of her neck. There's a long band of raised skin disappearing down into her shirt. It's even broken in a couple of spots, dotted with tiny red globes. "You tell them to stay the hell away. I don't need them, and neither does my boy. We'll get on just fine without you."

She stands as the van pulls up. I try to do the same but the crutch slips and I lurch forward into her. Her hands grab me, holding me in place. I can feel the jitters in her. And yet she's strong.

"My knee," I say. "Sorry."

She doesn't say anything. Instead, she turns to the van and waits.

Moko steps out of the driver's seat, a cigarette in the corner of his mouth. He's staring, his shaded eyes dispatching the same message from the marae. For a moment I wonder if he'll cross the space and move me off, but he doesn't. Past his shoulder, more people are emerging from the van. I recognise most of them from Bradley's party; the mums gathered in the kitchen while the kids played pass the parcel, their hubbub easing as I came near.

Then there's Sheena. Hair wild at her shoulders, her cheeks puffy from these last days, she's halfway out of the van before she sees me. She stops where she is for a moment before she steps onto the pavement. There are so many hands waiting for her.

"Sheena." I move forward but Queenie steps between us.

"Kāore." Her voice is firm; she holds a hand up flat. "Wait."

A man moves to the front of the group, and the others fall in behind him. His collar is open, showing a thick square of pounamu wound with cord. I try to remember the word. A tohunga. He begins a chant, the words smooth and fluid, a reassuring rhythm to brace us against the thing we are here to mark. There is a structure here, a process. This is nothing new, his voice seems to be saying. Others have borne this before.

At the side of the group, I wait for people to pass, Sheena bundled among bodies holding her close. I could reach out and touch her but I hold back. Moko and I move ahead side by side, the last of the group, walking slowly up the cracked path to the verandah. I can't see his eyes. His hands hang in fists at his sides, telegraphing his mood. We're too far back to hear the karakia, especially with my ear the way it is, but it's there anyway, the cadence mingled with the breeze coming over the long tufts of dry grass. There are eyes on us from over the fence, always watching.

The others slip off their shoes before climbing the steps. I stop in place, one hand against the wobbly banister. There's no way I can reach my laces.

"Here."

Moko bends down to my feet. I start to protest but his fingers are already making quick work of it. He wraps a hand around my ankle and lifts, slides my old runners off and sets them with the others. Before I can say anything, he's helping me up the steps. I can feel the strength inside him, the easy grace.

"I . . ." Words leave me. "Thank you."

He moves inside and down the hallway behind the others, the necessary task completed, the courtesy discharged. The voices all rise together now, cancelling the empty air as they move from room to room.

Keith Mākara. A life noticed.

I lift the crutch up and through the doorway, the old smells greeting me as the karakia reaches my good ear. It's calming, somehow, like a blanket smoothed flat. From the outside the house looked so forlorn. Now, there is sound inside, and movement. People are here in every room, footsteps tracing every corner, and the windows open to the day outside.

What did we do in this house when Debbie and Billy were gone? I remember packing things up in boxes with Mum and

Dad, and Dad muttering under his breath at the state of the weatherboards outside, and what it would take to have them sanded and painted to get the place in a rentable state. What else did we say? How did we notice?

The tohunga moves back through the hallway to the kitchen. As he sees me, he nods over his shoulder to Sheena's room. A small gesture, but unmistakable. I move into the house, the difficult steps past the laundry room—boy and kitten, box pocked with tiny claw holes—and push open Sheena's door. She left it only half-closed. Forgetfulness, maybe, or invitation. She's alone in here, a forlorn shape against the messy bed, the daylight spilling inside as the wind plays through the closed curtains.

"Darling." I move forward a tiny step. "Can I sit? I'm going to sit."

There's no response. She takes a messy breath inwards. I go to her then, leaning down onto the bed and setting my hand on her side. It's something, at least.

"Sheena." A bed can seem so vast with just one person. Whatever I thought of Keith, I know what that's like. "I'm sorry."

These are the smallest words. Voices murmur behind me, and the frame of the house shifts with the weight of bodies. I can only see the edge of her face. How yellow the lamplight in the shed was, and how pale and lost she looked on that stool with those burning smells hung through the air. She takes a breath, and my hand rises with it.

"He wouldn't look at me."

"What's that, my love?" I lean closer on my good side.

"The whole drive back." Her voice is barely audible. "The detective. He wouldn't look at me." A long breath leaves her body. "He knows what he did."

Hayes. The kindness in that face behind the pistol, and the concern. A terrible decision. A hand moving through torch-light, and eyes pleading. Factors weighed, then a sound to end the world, and that weight across my legs.

No longer responsive. Shoulder, chest, and abdomen.

"I'm here, girl." I move my hand over her side. "Just tell me what you need."

A long gust pushes the curtains sideways, letting enough daylight in for me to see her drawers. The Ngaio Marsh book, and the plastic bag. Those little crystals and all they've done. She lies still. A scrap of information plays through my mind, the glint of sunlight against a window.

"What did you mean, up there?" I bring myself closer. "When you said Keith knew things?"

I wait but there's no response. My hand moves up to her shoulder, pressing against her in our old way. Aunty and niece.

"Sheena?"

"I can't." She's whispering to herself. "I can't."

Footsteps sound behind me, louder than the others. The door swings open wider.

"That's enough for today." It's Moko.

"Someone needs to stay with her." I wipe at my eyes. "She shouldn't be alone."

"She isn't, Aunty." He moves up to the bed. "Here, let me help you."

I take the hand offered. "I'll be back, my love. I'll be here."

Moko guides me through the others to the verandah. Again, without asking, he helps with my shoes. Sliding his sunglasses off and into his shirt, he lets me see the feeling in his eyes. For Keith, and for Sheena.

"We'll stay with her." He speaks low, helping me down the stairs to the path. "You just keep them on track. Those kids need you."

"Me?" I shake my head. "I'm out of the loop, mate. They've as good as canned me."

He fixes his eyes to mine. "You have to do what you can."

The breeze picks up around us; a few tentative drops of moisture come down over my face. Behind Moko's broad shape, the sky is darkening, the blue day turning to bruised purple.

"Up in the forestry, she said Keith knew things. About Bradley, and the others." I look into Sheena's window, then back to Moko. "Do you know what she meant?"

His features remain impassive. He stares back at me for a long while, weighing his words. "It's not my place."

He turns and steps up and into the house, leaving the door open behind him. Soon, I hear his voice join the others. At the end of the path, the basket waits on the fence, the plastic bag shifting in the cool air. I carry it to the verandah, setting it inside the circle of shoes, out of the rain.

IN THE MORNING, the last straggling clouds slide away, leaving everything lush and full. I'm up early, the crutch left by the front door, digging carefully for the first of my potatoes. The radio plays low through the open window of the kitchen, the easy listening station. Everything's easier with a project. Sheena, Bradley, the meeting with Ambrose: every lump brought out of the soil pushes it further away.

"All right, girl." Patty appears behind me. "I'm off. You all set?"

"Yep." I don't need to turn around to see her. She'll be wearing her work blouse with the blue stripes tucked into her jeans, a thin cardigan across her shoulders, hair carefully in place. She's had the streaks touched up again, little veins of bronze and gold swept through. "See you tonight."

She nods, watching me. "I can always help out, you know."

"With the spuds?"

She grins. "With a lawyer. There's no way it's above board, what he's doing. You've been there thirty-five years, love. You should at least have access to the files while they're doing the audit." Her eyes are hard. "I've got an old uni friend who does employment stuff. She'll give you a rate. Hell, I could cover it myself. It's the principle of the thing, Lorraine. That bastard can't just . . ."

"Take it easy." A sharp ache rolls through my knee; it'll take another hour to earn back some ease. "I'm sitting tight for now."

She folds her arms across her chest, gentle with the blister on the inside of her wrist. It's mostly healed, leaving behind a pink bar of new skin.

"Think about it, at least."

I wave her away. "You'll be late."

The Fiesta sputters, then recedes into the mouth of Rickett's Circle and out into the main road. A poky little car, a divorce brewing, and she's offering to cover my legal bills.

I push the fork into the soil with my good foot. Patty's been telling me to wear gloves so the handle doesn't rub, but I like to feel my work. This is Frank's old vegetable patch: a neat square of earth marked off with some sleepers from the old railyard, two trips across town with the Morris so the roof didn't buckle. He was never much for flowers, Frank, but vegetables—he even managed to coax basil out of the ground, despite the hiding it took in the windy months. Whole evenings he'd spend out in his patch, a smoke hanging from the corner of his mouth, those big knobbly hands touching the plants, speaking their language.

I met Frank on horseback, down by the river on the old farm. Things like that used to happen when I was a girl, before Dad sold up and moved us to town. It was a Sunday— my mother always gave me and Debs an hour to ourselves between the morning cleaning and lunch. Sometimes Debs would come with me on my rides, but not this time.

Frank had his dog with him, an old huntaway, her eyes gone rheumy, always barking at shadows and strange sounds. Samson, our mustering horse, was mostly Clydesdale; he wasn't fussed about some toothless milk-eyed bitch nipping at his hooves. He just kept up his plod to the riverbank, our usual Sunday ride, even while Frank came running over with chivalry written all over him, trousers rolled to the knees, calming his dog as if she might take us down. I remember how he stood with a palm above his eyes, shading himself to see me, not a bit worried about being caught trespassing.

"It's Lorraine, isn't it?" His eyes moved over my legs, drinking me in. "You're Mickey Henry's youngest."

Behind him, under the long braids of the willows, a knapsack moved against the stones and an inky black shape shook itself loose, the eel's mouth open and tasting the air for a way back to the water. I'd heard a new family had moved into the cookhouse on the old McPherson place next door, a Māori shepherd with his wife and their two boys. This must be their eldest.

"You ask anyone if you could take those eels?"

He turned, feigning surprise. "I was gonna."

"You were going to."

He set his hands to his hips. "There's some bloody big huas in there, I'll tell you that. Wanna see?"

"It's our river." I kept on staring. "I know what's in there."

I had a good five feet in the advantage, up there on Samson's back, but he held his eyes to mine. "You smoke?" He patted his pocket and gave me his first proper smile. I saw the lovely full shape of his teeth, each one its own tall glass of milk.

"My mother." I shook my head. "She'll smell it."

He waved his hand. "Here, I'll show you."

Making sure nobody was looking, I swung down to the spot next to him, the grass soft under my feet. If they'd known I was out here with this boy, Mum and Dad would've flayed my arse with the shaving strop; Debs had taken a good hiding earlier that summer for chatting to one of the forestry workers behind the workshop, and he wasn't even brown. Frank rolled a cigarette with quick hands, striking a match and setting me downwind so the smoke ran back into him. The air between us filled with bluish vapour, his eyes watching me through it. On even ground my head only went to his chest; I had to look up to see him.

"Cut through the line of gums to the old forestry track when you leave," I said. "No one will see you that way."

"What if I want them to see me?" He inhaled and set the smoke to my lips, the paper damp from his mouth. "What if I want your old man to know I've been talking to his daughter?" I coughed with the taste, making his dog jump at the sound. "Don't worry." He showed me those lovely teeth again. "I'll be careful."

I remember the sun, the way it framed his face in a burning white shimmer. Behind his shoulder, the river murmured low and soft, and a breeze moved through the willows in a long hush. There were so many sounds. For a moment I thought he might kiss me, and my heart gave a twist, slow and lovely.

"I should get back," I said.

"You'll want a leg up." He nodded to Samson, the horse snorting softly as he picked through the long grass for the softest shoots.

"The old track." I spoke over my shoulder. "Don't forget."

In three long strides, I had my hand against Samson's broad flank, the muscles marbled and quivering, his hide like my very own map of the world. Dad had practised the mount with me and Debs until it was second nature: I sprang high on my toes and latched myself to the horse's side, one hand full of thick mane, sliding my hips up and over. Like climbing a wall, Dad said.

When I looked down, Frank was whistling through his teeth. Behind him, the fugitive eel twisted across the gravel, heading for the river. It didn't matter; there were always more eels.

"You're some girl." His face was a scone in the oven, rising and ready.

Some girl.

I still think about that.

A car door slams behind me, jolting me back. It's nice there at the old river, Samson like a furred mountain between my knees. I'm not sure I've ever felt the same command I felt on his back, that sweet sense of momentum and safety.

But the present is calling. "*Lorraine.*"

I turn with my good ear, squinting into the sun. It's Hayes, his suit as rumpled as ever, beads of sweat pooled in the cleft of his neck. Seeing his face is enough; for a moment I hear the shushing of the pines, and Keith's ragged breath in my ear. It's only a moment, a flash of nerves. Then it's gone.

"What are you doing here?"

I stab the fork into the soil. He's holding a cardboard box against his hip, the lid taped shut. He wipes at his brow and looks back to the road.

"You have a second?"

"Come on, then." I nod towards the house. "You could use something cold."

Hayes sets the box under the kitchen table, looking through the window to Patty's place. He's restless but it's probably just the heat. I click on the overhead fan, and the blades chop the air.

"I had to wait to make sure you were alone." He shucks off his jacket, watching as I scrub my hands in the sink.

"My neighbour? She's on morning shifts this week."

"I noticed," he says.

His eyes rove around the kitchen. A detective's tic, I suppose. I dry my hands and pour a couple of glasses of cordial from the jug in the fridge, dropping in some ice.

"You want to sit?"

He takes the glass and drains it, then perches on the seat at the far side of the table, watching me. The radio is playing the Righteous Brothers, a melody as comfortable as old clothes. It's a familiar song, so familiar I'm not sure if I'm hearing it or just thinking of it.

"Do you have any idea what ran through my head when I came back to the cars?" Hayes's hands are shaking; he clasps them together as if squashing something. "Anything could've happened to you, Lorraine."

I focus on the Formica patterns under my hands. "Sheena. I knew she was up there. I had to go."

"A man is dead, Lorraine." His eyes hold me, two wires strung tight. "Do you know what that's like? To . . . do that?"

He leans over the table, pale and shaking. First Sheena, now him. Everywhere I turn, there's another hurdle I've careened into. Maybe I should leave everyone alone, just stick with my new potatoes and my evening gins.

"I'm sorry, Justin." My eyes are wet; across the table, Hayes turns into a smeared impression of a man. "I don't know what's happening, lately. Ever since Bradley was . . . I . . . it's shit. It's all just shit."

I cover my face with my hands, and everything turns dark. There's the squeak of a chair; I feel him next to me, his hand on my shoulder, his fingers steady. I wipe at my eyes and set a hand over his. He's looking down at me, the air from the fan tickling at his ragged hair. The anger drains from his face like dishwater, letting warmer colours back into his eyes.

"Nobody in that station knows a useful fucking thing, Lorraine." He gives a half-grin. "What would I do if something happened to you?"

"Well." I cough. "It doesn't matter now, does it? Ambrose made sure of that."

"The audit?" Hayes sits back down. "That's just head-office stuff. The commissioner had a few questions about what the station file clerk was doing out in the field, and Ambrose didn't have a good answer. He's just trying to look proactive, that's all."

"Proactive?" My mouth falls open. "He's as good as fired me."

"You don't know that yet."

A mewl sounds from the lounge doorway. Tilly steps up to Hayes, tail high and interested, and presses her whiskers against his legs. He moves his fingers through the fur at her neck.

"She hates people, usually."

"I'll count myself lucky, then." He reaches for the box, lifting it to the table. "Listen." He clears his throat. "Whatever else is going on, I still need your help."

"My help?"

You have to do what you can.

He picks at the tape and pulls it off in a long strip. "Dion's a good guy but he's not exactly winning awards for initiative. It's mostly Ambrose himself on the case, and . . . you know." He reaches inside and brings out two tall stacks of papers tied with twine. "These are copies of everything you've seen already. These"—he pats at the second stack—"are our new reports. Since Mataikona I've been pulling anything even vaguely related to the Kīngis and the Larkins, or anything we could've missed on the first pass."

I reach out and pick through the papers. There are photographs, maps, even interview transcripts I haven't seen before. Some of it has come from further afield: Hawke's Bay, Taranaki, the East Coast.

"It's probably irrelevant," says Hayes. "But given the dead end we're at, we need to look wider. It's all about fresh eyes."

"Are these mine?" I hold up a packet of photocopied scribbles.

He nods. "I dug them out of the desk. The originals are still there, where you left them. So long as Tania doesn't get too enthusiastic with her tidy-up."

At the bottom of the pack, there's a manila folder wrapped in a thick rubber band. Inside, the pages are watermarked for head office.

"It's their write-up on the shooting," says Hayes. "You, ah . . . you'll want a stiff drink with that one."

I flick through the pages, glimpsing a photograph of Keith sprawled on the ground, head angled away from the camera, dark stains through his clothing. His shotgun lies next to him, the barrel catching the flash of the camera. My breath sticks, and it takes a moment to come back to myself.

Hayes scoots closer. "I don't have to tell you what I'm risking doing this." He nods through the window to the old Wikaira place. "You need to keep it under wraps."

"I will." I wipe at my eyes. "Trust me."

He grins and sets his hand to my arm. "Anything you find, anything at all, just call my mobile. I might not answer right away but I'll find time."

"Okay."

The house is silent around us. I hold him in my eyes, this ragged heron of a man, bright-eyed and unshaven. The fan sends cooler air down against the back of my neck; there's a gap between the songs, a comfortable silence.

"Well." He reaches for his jacket. "I'll hear from you."

I turn my attention back to the files. With a last scratch for Tilly, he moves to the doorway. I go to stand but he waves me away.

"I can see myself out. You just get reading." He stands in place, his fingers playing at the edge of his jacket. "Your niece. Is she . . . how's she been doing?"

I shake my head, and he seems to understand. He steps outside, his thin frame moving through the bright daylight.

My hands reach into the pile of papers. I look at the clock: six hours until Patty gets back. Maybe seven if I'm lucky. I boil the jug for coffee. Everything in the room feels sharp and immediate; my legs are steady beneath me, holding me firmly to the floor. The potatoes will have to wait.

WHEN I LOOK up from the papers, it's already gone three o'clock. I've drained two stout plungers of coffee, the thick brew sluicing through my body, and now my stomach is crying out. I set a couple of eggs to boil and peel a mandarin while I wait, treading a circle in the kitchen and mulling over the new information. There's the low murmur of the radio, and between songs, the trill of cicadas on the lawn.

The details weren't too surprising at first. A bunch of head office commentary on the shooting, and all those Wellington questions as to whether Hayes and Ambrose followed correct procedure by heading up the logging track without calling for another car. All above board, apparently, given the information Sheena gave them. *Use of force deemed justifiable in the circumstances.* It's even backed up by a statement from yours truly, half-conscious and drugged up in that poxy hospital bed.

A man kills another man. *Use of force.*

The next folder holds the file on Les's arrest. One of our unmarked cars pulled him over near Mount Bruce in the early hours, likely on his way to a deal with some East Coast guys. There's something in there that didn't make it to the papers— apparently the patrolling officer thought Les might be reaching for a weapon when it was just a drumstick from a box of Country Fried Chicken tucked between the seats. That stuff's half-price after midnight from the Gull next to Farmlands; everyone knows that. Still, there was the sawn-off twenty-two under the driver's seat, and eighty grand's worth of powder wrapped in tea towels in the back. Sometimes a little paranoia is justified, I guess.

Where things really get interesting is the appended files on the Kīngis and the Larkins, and the strange web of gang connections enmeshing the families. There are transcripts of the follow-up interviews Hayes and Ambrose held with Queenie Larkin and Cath Kīngi, and damn near every sentence makes me want to run to the file-room stacks. I'm reading one coincidence after another, feeling more and more like a bird dog pointing into sagebrush.

For example.

After five pages of nothing but terse responses to Ambrose and Hayes, Queenie mentions something about Hēmi enrolling in the last Marist Rugby Club training weekend over on Dixon Street. My mind jumps to the second shelf from the back, the bottom row. It was one of Dion's files, full of his usual spelling mistakes, about a minor dust-up between Jason

Larkin and a patched guy at scrummaging practice. Nothing too major: a chipped tooth, a sprained wrist and no charges. Nothing definitive, but it helps paint the picture.

Further on in the Cath Kīngi interview, after what must have been an interminable hour of dead-end discussion—Precious's cousins visiting from Hamilton, her best friends at school, her mealtime habits—there's mention of a trip to the Bucks Road swimming hole near Featherston last Christmas, not long before she went missing. Something about it sets my brain itching. When Sheena turned up with Bradley at my doorstep late last year, pale and shaken up from what she'd seen Keith do to that prospect out front of her place, she mentioned something about him losing his rag one day at a swimming spot on the Tauherenikau. She'd been swimming with Bradley, she said, when Keith and Les saw someone pull up to the carpark and took off after them, leaving Sheena to hitch a ride home. Could it have been Bruce Kīngi? Would Cath have mentioned it if they'd had a run-in? She talks about the Bucks Road spot like it's a regular thing, which makes sense: they're down Underhill Road, right where the road turns to gravel. The river's only a short drive from there.

None of the details are conclusive on their own, but put them all together, and I get the sense the Larkins and the Kīngis had a longer history of running up against the Mongrels than they let on. It's not exactly novel: half the families in this part of town have some sort of connection, and the threat of violence hangs over the streets like the low hum of electricity. There was Jason Larkin's black eye after

Hēmi went missing, and my conversation with Keith on the night of Bradley's party.

Still, Keith wasn't one to spend his energies where they weren't justified. You don't get to occupy the king's table at Value Roast through violence alone. It takes a dash of clemency, too. But maybe the chief's theory deserves more time than I thought.

I read on through the remaining pages, scribbling notes to myself on any detail that clicks. After a summary of Bruce Kīngi's work history—road crews and metalworks, mostly, then driving trucks for a haulage outfit in Carterton—there's a long discussion with Cath Kīngi about how well Precious was doing with her classes. Gifted, she says, especially with her reading. Good school reports—her teacher used to write the nicest things about the girl's potential.

Tilly leaps onto my lap, staring up at me with her saucer eyes.

"What's happening, girl?" I give her a scratch in her favourite spot. Behind me, my good ear registers a frothing bubble from the eggs. Christ. They'll be boiled rocks by now. I take the pot off the boil and let them cool. Maybe some mayo and chives, a snip of dill from the planter outside. Herbs save everything.

"Come on, then."

It wouldn't hurt to feed the kittens a little early; that way it'll be fine if I forget later. I bend down with a grimace, spooning out enough jellymeat for Tilly and the three kittens, patting them as they eat. Four mottled shapes, and the fifth, Patch, still out there somewhere. With Bradley, I'm hoping. I move my fingers through their fur, whispering to them. They're still gangly in the legs but they'll be hunting soon enough.

Through the doorway, I hear footsteps in the kitchen.

"Pat?" I check my watch. Four o'clock; she's not due back for another hour yet. And anyway, I didn't hear the Fiesta. "Who's there?"

There's a heavy stumble, and a chair scraping against the floor. A voice sounds out, one I don't recognise. I look to the shelf and grab one of Frank's old carpentry mallets, the wood tight in my hand. Creeping ahead, I peer into the hall and catch an eyeful of dark hair slumped against the tabletop. It's my niece, sprawled in my chair, her arms out over the papers.

"Sheena?"

Her eyes stare through me. "Still keep the spare key under the cactus, eh?" She lifts a hand; a fresh droplet of blood rests on the tip of her finger. "Fuckin' thing."

"Jesus, girl." I set down the mallet and move up beside her with outstretched arms. With a start, her hand flies up and knocks me back.

"No." She looks me in the face, lifting what's left of a smoke. It takes her a couple of attempts to find her mouth. "You stay there."

Her eyes are laced with red. There's a rank smell like a floor left wet too long. I pull a chair closer to her, trying to gather the papers without drawing too much notice.

"Been busy, eh?" She nods to the Gordon's bottle on the

bench. "Busy having a lovely time with that neighbour lady. A nice wee time, the two of you." Her eyes narrow. "I'm glad someone has company."

I reach for her hand. This time, she lets me touch her. Her skin is hot. "Where's Moko?"

A slow shake of the head. "It isn't true. What people are saying."

"What do you mean?"

"Me and him." She shuts her eyes, and her head slides back against the wall with a loud clunk. I wonder when she last slept. "It isn't true."

"How about I boil the jug, eh? You have a lie-down, and I'll make us a brew."

A fleck of moisture slides from the corner of her eye. "They were mates, him and Keith." She sniffs. "I'd never."

"It's okay, Sheen."

I reach forward and try to fold her into me. There's a tremble in her chest, the low whir of something building. Her eyes fly open then, huge and red, and a low snarl fills the space between us. She shoves the table, standing so abruptly that the whole kitchen shakes. The papers fly to the floor along with my coffee plunger.

"Don't you fuckin' touch me!"

She falls back against the fridge; something heavy topples inside.

"Okay, girl." I hold my hands open wide; my mouth doesn't seem to work. "It's okay. Just . . . why don't you sit down? We can . . ."

Before I can say anything else, she lurches into the doorway and out into the sun. I call after her but she's already gone, stumbling down the side of the house to the footpath. I move as fast as I can manage, stepping into my old runners with no time for laces. Up ahead, she falls forward into my gate with a heavy clunk. The wood splinters against the hinges, leaving it hanging askew.

"Jesus, Sheen." I move to her side and try to lift her up. "Here, let me help you."

"No." She's muttering to herself. "No, no."

Eventually I get her upright again. There's a scrape on her arm but it's not bad. She's lighter in my arms than I remember; I'm not sure my basket made it to her.

"Home." She sobs into my ear, her hair across her face. "Home, Aunty."

"All right," I say. "Easy now."

We move ahead in a slow crawl from mailbox to mailbox. At the end of Rickett's Circle a milk tanker comes past, its silver cylinders shining like two giant spoons. The driver stares down at us from his cab, one arm folded against the open window, his skin toasted to a deep red. He doesn't wave.

By the time Sheena's place comes into view, my hip is crying out, and my bad knee feels like it might buckle. I keep my hand steady around her shoulder, trying to move with her weight. She's muttering again.

"Keith . . . him and Les, they kept asking and asking . . . for ages, and . . ."

"What's that?" I look her in the face. "What did you say?"

"They were selling." She blinks into the sunlight like something newly born. "To Bruce."

"Bruce Kīngi?"

"Eighty points a week." She wipes a palm across her cheek. "More, some weeks. Jase and Queenie wanted to come in, too. But Keith, he . . ."

"He what, girl?" My mind is racing. "What about Keith?"

"He never liked Jase," she mumbles. "Can't say why."

She totters ahead to the end of her path, leaving me standing in place. I feel unsteady myself; it's all I can do not to topple over.

"Sheena, wait."

She disappears through her front door, leaving it hanging open. I take the steps one at a time, though in truth, I can't feel anything under me; it's all moving so quickly. Inside, there are dishes stacked in the sink, and a pile of sleeping bags on the lounge-room floor. In her room, I find her sprawled on the bed, face pressed into the pillows. Gradually, my eyes adjust to the dark; there are scorched bulbs on the floor next to the bed; a lighter on the bedside table. A new vein of anger flashes through me.

"Damn it, girl." I reach a hand down to shake her. "You can't stay like this."

"Leave it," she says. "Just leave it."

I stand watching her for a moment, wondering how to help. There's no time; I need to call Hayes. I pat my pockets for my phone. I've left it behind.

"I'll come by later, okay?" There's no answer but I can

hear her breathing. That's something. "Just . . . don't go anywhere."

I step back out of the room, past Bradley's door, left ajar. Boy and kitten. The world is so big and so strange. Stranger by the minute, as it turns out.

On the way home every step feels far too slow, as if I'm running in a dream.

Eighty points a week. That's decent money in anyone's books, even if you're keeping the odd bag for yourself. Yourself, and your missus. Queenie and Jason Larkin too. I had my suspicions, and now I have a whole lot more.

The street slips past in a blur of summer heat. Up the path and through my busted gate, my lips moving as I walk, as if the information will fly away from me. The Fiesta is in Patty's driveway. My front door is still open; I hear a rustle inside.

"Hello?"

"I wondered where you'd got to." Patty looks up from the table with bright eyes. My skin feels tight; there's new moisture rolling down my back. "I scraped the coffee grounds off as best I could." She taps at the pile of papers, the top sheaf stained dark. "I knew you had it in you, girl."

"What are you doing?"

"Hmm?" A confused grimace. "The door was open, and I just . . ." She frowns. "Is something wrong, lovey?"

I move forward and grab the box. "That's private." An edge has come into my voice, sharper than I expected.

"I know, I know. But it's only me." She takes a step backwards. "I thought I'd clean the mess up, that's all."

"You're sure?"

Her eyes linger on the table. "All right, I looked. But only the coffee pages. It's so fascinating, that's all. You can read all the books you like, but it doesn't compare. The reports, and the way they write it all up. I always wondered." A smile plays across her mouth. "Before I forget, this was in your mailbox."

She hands me a thin white envelope. *Pinnacle Consulting.* It's postmarked for Auckland. The audit. There's no room in my brain; I feel like a circuit smoking under too much current.

"How did you sneak them out, anyway?"

"What?"

"The papers, girl." She sets a hand to my elbow in conspiracy. "They took your swipe card, right? How did you . . ."

"Stop. Just stop." I toss the stacks into the box and flip the lid closed, making her jump in alarm. "If anyone knew I had this stuff, it'd be a major fucking ordeal. Do you understand?"

"Lorraine, what's happened?" Her face clouds over. "Did something . . ."

"Tell me you understand."

Chastened, she looks to the floor. "I'm sorry. I . . . I'm happy you're still involved, that's all. After everything with Keith. Now you're back in the swing of things." She lifts her eyes to mine. "I know what it means to you. To your niece, too."

I stand beneath the twisting fan, feeling the air on my skin. *Your niece.* Six months I've known Patty, and she still won't call Sheena by her name.

"Listen." I sigh. "You know you're welcome here whenever you like."

She frowns. "What do you mean? Why are you so cross?"

"I don't want you going through my things." I gesture to the table. "You should've known bloody well these were private."

With a quick hand, she brushes her hair into place; her bracelets jangle as she moves. "I'm sorry, Lorraine. I think I've upset you." She reaches for her bag. "I didn't mean to stick my nose in. It's just always fascinated me." A new silence unfurls between us. I watch her fiddle with the handbag straps. "Maybe I should go."

She waits for me to protest. Then, clutching her bag, she steps outside, her shoes clacking down my path and onto the lawn.

"Christ alive."

I place my hands on the tabletop and stand as still as I can, breathing low. When she's out of earshot, I reach for the phone and call Hayes. It goes to voicemail the first time. On the second call, he picks up, whispering.

"I'm out with Ambrose," he says. I can hear cars in the background, and the sound of his footsteps. "We're checking in with the guys from the unmarked units. I can't stay on the line too long."

"They were selling to Bruce Kīngi," I say. "Eighty points a week."

"Who?" There's a stunned silence. "Keith? Who told you that?"

"Sheena." I look across to the wall. The way she'd slumped

against it, like a puppet with her strings cut. It hurts to think about.

"Jesus, if they were all in on the same deals, then . . ." I hear him muttering under his breath. "I can be there in an hour."

"No." I stare across the lawn to Patty's house, the afternoon sun framing everything in clear crisp lines. "I'll come to you."

Later on a lady came. I dunno how long I'd been there.
Long enough for the flood to go away after the storm
anyway. You could see her coming all the way from the
driveway where the road goes under the trees. Mr. P kept
some binoculars by the sink so he could see people. He
showed us how to use them too. The afternoon the lady got
here Mr. P took us over by the potatoes to shoot at the
rabbits. He said the rabbits eat the vegetables we want to eat
so we have to keep the rabbits sorted. He told us how his
people brought the rabbits over in boats. They didn't mean
to do any harm but it all went wrong and now there's too
many rabbits. He looked like maybe he was a little bit cross
when he talked about his people and our people.

We all lay down in the grass with the rifle and waited.
We had to keep real still he said like a statue or a big rock.

He put the barrel between the fence wires to keep it steady then it went off and Precious was the first one to go over to get the rabbit from where he shot it. She didn't mind. She said she'd done it at her uncle's but I didn't like to see them. Their eyes were all shiny and they had blood around their nose.

When we were finished Mr. P said he had to go into town and the lady went out to the car with him and I could hear them fighting through the window. It made me think about Mum and Dad and wonder when they're going to come out to meet us. Maybe bring Manaia. Precious could've been thinking the same thing about her mum and dad. She held my hand while we listened.

We played some games with the lady when Mr. P left but I could tell she was upset. Her hands shook and she didn't even notice when Precious changed from the silver shoe to the silver dog. I thought about asking what's wrong but I didn't really know her and I didn't want to make her cry again. Then we ate some soup. It was the same soup as when I came here the nice tomatoey one with bits of the new carrots and some hot bread we made together. That seemed to cheer her up a bit. When we went to bed she read a long story while we had the lamp still burning. Precious chose it the one about the hunchback and the fishbone. Mr. P explained to us once what a hunchback is and why there aren't so many around anymore. The lady was okay at reading but she didn't do the voices or any of that stuff. It was still nice though.

Then when Mr. P got back Bradley was downstairs. It made me think Mum and Dad and Manaia might be there too but Mr. P told me they were coming later. Bradley was holding something in his hands that I couldn't see what it was but then it made a little sound and it was a kitten. Bradley said its name was Patch. Precious wanted to hold it but Mr. P told her let the kitten get settled in first and maybe Bradley will let you hold it later. Bradley kept staring at the lady and I thought maybe something was wrong.

We sat down at the table and Mr. P gave us a bag of chips each. The kitten was trying to get out of Bradley's lap but he held on tight to it. He wouldn't stop looking at the lady. Then Mr. P went to stand next to her by the bench and he was making his shushing sounds and telling her she'll be okay. I didn't know if he was talking about Precious. Probably not because Precious was there with us. The lady wiped at her eyes and tried to show us she was smiling. She wasn't though. Not really.

Then she said to Bradley oh you must be hungry. She poured a bowl of the soup from the pot on top of the stove where the wood was still burning. I had had my soup already at dinner but I felt a bit hungry still. I was going to ask for some after Bradley had finished his or maybe he would leave me some because he didn't always finish his food even at school and Kellen always took it for himself. The lady carried the bowl with just her fingertips but then when she got near Bradley he put his arm out and knocked it over. It was on purpose I think and the kitten fell on the floor and ran away. The lady yelled a bit and Mr. P poured water at the sink and said hold still. Precious followed the kitten and tried to catch it in the next room. It was dark in there because the lamps weren't burning but she knew where everything was.

It was ages before everyone got quiet again. I had my hand in a bag of chips but I didn't want to move or make the crinkles. The spilled soup made little steam clouds on the tabletop. The lady had tears all over her cheeks and her eyes looked funny. It was like she was sad and angry at the same time. The water was making noises in the sink and the bugs kept on hitting the window meshes. Precious was calling out to the kitten saying puss-puss. Puss-puss.

IT'S BEEN A while since I've bothered with the bus. Turns out the old timetable I've had pinned to the fridge since Shipley is still good: right on time, the lime-green box wheezes to a stop on the corner by the dairy. The fare's steeper than I remember; on the upside, the seats smell better. I've left the papers wrapped up tight in a box tucked in the back of my wardrobe cupboard—padlocked to keep Patty's curiosity in check.

"Solway Park." The driver calls out over his shoulder, smiling as I descend.

I cross the road from the John Deere saleyard to the tennis courts, the grass springy and inviting, then up the stairs and into the chilled air of the Copthorne reception. I tell a girl at the counter I'm meeting someone, and she points to a horse-shoe of plush grey couches. There's complimentary coffee and biscuits; I help myself to a Cameo Crème and catch up on the city papers. Nothing on Bradley or the others—the shooting drew the headlines for a few days but it's been quiet since. New stories, fresh heartbreak.

The clock hits six, and a bunch of conference types stream through the lobby, finished with their workshops and heading for the bar. Then, the rumpled arm of a jacket comes through the sliding doors.

"Sorry." There are deep crags under Hayes's eyes. "Tania managed to lose an evidence box. We had the whole bloody station checking the rooms out back."

"Is that right?"

He gives me a wry grin. "Don't look so pleased with yourself."

We move into the expensive hush of the hallway. "A budget under review, and we put you up in here, eh?"

"I know." He fishes around in his pocket for the room card. "I told the chief the Highwayman would be fine but he insisted."

We step into what I'm sure is the wrong room. It isn't just that the bed's crisp and flat; you get that in hotels. But there's nothing to suggest anyone's been here for ten minutes, let alone a few weeks. Then I see an open bag of toffees by the bed; a shoe poking shyly out from under the desk.

"So, your niece, eh?" He gestures to a seat and clicks the kettle on, shucking out of his jacket. "What did she say, exactly?"

I tell him about Sheena's visit, sparing the lightbulbs and

the red spiderweb through her eyes. A shiver moves across my shoulders; we'll have some work to do getting the place back in shape for Bradley.

"Sounds like she's in a real state." Hayes sets a coffee down on the table. Milk and two sugars; it's what the day calls for. I try to take a sip but my hands are shaking.

"First our boy, then Keith." My head falls into my hands. "It's no wonder she's falling apart."

I hear him pull a chair closer. A hand comes to my shoulder. "He was armed, Lorraine. With enough puff in his system to fry a bull." He squeezes me. "I know what he was to your niece. But it's a lucky thing you came out of there at all."

I move my hands away, letting him see me. "I don't feel lucky. Not lately."

"You're not alone there." He sighs. "My wife called this morning. Our eldest got into Medicine at Otago. They're out celebrating right now, and look where I am."

"That's fantastic, Justin." I lift the mug to hide my expression. Other lives, other possibilities.

"She asked when I might make it back home. She knows the case we're on, but still." A new weariness comes into his smile. "I've got a little something, actually. If we really wanted to toast my boy, I mean."

"Sure."

With his usual elbow grace, he leans into the cupboard and brings out a bottle of Jameson's. There's a generous slosh for us each.

"To your boy."

"And to Sheena." He holds my gaze as he sips, then sets the mug down and stretches his arms up high. "It'll get easier, Lorraine. Trust me. We've got a few more pieces of the puzzle now." Outside, I can hear the steady thwack of tennis balls and a woman's commanding voice talking about the angle of the wrist, the follow-through.

"You're not going to bring Ambrose in on this, are you?"

"Not yet. At this stage it's only hearsay anyway. He doesn't need to know you're in the mix, still. Not with everything else going on."

Everything else. The audit, and that envelope from the consultant. All those lines about streamlined functions and operating models, the words shifting like mercury under the eye, giving the semblance of meaning but saying nothing. Thirty-five years, and it's the work of an afternoon to streamline me right out of a living.

"What about Les?" I ask. "Any chance he'd confirm what my niece said?"

Hayes shakes his head. "He clammed up tight after Keith. He wouldn't tell us if his leg was on fire."

He takes another long sip and nods to the bottle. "It's become a bit of a habit, this. Some days it's the best thing I can find to think about."

"Hard-drinking detective, eh?"

He laughs, a strangely boyish sound. "Every stereotype starts somewhere."

There's a question running through my head as I watch him, a train clacking against the tracks, gathering momentum.

"That moment, with Keith." I pause for a moment, choosing my words. "When he looked sideways, and you . . . you pointed for me to drop . . ."

The hand on my arm, the dry needles under my feet like a strange carpet.

There's only the tennis sounds outside, and the fan turning silently above us.

"They train you to do it, but it's never like anyone says." His voice is low. "It's a terrible thing, Lorraine. The most terrible thing there is, I think. But he could've killed you." He reaches for the bottle. A shrug; a sip. "I mean, I don't know how you put a value on a human life, but in that moment . . . Well, it just seemed to me yours was worth quite a lot."

Blood rushes inside my ears. I feel the salty air coming over me again, the ocean shushing up through the pines. The white floating dots of the crayfish buoys caught in our headlights at the bend, and the gravel curving away into the dark. Somewhere to the south is the lighthouse, tall and steady and protecting.

"You have all these people, Lorraine." I feel his eyes on me. "Your niece and her boy"—his eyes flicker as he says this—"and that neighbour of yours. Shit, even Ambrose and the rest of his clowns. They're taking from you, taking all the time. They take so much, I wonder what's left for yourself."

I sit frozen in place. Each one of his words is a key in a lock, a stone sinking to the bottom of a deep lake. It's this room. Everything in here—table and bed, those tiny soaps by the sink—the kind of anonymity I haven't found in so long. Maybe people can only be truly honest in hotel rooms, beyond the reach of the outside world with its histories and suggestions, its expectations. The mug is at my mouth, and I drain it away.

"Jesus." My lips move slowly. "How much did you put in there, anyway?"

He returns my smile, eyes intent on my face. "Just enough."

"Well." It would be so easy to stay. Talk; maybe take him up on whatever offer is in the air. "I'm going to have to leave you to it."

A nod, slow. "Let me give you a lift, at least."

I raise a hand. "It's fine. I could do with the walk."

"The walk?" He eyes my knee dubiously. "It's quite a way to Rickett's Circle, isn't it?"

"Just give me a call before you drop any papers around, all right? I'll make sure I'm on my own."

"Righto."

He sees me to the door, and the long hallway takes me away.

Outside, the air is still sticky though the sun has dropped behind the hills, leaving just a low glare over the town. I set a good rhythm for myself and I turn his words over in my head. Beside me, cars and trucks stream past, their tyres shushing against the road. I let my mind drift: the forestry and the hospital, Patty leaning over the papers, and Sheena on the night of Bradley's party. It's uncountable, how many times I've run through that afternoon. Kitten, box, cake. The eel girl shoving the boy in the face, and the circle of women so silent as I approached. Sheena's shattering expression when I told her I'd be back to collect Patch; Keith pulling up next to me on the footpath.

What did I miss that day? Was someone watching from the street? Was that red station wagon anywhere nearby? What strange face saw me, this grey and rounding woman in her best blouse, walk away with wet eyes?

After a while, the streetlights flare on, the golden cones of light pointing the way home. I cut between KFC and the Fresh Price carpark, dodging the drive-thru line snaking out into the road. In one corner of the carpark, a white Toyota is parked across two spots, the doors wide open and the radio on. Two little girls, they can't be much older than three or four, leap out from the back seat, chasing each other. I look into the car to see who is with them. There's no one around. The running girl squeals and darts backwards between the cars, her quick legs carrying her straight out into the path of a reversing ute, her head too low to be seen.

"Hey!" I break into a run. "Stop!"

The girl freezes in place, and the ute's brake lights pop on, the bumper just short of striking her tiny body. She stares up at me as I come to her. I bend down and pick her up, light in my arms, and reach out a hand for the other girl to take.

"Shit, lady." A sunburnt guy in a Billabong singlet steps out of the ute. "The fuck are you thinking, letting 'em blast around like that?"

"They're not mine."

He looks to the girls, then to me. It should be evident. To

my side, a voice lifts through the din. A stout woman is pushing a trolley to the Toyota, her eyes squinted in suspicion. She's younger than Sheena, early twenties maybe. Before I know what I'm doing, I'm planted right in front of her.

"Are these your girls?"

She lifts a pair of shopping bags into the back seat. "Put her down. Jade, get in here now." I set the girl down, and they both climb into the front seat, quiet and watchful. "What's the problem?"

"She was almost knocked over, you silly cow! Who leaves kids that young in a busy carpark?"

She turns to the guy in the singlet. "You should watch where you're fuckin' driving, mate."

The guy frowns back at her in disbelief, his mouth hung open. He pushes his cap back on his head, looking to me for support.

It's like I'm watching myself. Without willing it, my palm flies up and cracks her in the mouth, harder than I knew I could. Despite the noise around us, the slap carries through the air, like a branch snapping. The woman steps back, turning to me in disbelief. In the front seat, the two girls are watching with wide, dark eyes. They're so small, and the world is so large. My hands grab at the woman's shirt, shoving her back into the Toyota; there's a heavy thud before she hits the concrete.

"Jesus, take it easy." The guy moves in front of me, lifting his arms.

"Don't you dare leave them alone." There are tears falling

across my cheeks; the woman stares up from the ground, her stunned expression turning to anger. "Don't ever leave them."

There are other voices now: sarcastic laughter, and young men egging us on from the drive-thru line. I hear someone talk about calling the police. Wiping at my eyes, I turn away and head for the corner, my body suspended in the streetlight, the car radio still blaring behind me.

I GIVE UP on the idea of sleep at around three or four in the morning, after hours of tossing against the covers. The sound of my hand hitting her mouth. Those two girls watching. She was close enough to Sheena's age, that woman. And those little ones; it wasn't so long since Bradley was their size.

A week. It's been a whole week.

I get out of bed and brew a plunger of coffee, throw some water on my face, and spread the papers out on the bed in the spare room; that way, I can always lock the door if Patty comes around. I read over yesterday's notes, waiting for anything new to jump out. There's a voice in my head, talking to me as I read.

They're taking from you, taking all the time.

On the bed, my phone vibrates with a call. It's Justin.

"Speak of the devil."

"Hmm?" I hear the chime of a spoon in a mug. "What's that?"

"Never mind," I say. "Little early, isn't it?"

"I thought you'd want to hear this." He clears his throat. "I did a bit more poking around on Bruce Kīngi. Turns out one of the gang-liaison guys over in head office was looking into something a couple of years ago. A stabbing in Upper Hutt."

"A stabbing? Bruce Kīngi?" My mind flicks through the stacks. "That doesn't ring any bells."

"No, he wasn't the suspect," says Hayes. "But one of the cars impounded during the investigation was registered under his name. An old Ford station wagon." I hear him take a sip and swallow. "He claimed it'd been stolen but he hadn't gotten around to filing a report. It's nothing that would show up in his files but it could point to a connection."

"Got it." I write down the details.

"I was thinking of having another chat with him. With Cath too." A pause. "Actually, I was thinking you might want to be there."

"Me? At the station?"

"That'd only get people talking. I was thinking their place, Featherston." Another sip. "Later this morning, if you can."

There are rocks in my throat. "Ambrose'll never go for that."

"He's got his hands full, the audit and all. Look, you know the files better than anyone, Lorraine. You can help me with their story, make sure there aren't any holes anywhere."

I lean back against the wall. My eyes are sore, and my hand still stings. I look down at the papers, seeing a photograph of the Kīngi house: a leaning cottage crowned with rusting iron, and the thick green shoulder of bush looming tall over everything. I can already feel that South Wairarapa wind on my arms, strong enough to strip trees bare.

"Are you there?"

"Okay." I clear my throat. "I'll come with you."

"Great. I'll be there just after nine."

The line cuts out. I stare at my scribbles on the pages, wondering where to start. Draining my coffee, I stand under the shower, the water as hot as I can stand it.

Later, there's a knock on the door. I check my watch; it's not long past eight. Too early for Hayes.

"Lorraine?" Patty's voice. I hear the front door swing open. "Are you there?"

"Coming."

She's in the kitchen, standing by the table, holding something at her front. "I got some of that marmalade you like." Hands outstretched, she moves forward, offering a jar tied with yellow ribbon. "The one with the thick peel. We had it with that grainy bread, remember?"

"You went all the way to Martinborough?" I shake my head.

She offers a tentative smile. "It's for yesterday." Her eyes go to the floor. "I know I overstepped."

I take the jar and turn it over in my hands. "You didn't have to, Pat."

"You look nice," she says. "Heading out somewhere?"

"Sheena's. Thought I'd help her clean up a bit."

"She'll be glad to have the help, I'm sure." She still can't meet my eye. "I drove past the place last night, and it looked like a bloody bomb had gone off. The front door was left open, even."

A long shiver runs through me. "Did you see anyone there?"

"Just that big guy, the one from the marae. The service."

"Moko?"

She nods and looks outside across the lawn to her car. Her eyes are busy. "It's the finals on *Villa Wars* tonight, you know. I was thinking I could pick up some dinner on the way home."

"That'd be lovely." There's a new quality in the air between us. I wonder if it's everything with the papers, or something else.

I watch her move down the path and across the lawn to her driveway. Her shoulders seem bunched together, somehow, like she's imagining a great weight bearing down. There's the tinny rattle of the Fiesta as she reverses into the road.

I'm in the front seat, watching Justin drive. It's strange, seeing him in his sedan, unmarked so as not to draw any attention at the Kīngi house. You'd never think this was the same guy swearing behind the wheel up in the pines, increasingly frantic as the track narrowed to a shelf of crumbling earth. He looks relaxed; he's even shaved.

"What?" He looks sideways.

"Nothing." I try not to grin. "They know we're coming, right?"

"I called earlier," he says. "It can stress the mother, showing up out of the blue."

The mother. Is that how he talks about Sheena when I'm not around?

We come to the end of the straight before Featherston, and the dark green ranges lift high in the background. I haven't been through here in months, not since we took Bradley over to the Hutt pools back in December when we all needed cheering up. It's a clear day, at least, though the wind still tilts the car to one side.

"What'd you tell Ambrose?"

He sets his coffee between the seats. "A few things to chase up back in the city. Not a lie, exactly. He's not one to ask too many questions. Not right now, anyway."

"What if we get something?"

"Shit." He grins. "He'll be so chuffed with any new leads, he won't think to ask who was with me. Not with the kinds of questions he's been getting."

We slow down as we enter the town, and I try to decide how much to believe him. Even if the chief did find out about me being involved, what's he going to do? Sack me?

Outside, there's the cenotaph and the fish and chip shop, and the old bank, its art deco façade shuttered for good. At the skate park a couple of truant kids sit on the edge of the ramp with their feet dangling, watching the passing cars with listless eyes.

"You all right, Lorraine?"

I take a long breath. What would he say, knowing I've been going around slapping strangers in carparks?

"Fine. Tired, that's all."

We take a right past the train tracks. The streets start to taper off, the sections getting larger and wilder. Past the rugby club, the seal turns to gravel. There's a sign for the Bucks Road campground up ahead, and the swimming hole Sheena mentioned.

"It's coming up on the left, here."

At the end of a narrow driveway is the cottage from the files, its low shape bordered by thick trees. The driveway is stacked with old cars, metal shapes rusting in a long row. I can feel my heart in my chest. Justin must notice it too.

"It's all right." He sets his hand on mine for a second. "Just follow my lead. If something doesn't sound right to you, say so."

We pull to a stop in the only free square of gravel, the hood nearly touching the bumper of a truck with a yawning gap where the windscreen should be. I slide my bag around my arm, my notes ready, and step out into the wind.

Cath Kīngi is at the door already. She's a tall woman, long in the arms, with thin fingers clutching the glowing stub of a cigarette. Hayes offers his hand. "Bloody windy today."

She takes it with some reluctance and eyes me from the doorway. The skin around her eyes is stretched and taut; there's the same weight in her expression as I saw in Sheena's, only more of it. She looks between us, as if she's snagging on something.

"This is Lorraine." Justin makes room for me. "Lorraine Henry. She's come along from the station to help me out."

"Henry," she says. "Not the Henrys from out near Flat Point? Mickey and Sal?"

"That's the one." I feel myself squinting. She can't be more than five years older than Sheena. Mid-thirties at the most. "Mickey was my dad."

"Right, right." A grin of recognition blooms around her cigarette. "My cousins used to shear with Debs and Billy. I'll bet we met at a party or two, back in the day."

"Probably." I search her features for the kid she would have been. Then, something sparks. "Ben and Trapper Kīngi, right? Trapper used to press, I think?"

She nods. "I used to rousey with them every holidays. They got me started nice and early." A shadow crosses her face. "Bloody shame what happened. I had a lot of time for your sister, you know."

"Yeah." Even now, after twenty years, the words stick in my throat. Fortunately, Justin jumps in.

"We had a couple of things we wanted to run past you."

"You said on the phone." She glances at me and turns into the hall, leaving us to follow.

Inside, the air is stale, like forgotten onions. I risk a few glances into the open doors as we go. The first two rooms are empty, the beds stripped, the mattresses the colour of teeth. I don't know what I'd expected to find; it's not as if they'd have their wares sitting out in the open in a nice little pile, even if they were selling. Instead, there's a car transmission pulled to pieces on the coffee table in the lounge next to the fireplace, the rest of the room patchy with clothes and plastic bags. The walls look like used baking paper; it's like someone's had a bonfire inside.

It looked like a bloody bomb had gone off.

I clutch my bag tight in my hands.

"Tea?"

"We're fine, thanks."

With a relieved look, Cath nods to a couple of spare chairs. There's just enough room on the table for my notepad; I get myself settled between stacks of laundry and newspaper.

"Bruce around this morning?"

"He's on a run up to Napier." She sets down an ashtray and pulls out a pack of Bensons, offering me one. I hold up my palm for no. "Back later tonight, he said."

Justin nods to himself and sets his hands at his front. "What's he hauling?"

"Framing timber, I think." Cath looks between us again, annoyed. "Listen, do you have anything on my girl? Because getting a call like this . . ." She clicks over her lighter and takes a long drag, eyeing Justin. "It's been bloody ages."

Twin plumes of smoke exit her nostrils.

"We're making progress," says Justin. "We've had a number of interviews with local contacts."

"Yeah?" She plucks the cigarette from her mouth with a dubious smirk. "I think I saw that on the telly, that stuff in Mataikona. That interview didn't go so well, did it?"

At the mention of Mataikona, a shudder rolls through me. I grip my pen tight and wait for it to pass. When I open my eyes, Cath is staring at me.

"Shit, that was you, wasn't it? Both of you, up there?" She looks between us. "The news was saying . . . Jesus, she's your niece? The woman, with the missing boy?"

I nod.

"He's family to you, right? Bradley?"

"That's right." I lift a wrist to my nose. I try to hold it together but I can't. Despite what we're here to do, there's so much sympathy in her, so much recognition.

"Oh." She sets a hand to my elbow. "I had no idea."

I look at Justin, and he gives me the slightest nod.

"We need to ask a few things." I sniff, trying to gather myself. "About Bruce."

"Sure, sure." She lets go and picks up her smoke. "What about him?"

"He had an old Ford, right? A station wagon, silver? This would be a while back now."

"Had a few, actually." Cath sighs, nodding through the scratched window to the driveway. "Still does."

"One was seized after a stabbing. A gang thing, over in the Hutt."

"A gang thing?" She leans back in the chair. "A few years back, you mean?"

"That's it," says Justin.

Her eyes flicker. "Someone nicked it from outside the depot," she says. "Two, maybe three months before they impounded it. He was up the Kāpiti coast on a construction site. He only heard about it when the cops called."

Justin leans forward. "He never filed a report, right? For the car?"

202

"Wasn't insured." She purses her mouth. "Not worth the hassle."

I wait until I catch her eye. "Did he ever have much to do with any patched guys?"

"Bruce?" Cath ashes her cigarette with calm fingers. "No more than anyone else around here. Had an uncle go that way but that's about it."

I watch her as closely as I can. "He never ran into Keith Mākara?"

She stares back at me. "He's the guy who got shot, right?" She looks to Justin, then back to me, as calm as anything.

"That's right."

"Not that I know of." She shakes her head, eyes still fixed on me. It's enough to make me think maybe Sheena's got the wrong end of the stick. "Why, did he have something to do with it? With our girl, or any of that?"

"We're looking into every possibility." Justin's voice is careful and weighted. "There's a chance Bruce and Keith might have run into each other, maybe."

Cath squints for a long time, then leans back. "I don't think so, eh." She turns her head and looks at the phone, the scratched plastic hanging in the middle of a strip of flaking wallpaper. "You can call him if you like. He'll say the same."

Her movements are easy, her voice unrushed. I look to Justin; time for something else.

"Back in December, you mentioned something about heading down to the swimming hole," I say. "The Bucks Road spot, with Precious."

"Oh, sure." She takes a drag. "My girl loves that place.

She'd walk down there on her own if we let her. These roads, though. Everyone's always tearing down there at a million miles."

"Bradley loves it too," I say. "Can't stop going on about the waterfall. My niece takes him down there all the time. They were there one weekend in December, actually. Keith, too, and some of his mates." I let her take in the information. "Some other patched guys."

"We see some guys down there sometimes, sure." Her eyes are still clear. "Like I said, we bump into them every once in a while."

"Do you remember seeing any sort of argument around then?" I ask. "A patched guy, and someone else?"

"Last Christmas?" She sits back in her chair with a pensive expression. "That's going back."

"You mentioned in your statement that you were down there with Precious pretty much every weekend." I watch her face. "It was a hot one, too. A real stinker."

There's a tiny glimmer of recognition in her eyes. "There was one day, I think. We'd just arrived and set up in our usual spot. It was busy as, the whole bloody town down there. Our girl was bugging me about jumping from the high ledge. The older kids were doing it, you know? Then someone started yelling. Some guy in a singlet, and a mate of his. He was really giving it heaps. Reckon that was Keith?"

"Sure," I say. "He could do that."

She gives a wry grin. "I've got it now. The big guy, he took off with a mate of his, and there was some kind of bust-up in

204

the carpark. I wanted to see what was going on, so I asked Mr. Prendergast to watch Precious and her mates."

"Mr. Prendergast?"

A frown. "Hmm?"

"The guy you asked to watch the kids."

"Oh." She nods. "That's her teacher. Her old teacher, I guess. Retired not too long ago."

"He was at the swimming hole too?" asks Justin.

Cath shrugs. "It was thirty-six degrees, mate. And no wind, for once. That kind of weather, everyone heads down there."

"What's he like?" I lean forward. "Mr. Prendergast."

"Nice bloke." She nods again, and the skin around her eyes relaxes. "Precious loved his classes, eh. He was always great with her, with the numbers and that, the maths. He used to give some of the kids more time after school, to make sure they kept up with the harder stuff. Even came around here once or twice, to visit."

"He retired, you said?"

"In December, yeah. It was his last year in Featherston. Went off to run his farm, I think. School had a party and everything, invited all the kids from over the years." Her expression brightens. "He asked Precious to give a speech. You should've seen her."

Justin flicks open his notepad. "Do you remember where the farm was?"

She stubs the cigarette in the ashtray. "Somewhere out Martinborough ways, I think. Near the coast?"

There's a pause. For a moment, there are no sour smells in

the room, and no surfaces mottled with grime. There are just the facts, stacked together in a growing pile.

"Well, then." Justin gives me a nod. "That's about it for today, Mrs. Kīngi. We're grateful for your time."

"Really," I say. "Thanks."

I climb to my feet, my knees stiff from sitting. Cath ushers us to the front door, standing to the side to let us out. It's a relief to breathe fresh air, even with a gale blowing.

"We'll be in touch," says Justin. "If you remember anything else, give us a call."

We step off the deck and into the car. Cath watches us from the steps.

"You did great." Justin reaches back between the seats, looking into the road as he reverses. "Really great."

I wave to Cath right as we leave her sight. Despite her height, she looks like someone sketched in miniature, the tall maw of the ranges ready to eat her up.

"You're sure?"

"More than sure," he says. "It's tough, building that kind of trust. Maybe you should be the one to follow up any other details with her and Bruce."

He pulls into the road in a crunch of gravel. After a few minutes comparing our impressions, we come back into Featherston, the main road dotted with traffic heading back and forth over the ranges. Heading left on the way back to Masterton, Justin pulls off the road just past the skate park. The same two kids are there, in the exact same spots, like a still life sketch. They watch us turn the corner.

"What're we doing?"

"We've spoken to everyone else who knew Precious." Justin nods through the glass and shifts down through the gears, stopping in the generous shade of an oak tree. A set of school gates reads *Featherston Normal.* Past the fence, the kids have just been let out for morning tea, and everyone is running around in the usual melee of elbows and scuffing sneakers. My hand aches. I rub it absently, hearing the shouts of abandon from those two girls again. A thin-lipped woman in a purple cardigan bends down to a boy, wagging a finger in his face.

"Let's see if we can find an address for this Prendergast guy, eh?"

IT'S NOT FAR to Martinborough; just long enough to get my head around the address the school gave us. I really shouldn't read the map in the car, though. Even with Justin taking it easy on the corners, those twisted white lines of the roads spreading out against the paper soon send the familiar yellow bloom in my guts.

"You all right?" asks Justin.

I take a long breath as the town square comes into view. "I think so."

"A coffee, I'd say." He looks at his watch. "We've got time."

We pull in opposite the only hotel. Growing up, Dad used to take me and Debs on drives here to get ice cream, though the hotel was no place to linger. All the farmhands within an hour's drive would descend on a Friday night, and barely an evening passed without a cracked jaw or fractured eye socket.

Things have changed, though. Now the only hardship facing the drinkers in the Martinborough Hotel is deciding which pinot will most impress the city colleagues.

"Flat white, right?" Justin steps out of the car and stretches his arms.

"Two sugars."

He disappears into the café, and I walk up and down the footpath outside, calming my stomach. The place is doing a decent trade for a weekday: a table full of dears in the window has ordered an early soup lunch with soft bread for the dentures, and behind them a young couple with a sleeping baby are slicing into eggs Benedict. Justin jokes with the girl behind the counter, his expression open and easy. She slips a cookie into a paper bag for him. Past the till, I see a pyramid of marmalade: the jars stacked in a shining monument, waiting to be purchased by apologetic neighbours driving an hour's round trip just for the special kind of thick peel.

Justin steps back out. "What's so funny?"

I shake my head and take the coffee. "It doesn't matter. Here, look." I point at the map spread out across the hood. "This guy must be out near Hinakura."

I set down the scribbled piece of paper. *S. Prendergast*, it reads. *Hikawera Road, Rural Delivery 6, Martinborough*. There's no phone number listed. My fingertip traces the road from where we are, the thin white markings coiled intestinally inside the different shades of forest and pasture.

"Just looking at the bloody road makes me feel crook."

"We'll take it slow." He slips his sunglasses back on. "Come on."

With the map folded, we pull through the main square, the trees throwing spackled shadows over the car. "How do you want to play it with him, anyway?"

"It's just like with the other teacher interviews," he says. "His impressions of Precious, anything noteworthy about the family. Then we'll go from there. We've got the swimming-hole angle too. Maybe he'll remember something about Bruce or Keith, something we can use."

I sip at my coffee, my thoughts drifting. "How often do you get anything useful from them?"

"Teachers, you mean?" He waves a hand horizontally. "Nine times out of ten it's a wash-up. You saw the transcripts."

I did. Page after page of Ambrose and Dion going back and forth with these well-meaning, oblivious people, talking about these kids as if their existence had only truly occurred to them since the headlines started. *Hēmi Larkin? Oh sure, nice kid. Energetic, and, uh . . . yeah. Hard to get him to focus sometimes, especially in the afternoons. A terrible thing, what happened. Terrible.*

It was the same with Bradley's teacher, the same empty platitudes. She'd called our boy stubborn, though, which gave me some satisfaction. A little stubbornness can be useful, especially in Masterton.

"Maybe it'll be different." I'm allowing myself a little optimism. "If this guy saw Precious as gifted, and if he was spending extra time with her and everything, then maybe he'll have something more to say."

"Maybe." Justin shrugs. "It's not the worst day to be out here anyway, right?"

We come past the golf course and over the river, the sunlight striking the water in a thrown blanket of gold. I keep reminding myself to keep my eyes on the road; it's best for the stomach.

For a while we're quiet. The corners keep turning, the car steady and gentle beneath us.

"What was she talking about?" I feel Justin's eyes on me. "Cath—about your sister and all?"

I look away. There's the old grey feeling.

"It's fine if you'd rather not." He lifts a hand from the wheel. "Just curious."

I take a deep breath, counting the dashes of paint slipping under the car.

"They were coming back from a job, up past Dannevirke. A fortnight of summer hoggets on the station at Rolling Downs."

A tightness seeps into my body, a sleeping animal settling in for decades inside my chest. It's always this way.

"The driver, a presser from up north, hit some gravel on a corner south of Eketāhuna and flipped the van into a dam. Two guys in the back managed to walk away. The rest drowned before they could get them out."

Breathe.

"My sister broke her neck in the crash. It was quicker for her."

"Jesus." Justin shakes his head. "And Sheena, she must have been . . ."

"Ten years old."

The afternoon's still there for me, waiting whenever I close my eyes. One of the switchboard women had come into the staffroom looking for me, her face like a bedsheet. I went over to Sheena's school to wait outside the gates. She'd been staying with me anyway, the usual thing when Debs and Billy went off for any long work. Her eyes lit up to see me outside; a walk home meant a treat of some kind: chips or juice, maybe even chocolate. She knew how to work her Aunty Lo, even then. We set off towards Rickett's Circle, words streaming from her mouth: schoolwork and friends, all the urgent updates of her age. Meanwhile, I had a thick chunk of granite lodged inside me. It didn't take her long to notice; she fell quiet before the end of the street. I remember kneeling next to her, pressing her thin body tight to mine while the older kids watched us from across the road.

"She came to live with me," I tell Justin. "It was the easiest thing."

Around us, the road twists and spins through the countryside, the flatter land turning into broken peaks of scrub and hillsides scarred with slips. On and on we turn, until it becomes hard to tell which direction is which.

"You've had your fair share," says Justin. "I'll give you that."

I close my eyes and let him drive. There's only so much a person can ever say.

It's not long before we're out of reception. My phone shows a flat line where the bars should be, and so does Justin's. It's no wonder: we're deep in the ranges now, the craggy peaks high around the car, nearly blocking out the sun. When I wind down the window I can smell salt in the air.

"The coast must be just over the hill," I say. "We're getting close."

"Thirty-five clicks since Martinborough." Justin peers into the dash. "Thirty-six, now."

I point ahead. "There."

Right before the next corner, a turnoff leads through a copse of mānuka. Justin slows down and pulls over in a plume of dust, reaching for the map. His finger traces the looping white scribble, coming to rest exactly where we must be.

"This must be it, right?"

We pull into a long straight road that needs grading. There are no markings on the fenceposts, and nothing to suggest where we are. Justin weaves around the deepest potholes, letting the belly of the car scrape through the minor ones. Behind the fence, a mob of ewes scatter, startled by the engine. We pass through a cattlestop, and the metal slats throw low vibrations into our feet. After a while, a farmhouse comes into view; two storeys with a verandah deep in shade.

"Nice spot," says Justin.

Past the end of the driveway there's a hayshed with its doors closed tight. In the nearest paddock, a couple of horses lift their heads from grazing to stare at us.

One of them, a tall fellow the colour of dusty earth, trots over to investigate, his head leant across the fence as far as the wires allow. The barbs are already coated with his hair; he's been scratching. We pull up on the grass beside the gravel, and Justin cuts the engine.

"Just like with Cath, okay?" He slips the keys into his pocket. "We'll start general, then see what he has to say about everything down at the swimming hole with Bruce and all that."

I nod, and we step out of the car. Everything is quiet. The farmhouse door is closed, and there's not even a breath of wind through the pines at the edge of the shelter paddock. I can't help myself; I step over to the red horse and give him my hand, letting him know me.

"Hey, beautiful boy." His breath is warm on my palm. He blinks at me with dark eyes, letting me scratch at his neck. I reach up to his withers. He's a big lad, not far off old Samson's height. He snuffles his nose into my shoulder, his lips nibbling and probing. "Looking for treats, eh? Can't help you, sorry mate."

"I'm going to check the house," says Justin.

I tuck my bag closer around my arm, stepping across the gravel driveway and onto the lawn, the grass plush for the season. The upstairs windows of the farmhouse glint in the sunlight; for a moment I see something move up there, then it's gone. A bird, probably, or a passing cloud.

Justin is knocking at the door and calling out, but no one answers. It's like we're held in a cupped palm, the ranges hiding us from view.

"I'll see if anyone's in the shed."

"All right." He's peering through the nearest window. "Don't go too far."

There are tyre marks in the gravel, not too old, from the looks of things. Between the farmhouse and the hayshed, there's a wide vegetable patch, the kind Frank would have dreamed of. Tomatoes hang in blood-red globes inside a green thicket of stems, and trays of fat zucchini lie waiting to be cut. It's an organised operation: from where I stand I can count three types of netting, and special coverings for the beds of berries. There's even a band of steel mesh dug low into the ground for the rabbits. Behind the farmhouse is an orchard: apple trees and plums, and a handful of olive trees.

Someone's put in a good chunk of time out here. A retirement project, clearly. This Prendergast might even rival Keith for his green thumb.

By the hayshed door, there's a hook with a lamp hanging under a metal awning. Kerosene. I haven't seen a kerosene lamp since I was a kid; we only used to bring them out if the wind had blown the wires down.

I'm reaching up to it to check it out, remembering the way Dad used to squint as he soaked the wick, when my eye catches a quick flash of orange at the edge of the shed. It disappears out of sight but not before I've seen a tail. First the tall red horse; now a ginger cat. Even if this is all the drive comes to, it won't have been a waste.

"Puss-puss," I say. "Here, puss."

I step to the corner of the shed on soft feet and stare around the side, looking for anyone who might be watching. There it is, crouched low behind an old plough with blades rusted into the earth, its attention fixed on something. There's a furtive leap, and a playful batting of a paw, white-socked. I move closer, still murmuring.

"What have you got there, puss?"

The cat lifts its head in my direction. In the sun, its eyes shine like new fruit, their pupils wide with the hunt. There's something in its mouth, a stout grey-black ball, jerking and twisting. It takes me a second to recognise it: a tūī chick, its yellow beak opening and closing in silence, calling for a cavalry that will not arrive. Not in time, anyway.

I stare at the two animals, and the young cat stares back at me, alert but unconcerned. There's a splotch of deep white fur peering through the orange of its face, a creamy puddle inside a bowl of apricot jam.

The shape is unmistakable.

A laundry room. A cardboard box. A birthday boy with folded legs—a charming and stubborn boy, a beloved boy—wincing as those little claws, bigger now and capable of their own mischief, pricked him through his new shirt. Party sounds from the lawn outside. Sausage rolls and sauce. A mother with secrets.

The cat's name forms in my mouth but my lips are incapable of sound. The tūī chick, a round ball dimpled with half-feathers, paddles its tiny legs. There's nothing to be done; it's pinned too tight, and those teeth are too sharp. Those wide black eyes can stare and stare, but the die is cast.

Patch.

It could be no other cat. The cream splotch across her face, the white fur blazing through her ginger coat like truer colour, and those darling socks. The markings are too distinct, and too strange to be a fluke. *She's like a pirate!*

I reach out for something to grab but my hands find empty air. The world slows to a terrible fraction of a second: one I'll live inside forever.

THE YOUNG CAT bounds away through the long grass, the chick tight in its mouth, and everything seems to rush past me, all shapes melting in the hard sunlight.

Bradley.

Justin is standing in front of the farmhouse, staring up into the second storey, his hands on his hips. The air is much too still; it's like someone's drawn a plastic bag down over us. I must have made a sound, because he lifts a hand to his forehead, shielding himself to see me. There's the ghost of a grin at the corner of his mouth, a curious expression curdling into worry.

"What's wrong?"

"He's here!" My throat is filled with sand. "Bradley's here!"

There's a snap like air from a popped tyre. A hot buzzing rips through the day, a seam torn in the world's fabric. Justin's head jerks back. His hands go to his throat, his eyes white with surprise. Shaking, his fingers come away coated in red. He looks to me for an explanation, trying in vain to speak. A second crack sounds, and a puff of crimson coughs out from his shoulder, the gunshot spinning him down into the gravel.

It's a terrible thing.

It takes me some time to move, all nerves tangled and coiled. Then I'm on my hands and knees, crawling against the car, my thoughts collapsing in a long tunnel of panic. I don't know where these sounds are coming from; I barely know where I am anymore. I pull open the car door and tuck myself inside its cleft, and the window collapses in a rain of toughened glass, the chunks bouncing off my face and shoulders. A third shot. The driveway—seems like it's coming from the driveway.

"Justin!"

My voice sounds like someone else entirely. Crouching, I look under the car, trying to get a clear view. Justin's feet kick out against the stones, his tired shoes wearing ruts in the gravel but going nowhere. My handbag is there, too, its contents spilled out against the stones; I must have dropped it. There's a wet sound like a drain coming unclogged. In and out, a rhythmic sucking that gradually slows.

It's Justin. The sound is Justin.

Bradley. Batman. A tiny black bird.

I'm trying to speak again. Everything feels blunted, my fingers turned fat and thick, useless balloons attached to me, unmoving. I must be breathing but I can't feel it. Behind me, there are low clumping sounds like faraway drumbeats. I stay as still as I can and listen for movement. The horses are running along the fence, their heads high and scared, their hooves slicing the dry earth. I stare into the car, at the empty metal slot for the keys. His pocket—Justin's. Impossible to get to them now. There's the radio, but that's no use either; we're too far out of reception. My mobile is in my pocket, still, but without any signal it's just a useless piece of glass and plastic.

I look behind me to the house, searching for any nook of cover. The verandah and the doorway, the stilled squares of shining glass; so much ground to cover, the whole expanse of gravel open under the wide-eyed sun. Even if I made it, I don't know who's waiting inside. If I did find a phone somewhere—unlikely; there's no visible line into the house—the shooter would still get to me first.

"Bradley!" He could be so close. He could be in that wood-shed, or behind any one of those windows. He could be in the orchard. "Bradley, it's me! It's your aunty!"

Nothing. Maybe he's nowhere near; maybe I'm just yelling into empty space. Even if he was nearby, I wouldn't want to call him into greater danger. But some part of me knows he can hear me, somehow. There's a flicker of warmth inside my chest, a spark that can't help but catch.

I creep slowly ahead, peering around the edge of the open car door. Sweat slides into my eyes, salty and stinging. Past the hayshed, the fence stretches back to the cattlestop. A mob of ewes graze in the shade of a walnut tree, their cloudy shapes still and serene. A line of bulrushes mark a dam; maybe a creek. There are dozens of places a person with a rifle could be. Whoever it is, they'll get to me eventually. If I'm going to wait here I might as well throw my arms up in surrender and join Justin in the gravel.

Justin.

I peer under the car again. He's still now. The lovely bird-man, unmoving. His shoes point up into the empty sky; a red-stained hand lies at his side, bordered by the wrinkled fold of his shirt cuff.

I can't see his face. Maybe it's a mercy.

"Justin." I know it's useless. "Please."

My breaths come fast in my chest, like steam from an over-heated engine. I wipe at my eyes and stare past the edge of the car door, waiting for something to reveal itself. There's nothing; only the empty space, the trees and the branches, and the sheep tearing at the grass with their quick teeth. Everything is watching.

A low clomp sounds behind me. It's the red horse, his eyes blinking and interested, head leant far over the fence, neck resting on the barbed wire. He stamps his feet into the earth and raises clods of soil, snorting as if he means to get my attention. I look from him down the fence to the far end of the paddock, where the tall row of windbreak pines tapers into shadow. I can make out a gate, and the suggestion of another paddock leading up into the ranges. If I can get there, out of sight of whoever has the rifle, then I can find a way south over those hills. There's salt in the air; we're not far from the sea, still. There's a farm there, I remember, where the river meets the coast. Glendu Station. I went there once or twice with Dad as a girl. Someone will be there; someone can find help.

For me, and for Bradley. Wherever he is.

"I'm coming, boy," I whisper to myself. "I'm coming back."

I reach inside for the map, brush the flecks of glass off, and tuck it into the pocket of my jeans. Measuring the space between car and fence, I picture my hand against the horse's neck, and the way my legs will need to slide up and over him. He's a tall animal but I've done it countless times. Long before this hip started giving me trouble, but still. I've done it.

There's Dad's voice in my ear, and his hands at my shoulders, coaxing me up again and again, telling me not to be afraid of old Samson, or his hooves like big hairy hammers.

Your feet need to pop off the ground, girl. You're a spring. Imagine yourself up there, looking down at me. Imagine yourself on his back, then put yourself there. He's your buddy, he is. He wants you up there.

Frank at the creek with the eel sack twisting. His eyes holding me, and the blueish smoke wafting between us.

You're some girl.

I wipe my hands together, looking around the edge of the car once more. I squeeze my hands together; this is about more than just me. Bradley. And Hēmi, and Precious. With a long breath, I push myself away.

My feet are slow beneath me, my legs barely moving. My eye stays on the spot my hand will need to grab: the smooth part of his neck just under his mane. There's another sharp snap and, behind me, the sound of metal striking metal. The horse tosses his head back, wanting to run. But he stays where he is, watching me.

I love him. I love this animal.

I cover the space between car and fence, and my good foot finds the middle wire, my hand reaching high into his mane. I'm about as graceful as a collapsed bridge, but now isn't the time. My bad hip is yelling at me, damn near screaming. And yet, my foot finds the right spot. The horse, my new friend, my best friend, the world's very best thing, stands steady long enough for me to slide up and onto his back.

"Hey, up!"

It's been decades, but the old commands all come back. My heels dig into his sides, and he lurches forward, the sweet mechanics of his body taking me away from danger. There's another shot, and the sound of hot metal through the air past my shoulder. I make myself as low as I can on his back, dipping and rolling as he moves, the steady percussion of his hooves taking us across the paddock. My knees are tight against his skin, my feet loose and ready. I think I hear another shot; I can't say.

Air blows hard against my body. We're really moving.

The second horse, the red chap's paddock-mate, is running alongside us, a blur of brown and white, her head thrown high into the air, her nostrils like dinner plates. The three of us come to the thinner end of the paddock where the fences run into the shade beneath the pines. There's a steel gate coming up, its top bar about where my foot is. Clutching his mane tighter, I ready myself for the jump.

"C'mon, now! C'mon!"

I lean forward and speak into the horse's ear, spurring him onwards. He's digging harder, every sinew of his planetary back stretching forward and away. The gate looks piddly and low, a child's plaything, no match for this animal rocket. Beyond, a wide field stretches up into the foot of a pine plantation; I can make out a stout shed in the distance, the steel roof winking in the sunlight. There's a track leading up into the cover of the trees, pointing the way. The gate is close now, almost underfoot.

We're in the shadows of the pines. The sun won't find us here.

This time, I don't hear the snap. There's just the meaty thump of metal against skin, and a tearing sound like a rope giving way. The horse screams and lifts his head. His front legs drop, his neck twisting as he falls. Then I'm airborne, with nothing in the world tethering me. The height is improbable, the air moving faster than I can ever remember. My hands reach out ahead, grasping at nothing. The silver gate rushes closer, until it's the only thing filling my eyes.

The earth rips open. It's dark in here.

We were almost done with our reading. It was the chapter on how people make steel in a big factory called a forge and all the different stuff that goes into it the chemicals and all that. It was my turn to make a speech to the others. Three minutes minimum five minutes maximum. A kōrero Mr. P said. I was writing it all out for practice about the iron and the carbon then Mr. P went to the sink with the binoculars and his voice got real quiet and he was biting his fingers. I could tell from the side of his face and the sounds outside that something was wrong. Then he held the edge of the sink with his hands and told us it was time for raspberry. That meant we had to get upstairs all three of us me and Bradley and Precious. We had to close the special door like we practised. I wanted to ask what about my speech but he ran to the back door. Go upstairs. Quick. His voice was strange and hissy like he was mad even though we hadn't done anything.

We went upstairs into our room to the special spy cupboard that looked like just another part of the wall but it was a trick because inside there was a little room for us to sit in and wait until he came up to tell us the game's over. You just had to know where to press on the wallpaper. It was really cool.

I got in there with Precious but Bradley just stayed next to the window looking outside. Precious told him Mr. P was going to be real mad and he'd lose the game for us but he didn't listen. Then we heard a car stop in the gravel outside and we knew we had to shut the cupboard door no matter what. That was the biggest rule of raspberry. So we left Bradley there and shut the door and sat in the dark listening. After a while I could see Precious a bit just her outline. There were voices outside a man's voice and a lady's. It wasn't the usual lady and it wasn't Mum or Dad so we just sat and waited like Mr. P told us because that's how you play raspberry.

Everything got real quiet. I could tell Precious was making faces at me behind her hands trying to make me laugh so I'd break the rules and then she could tell Mr. P and she'd be the only winner. She liked to do things like that to show us she was the first one there and the best one because she knew Mr. P from before. I just sat there on the little wooden chair next to her and tried to stay quiet and then there was a louder voice from outside. It was a lady yelling out to someone else and her voice sounded funny.

The rifle went off twice close together and I thought Mr. P's shooting the rabbits again. It was in the potatoes maybe or maybe in the greens or the orchard. I didn't like

226

to think about their fur and their bloody noses or anything so I closed my eyes and thought of Mum back home and Manaia standing in his crib watching me with his hands reaching out.

I was worried a little bit about Patch. We hadn't seen her since before we started our reading. Mr. P said never shoot at a rabbit unless you know exactly where all your animals are just in case. I thought Bradley must be worried too. Maybe that was why he didn't want to come into the cupboard. Then I could hear the horses running and there were footsteps across the floor and Bradley tapped on the cupboard. Precious held the special latch closed and wouldn't let him in because of the raspberry rules but I whispered to her again and again to open it and after a while she did. The light hurt my eyes.

Bradley looked different. He was scared I think even though he didn't get scared. He told us he'd seen his aunty outside and another man and the man was lying down in the driveway and his aunty had climbed up the fence and gone off on the red horse and gone away.

It was against the rules to let anyone in the cupboard once raspberry started but we let him in anyway. We could tell he was upset. Precious whispered to him. She said it probably wasn't your aunty really but some other lady because people get lost all the time when they're driving. She said Mr. P will explain everything it's all part of the game. Bradley got real quiet. I think he was crying maybe.

Precious looked at me in the dark. She told Bradley she wasn't going to say anything to Mr. P about him not being in the cupboard right away for raspberry then we might all get the same treat at the end. I wondered if I would still have to make my speech about the forge and making the steel or if Mr. P would let it be something for another day.

We waited in there for ages and ages. I was busting real bad. I told Precious but she told me I had to hold on. She told me to think of dry places like a sandy desert but then I kept thinking of the sand at the beach and all the water sloshing around in the waves and how Dad would play at sea monsters and pretend the seaweed was alive and trying to get him.

Right when I thought I might have to just go on the floor Mr. P came back and gave us the special knock on the door. Three knocks then two knocks then one. Precious undid the latch and he was smiling but his face was all red and sweaty like he'd been digging in the garden or running real fast. He said well done you've all won and I could tell Bradley wanted to say something but Precious just held his hand and squeezed it and said we'd all stayed in the special cupboard the whole time just like he told us to do.

Then Mr. P put his hand on our shoulders like he did sometimes. He told us we were all good kids and special. We came out of the cupboard and I only just made it to the toilet in time. When I looked out through the window in the lounge there was nothing in the driveway except for some black stuff in the gravel. The brown and white horse was running around in the paddock flicking its tail with its knees high up and looking strange. I didn't see the red horse anywhere.

SOMEBODY WAS WEEPING. A man. The smell of pine needles was high in my nose, the rotting spice of greenery turning to earth. Then the sun slid through the sky, coming down through the branches in broken pieces. A tightness in my chest, a hollow in my head, and nothing feeling right. He stayed in the corner of my eye, a thin man, dark hair; kneeling next to the stilled dusty flank of the horse, his shoulders hunched forward. When I blinked, everything was red. Low clumping sounds of panicked hooves in the paddock, and a throb moving audibly through me, some bodily alarm being struck, warning of something demanding attention. Sharp pieces moved under my skin when I breathed, like a jigsaw not quite finished. I went under again.

~

My tongue is the first thing alive. It searches the insides of my mouth, that slick furred territory, familiar, each of my teeth like dear old friends. A counting tongue. The blunted canines, the workhorse molars at the back, everybody a little rattled. Bloodied but still standing.

When they're ready, my eyes crack open. It's shaded in here, wherever here is. Walls, I think. Not too tall. Concrete bricks and wooden rafters, the corners iced with spiderwebs. The floor is hard, and there's a chemical smell in my nose, the eggy waft of sulphur and salt. It could be hell. Patty might know; she spends enough time in the big old book to be on advisory terms. Anyway, hell doesn't have to be a big place, or hot. No reason it couldn't be a shed out past Martinborough.

There's a noise in here. A low groan, a sick animal. I set a hand to my mouth, and it stops. I am the animal.

When I try to sit up, pain boils inside my shoulder. My hand goes to my collarbone; there's something pointy in there, new angles where I don't remember them. It's sharp but it hasn't come through the skin. I draw the longest breath I can manage, letting my ribs rise as far as they'll go, and pat my hands gently to my sides. Just bruising there, I think. No breaks. The legs are okay, too; if I really focus, I can feel my toes moving. The hip is a toaster full of bees but that's nothing new. The old instincts must have taken over, all those drills with Dad about staying loose in the saddle, and tucking your body as you fall, hands over your head in a nice wee parcel. A smashed collarbone is small beer when you think about it. Not like Justin.

"Justin." My voice is a whisper. "Justin."

My eyes are filling up. A second. I just need to take a second.

When I shut them, I'm back in the car again, the road's angry black ribbon running out beneath us, and Justin's hand calm on the gears. His eyes hold me in a soft friendly pocket as the high broken ridges scatter past the windows, this reluctant country tamed by fences, dotted with the last straggling native trees too lonely and defeated to even bend to each other in the wind. The engine hums smooth and steady, and we have all the time in the world. He speaks to me, letting me know he is there. It's a moment I can live inside, something I can stretch to my exact dimensions, a woman-shaped instant, warm and cushioned. A son off to medical school. A bottle of Jameson's in a cupboard. Then the image begins to drain away.

I know what's coming. Here it is.

Those same dear eyes wide and disbelieving. The fingers slick with red, the wet sucking at his throat, a bottle unstoppered. The terrible metal coming through the air to reach him. I'm close enough to see the exact moment it registered in his face: mouth stopped mid-sentence, eyes seeing enough to truly panic. The sun hung like a stone above us. A second shot, and then the gravel under my knees, and the door and the glass and the horse and the silver gate rushing.

"Justin."

I let the rafters dance in a wet kaleidoscope. I need to be still, for a second. Just a second. The new angles inside my shoulder can settle, and everything can calm down. A second might just work if I can make it long enough.

Later, I'm thirsty enough to try moving again.

It takes real planning, and sparks keep shooting under my skin in little spasms, but I manage to roll to my side. I'm laid out on a bed of old fertiliser sacks, the woven plastic scratched and fraying. There's a door, a wooden frame braced with metal, and some shelves with plastic drums, their labels faded and peeling. On the far side of the shed, a stack of nitrogen fertiliser bags lean together in a white scrum. A thin window runs along the top of the wall near the ceiling, letting in a fading band of light. My own desk and a printer murmuring in my ear and I could almost be back in the file room. Providing I haven't been restructured out of a job, obviously.

No time to pine, Lorraine. Not with a mouth tasting of gravel, and blood shunting through my head fistfuls at a time.

There's a steel bucket in the corner, and a cracked enamel mug next to it. Thoughtful. Gritting my teeth, I climb to my feet. Every movement brings more of the yellow hurt into my shoulder. If I hold my arm just so, I can make it through. It's possible something's dislocated, but there's not much I can do about it. I dip the mug into the bucket and bring it out dripping with water. A brief smell, and then I drink. Clear, sweet liquid. There could be anything in it, but I'm beyond caring.

"Oh, Jesus."

I sound froggy, somehow, like something exhumed. But

Christ, that water. I take another two cups, leaning against the wall for ballast. It's enough to get my thoughts moving again. I try the door with my good arm: it's locked from the outside. I can see the deadbolt through the tiny gap in the frame, and the shadow of what might be a padlock. Even with a screwdriver, the hinges are tucked safely inside the jamb. I knock my hand against the wood. It's surprisingly solid.

"Bradley! Somebody!"

I know it's useless; I can tell from the sounds outside how far away from everything I must be. There's only the low trill of cicadas, and the echoing clang from my hand against the door. My hands go to my pockets but they're empty: no map, and no phone, useless as it was. I'm still wearing my fleece, which is something; the floor is bare concrete, and a few old fertiliser sacks are only going to do so much during the night. If I make it that far.

I check the shelves but there's only drench and engine oil, and a couple of old car batteries with rusted terminals. The shelves themselves are bolted into the concrete, the steel rods disappearing into the flat grey surface. They don't move at all, no matter how I pull at them. The ceiling's no good either; the rafters might look old but I can tell they're sturdy.

I measure the space with my steps. Ten feet by eight, I'd say. Hardly enough to be a long-term solution. This man, the dark-haired thin man, must have something else in mind.

Prendergast.

My eyes go to the window. The light's thinning now; it's getting on dinnertime. I drag the full bags of fertiliser across under the window, laying them down in steps. It's longer work than it needs to be. Once, I twist my shoulder just so, and the pieces of collarbone click inside my skin, the pain nearly dropping me. Another cup of water for ballast, and I climb my makeshift pyramid. If I stand on tiptoes, I can just see through the window.

A mossy fence bisects the expanse of brown grass to the row of windbreak pines. Far away, the glinting steel of the gate where I went down. I must be in the shed by the track, I think; the one I saw leading up into the hills. There are long shadows reaching over the grass from behind me, so that all fits. Past the edge of the pines I can make out the orchard, and a tiny corner of the farmhouse verandah, the steel awning shining in the low sun. I'm stretching upwards, the fingers of my good hand clutching the sill tight, when I see movement between the apple trees. A girl, carrying something at her waist. A basket, maybe. It must be heavy; she's leaning down with her arms around it, moving in little sumo wrestler steps up onto the verandah. Her hair is dark around her shoulders. She steps up and out of sight.

It's too far to tell for sure. And yet I know it in my chest. Precious. It's Precious Kīngi.

"Hey!" I slam my good hand against the glass, making the frame wobble. "I'm here! I'm in here!"

I'm drawing my hand back again when my foot slips from the top bag. I have to reach out with my bad arm to stay steady, and just that small movement is enough for all the blood to drop out of my head. I slide down with my back against the wall and white-hot shards of hurt marching up and down my side. It's useless anyway; I'm too far to be heard, even without the window in the way.

She looked taller than in her photos. Though at her age, three months is enough to put some real length in the bones. She looked healthy. And if she's out there, walking around with an apple basket, then Bradley could be safe, too. And Hēmi Larkin. But mostly Bradley. If Prendergast has any sense at all—and from the state of the place, he must do—then those kids wouldn't have seen anything in the driveway. He could have had them hidden away somewhere, those three, and any others he might have. Precious hardly looked like a kid who'd seen a man shot through the neck. Even from this distance, I'd like to think I could tell a thing like that.

I keep my back against the wall, and the sacks beneath me; that small burst of exertion has spent me. I set my head back against the concrete, staring at the shelves: the chemical drums in black and grey, the row of stout batteries. They're heavy, those batteries. Nice and heavy.

I sink into a soup of thoughts, drifting and swaying as the light ebbs away through the window, the amber afternoon turning to silvery grey. Tilly will be hungry by now. The kittens too. Patty will see I haven't been back yet; she'll come over to take care of them, surely. How long until she realises something's wrong, something big? How long until she thinks to tell someone? Ambrose, maybe, or even Sheena? A day? Two? Even then, it'll take some piecing together. Justin told the chief he was heading over to Wellington. Even if they start looking in earnest, they'll need to talk to Cath Kīngi to get the angle on Prendergast. If the news goes out, really goes out, then the chief might get a call from the principal at Featherston Normal, or the laughing girl at the café in Martinborough. Even so, it's far from a sure thing. By the time anyone makes it out here, Prendergast will have done whatever he plans to do.

"Patty." I bring my hands gently together, whispering low. "I need you, girl. Call the station. Call Ambrose." It helps to picture her, leant back in her chair in my lounge, Tilly on her lap purring and stretching, frowning at the clock. "I need you."

It's nearly dark now. There are other things to think about. For one, all that water going in one end has to come out somewhere; I've been busting for an hour. I heave myself up from my fertiliser throne and check the shelves for an empty container. There: there's a twenty-litre drench drum that's almost spent. I pull it to the floor with a clang and twist the cap off, then crouch and aim into it. Not my most elegant moment but it could be worse. I shove the cap back on and shift the drum against the wall. I won't have to smell it, at least. That's something.

I'm leaning against the shelf, wiping the sweat from my cheeks, when a glimmer of light comes through the window. I listen close. There: the spluttering cough of a car engine clicking over, something tinny. It's a familiar sound, but only barely audible; I have to turn my good ear to the door to catch it.

I climb the bags and reach up to the window, seeing yellow headlights pan through the row of windbreak pines. It must be turning around.

"Hey!" I bang on the glass. "Hey!"

I scan the shadows behind me. The batteries. Moving awkwardly across the floor to the shelves, I grab the smallest one. It's a real fright to carry; I have to balance it against my good hip just to climb the sacks again. It takes both arms to get it high enough, the pieces of my shoulder rubbing together like a sheet of cracking toffee. I reach back with the battery and tap at the window, and a splinter shoots through the glass. Tiny, but it's something. I close my eyes and lean back, turning my head away, and toss the battery as hard as I can manage. With a loud crash, a head-sized gap opens in the window. Cool air crawls across my face.

"Help!" I scream as loud as I can manage. "Help me!"

The headlights keep moving in their slow arc, then head away from the farmhouse. Whoever it is, they're in no rush. I scream again but it's no use; from this distance they'll never hear a thing, especially over the rattling sound of the engine. I keep my fingertips to the sill and pull myself higher, staring through the gap in the window to the house. The air is black; I can only just make out the edges of the pines against the stars, and the shorter shapes of the orchard trees behind the farmhouse. Then, hovering in the dark above the edge of the verandah, there's a new smudge of light. It must be one of the kerosene lamps, like the one I saw by the hayshed.

"Bradley." I speak through the gap in the glass, my eyes

salty with tears. It's softer than the headlights, a faint yellow glimmer blinking in and out. "I'm coming, kiddo. I'm coming."

In a few moments, the light disappears, leaving only the inky pool hanging across the field. There's no way to know what's out there, or who might be watching. I sink down to my knees, my forehead pressed against the concrete. With my good hand pressed over the jagged bump in my shoulder, I try to think. After a while, I pull the empty fertiliser bags into a lumpy approximation of a couch, and I tuck my knees up into my fleece. The broken window lets in a tolerable chill.

I stare at the ceiling and listen to the wind move through the trees. A morepork calls out, its two-note greeting like a radar blip through the night, steady and searching. The world turns. I must be turning with it.

HE'S IN THE room before I'm awake. A shadow crosses my eyes, half dream and half reality, and he's there: a thin apparition just past my feet, something heavy balanced in his hands. My blood speeds through my veins.

A rock. That's how he's planned it.

"Don't . . ." I scramble back against the wall, my good arm held up between us. "Please, don't."

He stands still in the open doorway. Behind him, the first light of day is coming across the fields, the gold breaking open the dark. The last time I'll see it; what a lonely feeling. My eyes adjust, and I can see his face, the eyes watching me evenly, the jaw steady and composed. I look again to his hands, and see the sharp black edges of the shape he carries, and the rusted metal terminals. The battery.

"Bit of extra ventilation, eh?" He nods to the broken

window, then crosses the floor and sets the battery back onto the shelf, calm and unhurried. "Not a bad idea. It's a little musty in here, I'll admit."

"You . . ." My voice is shaking; my eyes go to the door. A few steps and I'd be through it, out into the open air. Then what? "You fucking . . ."

"That's enough of that, now." He reaches under the bottom shelf and slides out a thick drum of motor oil, setting it in the middle of the floor with a clang. "I think we've had our fair share of drama."

With his elbows on his knees, he watches me from his perch. He's someone I could've seen in a thousand places: dark hair, thick but kept tidy, eyes crinkled with the long summer like everyone else's. His cheeks are burnt, the skin under his eyes dappled with flecks of red, forearms tanned to a deep brown. You could almost take him for any other farmer, if not for his clear, unblemished hands. Decades of paper and whiteboard pens instead of handpieces and fencing posts. Not much he can do about that now. A townie's hands, Dad would've said. Nobody worth the attention.

"Nice little setup." He nods to the sacks of fertiliser. "Not too shabby at all." I watch his face, saying nothing. With a brief shake of his head, he gestures to a basket by the door, then slides it over to me with the toe of his boot. It's covered with a tea towel, light blue, and worn with many washes. "Got a bite for you. Some bread, a little stew. A few apples from the orchard, and muffins from the kids."

"The kids?" My eyes water.

"Sure." His voice is calm personified, though the edges of his fingernails are torn and red with biting. Plenty going on beneath this veneer of composure. "They love baking. Bradley especially. We had a whole afternoon of it planned out, actually. A reward, for speech day. Banana bread, a few different cakes we could keep in the pantry, even some caramel slice, if we had time. Then you two came by."

Bradley especially.

Of course. My handbag, my phone: he must know who I am. Still, the boy's here. The birthday boy. Our loveliest boy, our treasure. A sob escapes my mouth; I can't hold back the relief. Then, before I realise it, I'm leaning forward with a snarl.

"Where are they? What have you done with them?"

He doesn't flinch. "Right now they're sleeping. Wake-up isn't until seven, seven-thirty on the weekends. Then there's the morning chores before breakfast, and our first class. It's history today. We're pushing on with the land wars. Te Kooti's return from the Chathams. They're really getting into it. Precious too, not just the boys."

A self-satisfied grin creeps across his mouth, turning him into a triumphant stoat. There's a thin cord around his neck, and peering through the open button in his shirt, the deep green shine of polished stone. Pounamu. The tohunga. Sheena's house full of voices and feet striking the boards. And no Bradley.

He has no place being close to that stone. Pākehā that I am, even I know that.

"What? I'm supposed to be impressed, just because you're keeping them at the books?" I lean forward and raise my good hand. "You took those kids from their bloody homes!"

"Their *homes*?" He frowns. "That's being generous, isn't it?"

I shake my head. Patty's words sound out through my head. *It looked like a bloody bomb had gone off.* No time for distractions. Not now.

"They're coming, you know." I spit the words across the space between us. "The others. They know where we've gone. They'll be here soon."

"Maybe." He holds my gaze, staring with his grey eyes. There's something shifting in them, like disappearing smoke. "Or maybe they didn't know what you two were up to, eh? Maybe you wanted to keep some things hushed up? The city detective sharing his reports with the filing clerk, the two of you out on the trail, chasing bad guys?" He raises an eyebrow. "You're pretty far out of your wheelhouse, I'd say."

I sit locked in place, the wheels in my head clicking over. I can't tell what he knows; it's like I'm swimming across a choppy lake, my head just above water. I can't even see the other side, and the wind is picking up. Before I have the chance to say anything, he's leaning forward, his whole body coiled in anger. For a moment I'm sure he's going to hit me; my good hand comes up between us, feeble and shaking.

"Do you know how many years I had that horse?"

I feel my mouth drop open. "The horse?" I watch his eyes. "You shot a man through the neck." A choked sob leaves my body. "You shot him, right in front of the house where the kids could see."

He shakes his head. "They were inside, just like we practised. They know what to do. As far as they know someone drove up here by accident. It happens."

"Where is he?" I picture Justin laid out on the gravel, his feet pointing out over the stones, the bright sky so open above him. "What did you do with him?"

There's another flicker of shadow in his eyes. "It doesn't matter."

We're silent for the longest moment. There are tears falling across my cheeks but I don't shift them away. It's the very least I can do, to look this man in his face. There's more I could do, and should, but I'd need something sharp for that. Or something heavy.

"And what about Keith Mākara?" I raise my voice. "Everything you've done, you might as well have killed him too."

"Keith Mākara? You're joking, right?" His eyes dance with spite. "I read the papers too, you know. That guy had you at gunpoint, Lorraine. Not to mention what he was doing to your niece, and to Bradley. The drugs and the parties, and the rusted cars all over the bloody street. All those other patched guys hanging around, the hordes of losers and sponges just lying around guzzling and fighting and kicking each other."

A cold certainty settles inside me. "Don't you say a word about my niece. Not a fucking word." I watch his face; he seems to understand.

"Okay. Listen." He leans back against the oil drum and takes a long breath. "Yesterday, with the detective, he . . . it couldn't be helped." He pulls his lips tight. "It's the last thing I wanted to do. But I'm not about to put those kids at risk. Not for anything. You must understand."

"Put them at *risk*?"

"Do you know how easy it was? Do you?" He looks through the door towards the farmhouse, chest puffed out. "How many people were at that party? And not one of them checking on the kids. Not your precious niece, not the neighbours, not anybody. I just walked inside. You know that, right?" He fixes his eyes to mine. "I came right in off the street and found Bradley's room. He hardly even argued. So long as he had his kitten, he was happy. I had a box all ready for her."

My head is spinning. I feel my eyes narrowing. "You brought a *box*? How did you . . ."

"You wouldn't even recognise him now," he says. "He must've been a good five kilos underweight when I picked him up. He's healthier out here. He's happier, too. And his classwork is making real strides." He shakes his head from side to side. "You know they hadn't even started him on his times table, right? His bloody times table!"

I keep my eyes on him, but I'm gauging the objects in the room. The basket and the batteries, the drums on the shelves. The window; if only I'd thought to pull out a chunk of glass, something sharp. It's too far now, and much too high.

"Is that the plan, then?" I squint. "Rescue every kid from

every struggling family in the Wairarapa? You'll need a bigger house, mate."

He's nodding along, as if he expected to hear this and he's pleased to be proven right.

"Such a lazy argument." He smirks. "Honestly, I'd expected more. Especially given everything with Sheena."

There's a stone in my chest. "What do you mean?"

"You know what it's like, Lorraine. You know how difficult it can be." He opens his hands in appeal. "What are we supposed to do when the ones we love can't get their shit together, eh? When they're fundamentally unable to take care of the most important things?"

My mouth feels frozen. There are things I can say but it's better to let him speak; I can hear the decades of teaching in his voice. The easy gratification of knowing more than his audience.

"It's easier to mock me than to take the question seriously, I suppose." His eyes are glassy with passion. "But with everything we've done to this country. All this land, the prison we made out of the Treaty, and those schools thrashing language out of the kids until it was bloody near gone. We're complicit. We both are." He raises a fist to his chest. "Our house is on fire, Lorraine. It's up to every one of us to decide what to do about it. Okay, it's only three kids. But it's something. There have always been those of us willing to do something over nothing."

Mangled shoulder or no, I can't help but let out a laugh. "Oh, sure," I say. "Of course you're doing it for them. Those wayward savages'll never save themselves, will they?"

There's a quick glimmer of hurt in his eyes. His jaw pulls tight, and he stands and dusts off his legs. "This is the best place for the kids, away from those families, away from the drugs and all that other shit." A new tremble comes into his features. "You should've seen them all, that day at the river. You've never seen such a hopeless bloody gathering."

Outside, the bleat of a sheep sounds out, lonely and distant.

"It's not for you to say." I hold my voice firm. "It's not for any of us to say."

"You've seen the files, Lorraine." He holds me in cold regard. "You know better than anyone what a favour I've done those kids."

In my mind, I'm walking the hallway again, Cath Kīngi leading us to her kitchen. The mildew in the corners, the wind blowing through gaps in the windows. There's that same sour smell, like food curling at the edges.

"You're fucking deluded, mate."

"Am I?" He looks out into the daylight, those early glimmers playing over his features. "They'll be up soon." He nods to the basket and turns to leave. "Get some food in your stomach. I'll bring something to strap up that shoulder. In the meantime, try not to move it too much."

"Then what?" I go to stand but my bad arm is giving me too much pain. "What happens after that?"

He rests his hands on his hips. There's an air of command in his posture; in his mind, he's in front of the classroom, herding all the facts into neat rows, a fount of knowledge for those rows of bright eager faces. A shepherd.

"We'll have to see," he says.

The door swings closed, and the bolt slides home. There's the click of a padlock, before his footsteps swish away through the dry grass. I clamber to my feet and grasp the windowsill so I can see him walk away down the fence line, stiff-legged and severe, tucking a set of keys smartly into his jacket pocket. Beyond him is the row of watching pines, and the tiny corner of the farmhouse peering out like hope behind the branches. I close my eyes and picture that soft smear of lantern light through the trees.

Bradley. He's there. Our boy. Our boy is just across the field.

As soon as Prendergast is out of sight, I slink back down to my perch and reach for the basket, doing what I can to keep the shoulder steady. There's a hole in my stomach I hadn't anticipated; it's all I can do not to swallow the bread by the slice. The stew is cold but it's lovely: good firm carrots, the potatoes falling apart in the gravy, and the beef peppered and tender. I'm nearly through the first muffin before I remind myself to slow down; there's no telling when he'll be back with more.

I take a cup of water and lean back against the wall to let my stomach settle. In truth, all that clear-eyed earnestness took me off-guard; I can't help but wonder what Justin would have made of it. Patty too, come to think of it. She was so fixated on the horrible state of the Larkin and Kīngi houses.

First things first. I reach up to the sill again, and my fingers find a loose piece of glass at the edge of the hole. With care,

I manage to work it free. A shard like a cheese knife: stubby, but with a curved hook on one end. I tear a piece from one of the old fertiliser sacks and wrap it around the thicker end, then tuck it inside my fleece, right under my arm.

There.

My eyes fall closed. I feel the wall at my back, its flat grey surface, the tiny grains and bumps in the bricks. I think of home, of Patty. Head set back against the pillows in her usual spot, legs resting up in front of her. Tilly will be up on her lap, cleaning her whiskers with her little engine going. She'll have called someone by now, surely. Sheena, or the chief. Someone. She must know something's wrong. She'll feel it, somehow. She'll know.

"Come on, girl." I tuck my good hand inside my fleece, my fingers playing at the edge of the glass. It's old but it's sharp enough. "Come and find me."

I CAN'T SAY if it's the adrenaline wearing off, or too much time in this cave with just spiders for company, but my shoulder is starting to feel like it's no longer part of my body. It's better under the wet tea towel, but not much. There are still pieces floating inside me, bone and cartilage suspended in a loose pulp.

I reach up to the window a few times during the day, praying for a glimpse of the kids in the distance and hoping the wind might carry my voice. But there's nothing, or at least nothing I can see. There's no Precious Kīngi with the apple basket, and no Prendergast with his stiff zealot's gait. As evening draws down and the lantern comes on through the trees, I give up my watch and settle in my usual spot, picking at the two remaining muffins. Stewed pear with cinnamon and cloves. Not bad.

The window lets in a thin square of day, a narrow searchlight shifting across the shelves and up into the rafters before it dwindles. It's almost dark; my morepork friend will be out soon. I let my eyes close, and I try to conserve my energy.

There are sounds outside.

The brushing of dry grass, and then a quick inhale of breath, something like surprise. I swing my legs to the side and move off the bags, standing on the inside of the doorway, the glass shard tight in my hand. Neck height: that's where I need to aim. I wait for the jangle of the keys, and picture him coming through the door, and the way I'll lunge forward and up. There's enough of a moon for me to find a good spot, somewhere that'll put him down for a while.

Breathe.

There's a quiet tap against the steel door, as if he's bumped into it. Then, another one, quieter still. I hold myself as still as I can, watching the air where he'll step through and inside. I can hear him fiddling with the padlock; he's taking a lot longer than I'd expected.

I'm ready.

"Aunty?" A whisper; a boy's whisper.

"Bradley?" I fall to my knees, staring through the tiny gap between door and frame. "Bradley! Oh!"

There's only a thicker patch of dark to suggest the presence of a person. I don't want to believe it; it's a joke, a trick played by a desperate mind. I'm dreaming. He can't really be here.

"I stood on something," he whispers. "I stood on a prickle."

Relief floods through me. A trick boy wouldn't say that. A trick boy would wear shoes, but not Bradley. For Bradley, shoes are just mousetraps with laces, prisons for his toes. He even tries to play rugby barefoot; the coaches have to threaten him with the bench just to make him wear boots like the other kids.

"There's glass," I stammer. "The window, I had to . . . oh, kiddo. You're okay! Are you okay?"

"I saw you," he says. "I saw you through the window, climbing the fence onto the horse. There was a man in the driveway, lying down. Hēmi doesn't believe me, and neither does Precious. Mr. P told us it was just someone come to deliver the mail by accident." He sniffs. "But I saw you. And there were muffins missing in the pantry, even though he said they had to last us till next week, and . . ."

"It's okay, darling." I wipe at my eyes. There's so much relief in me now, all those hours staring at my night-time ceiling and wondering. But we need to put our time to better use; Prendergast could get here any second. "It's all going to be okay. I just . . . can you see the lock, there? There's a padlock, right?"

"Huh? Um . . . yep. There's one up high, and one down low, here." The shadow moves, and there's a clank of metal by my knees. "I don't have any keys, Aunty."

"Is there a phone in the house?"

"There's nothing like that." His little voice sounds defeated. "There's not even normal lights or none of that."

"Listen, now." I keep myself as calm as I can. "I need you to run, okay? Run as fast as you can. These hills past the shed, there's a track there. You can follow it over and into the next farm, I think. It's Glendu Station. Glendu. It can't be far, maybe an hour at the most. When you get there, just follow the nearest road until you find someone. You call the police and tell them. You tell them what's happened. Tell them Justin's been shot."

It's quiet on the other side of the door. I don't know if he's heard me.

"Bradley?"

"I can't, Aunty."

My hands are shaking. "You have to, kiddo. You have to be brave, now."

"I can't." There's a change in the shadow; he must be shaking his head. "Not if you and Hēmi are still here."

I can't help but smile. He's being a lot braver than I might have been.

"The keys, then." I clear my throat. "Get the keys. They're in his jacket. The pocket on the left side, okay? Make sure you have them both, kiddo. You need both."

"He keeps his jacket in his room," says Bradley. "Behind the door, I think. He hangs it up. Or by his bed, maybe."

His bed. That fucking scum. "Listen to me. Did Prendergast . . . did Mr. P do anything? To you, I mean?"

"Like what?"

My tongue is heavy. "Did he touch you? You, or the other kids?"

There's a long pause through the door. My fingers are digging hard into my palms; every atom of me is ready to tear the bastard's head clean off. I swear I could pull this door off its fucking hinges.

"Only on my shoulder," he says. "Sometimes he pats me when I'm doing good with my reading. That's all. Like Dad does sometimes."

Keith's big hands. Tight around my forearm; gentle against my niece's cheek. Sometimes we know so little.

"You're sure?" Some of the pressure leaves me. "You're sure he didn't do anything else to you, or the others? Anything . . . anything not nice?"

Another pause. "He likes to pat us during class. Just on the back."

I exhale. "All right. Listen, kiddo. I need you to . . ."

"The neighbour lady tries to hug us a bit." He's so quiet, I almost can't hear him. "But she only comes out here sometimes."

"The neighbour lady? You mean someone from the next farm?"

"The lady next door to you," he says. "The lady with the colours in her hair."

I feel myself frowning. "No, Bradley. That's . . . you're thinking of someone else. That's Patty. She's in Masterton. Remember when she moved into the old Wikaira place, after Mrs. Wikaira had her heart attack?"

"It was her, Aunty. She comes out here sometimes, in her car." His voice is taut and serious, as serious as a boy can manage. "She came out yesterday, after I saw you on the horse. We came out of the cupboard, and Mr. P drove into town to use the phone, and then later she came out. They were talking outside. They were cross with each other. She was crying, I think."

I lean my hands to the door, its steel frame cold against my skin.

The in-between look on her face at the door, and the new distance in her eyes. Like I was someone new, someone different.

Thick-peel marmalade.

I know I overstepped.

S. Prendergast. Stuart. Patty's Stuart.

Patty.

"Aunty?" His voice is shaky and quiet, like something heard from far away. "Aunty, what's wrong?"

I'm on the floor, my knees against the concrete. There's a void hanging through my brain, a grapefruit scooped empty. I can't feel anything: not my collarbone, not my bad hip. I can't even feel the chunk of glass held tight in my hands, the edges cutting into my skin.

"Aunty?"

"It's okay, baby." I make the usual movements but my mouth makes no sound. I swallow, trying to make my tongue comply. "The keys. Just find the keys."

"I'll have to try tomorrow. I'll try, Aunty."

There are tears falling from my eyes. My whole body is shaking. "I love you, kiddo. We love you so much. Your mum, she . . . you won't believe how much she misses you. You'll be with her soon." It's like I've swallowed hot coals. "Now go. And be careful."

"I will."

There are more footsteps swishing away through the grass;

I stare through the door and watch the darkness change colour. Then I drag myself across the floor to the water bucket and jam my head inside. With the cool liquid holding my face I can scream. I scream until my lungs are empty, and then I come up to take a breath and scream some more, until there's nothing left inside.

The water fills with ragged noise, my hair sticking to my neck in wet clumps. At some point my body has had enough; I fall to the floor, eyes to the ceiling, measuring the exact volume of darkness inside these four walls, from the floor to the dusty rafters. Then, the darkness outside, the night's black net strung across the field, and the trees, and the farmhouse with its tiny sleeping bodies.

All the darkness in the world, all the darkness that has ever been. The whole inky void holding this scattered universe, every sphere and rock: it's nothing measured against the contents of these human hearts.

I DON'T SLEEP. I stare up into the rafters and pluck thoughts from my mind like river stones. What creatures might be hiding underneath?

All those afternoons and evenings, a thousand lemons cut for gin, all those trays of pork and cabbage from Leong's. The tea and the cake, the crispy potatoes, the biscuits. The chats about her shifts at the claims centre, and Ambrose. *Villa Wars.* Her divorce. Christ, why make up a thing like that? For sympathy? Sheena and Justin. The file room.

The file room. Jesus. Of course.

There's clarity breaking through me in wide chunks now: a calving glacier of impressions and understandings, the lies falling away in sheets. Her enthusiasm when Justin asked me to join the briefings, and the naked burning interest in her eyes after reading the files on my table.

How long? How long had those two had this in mind for me, and for Bradley? Was it there from the start? Were the pieces in place from that first afternoon?

The whole street was watching the old Wikaira place back in November, just to see what was happening with the market. Rickett's Circle isn't exactly Masterton's fanciest street but it isn't rock bottom, either. In any case, we were surprised to see moving trucks in the driveway only a fortnight after the rental listing went up. Old Mrs. Wikaira with her cress stew and fried bread on Sundays was barely in the ground, and now I had some new woman leaning across the fence by my cactus glasshouse, kind-faced, her hair enthusiastically lacquered with expensive colour. A few years younger than me: late forties, probably. Slightly on the short side, and a touch of softness creeping in at the middle. Pretty, though. Pretty enough for a person to notice.

"Hell of a day to bloody well move in, eh?" She lifted her eyebrows at me. "Someone had the toilets drained, and I'm busting. It's either your place or the lemon tree out back. Would you mind?"

I put down my pruning shears and dusted off my hands, nodding over my shoulder to the door. "Away you go. Just inside on the left."

"Oh, you're a darl." She stuck a hand into mine as she stepped through the gate. "Patty."

"Lorraine."

She crossed the lawn in a shuffle, not bothering to take her shoes off at the door. Not that my carpets are in showroom shape or anything, but still. In a few minutes she reappeared.

"That was a close one." She held a palm above her eyes, shielding herself from the no-nonsense sun. "Thanks."

"No worries at all." I shrugged and bent back down to the shrubs. It was late spring, and the garden gets out of control if you don't keep a close eye around then. Frank taught me that.

"Been down this way long, then?"

"A wee while," I said.

I wasn't looking, but I could tell she was nodding just to fill the space. Behind her, men were moving up and down the driveway, carrying couches and shelves. Had one of them been Stuart? Had he been watching from the very start, gauging this first interaction?

"Well, then." Patty had shuffled her feet, the grass bristling under her shoes. "I should probably get back. Those boxes aren't going to unpack themselves."

"Righto."

At the time, I couldn't say why she persisted. It wasn't like I'd been welcoming, or even particularly neighbourly. Yet she made the effort.

"Listen, how about I bring a bottle of Gordon's over tonight? That's your brand, right?" She must have seen some distance in my eyes as I climbed to my feet. "Not that I was prying or anything."

I gave my hands a soft clap and let the soil fall away. A look of pendulous hope shifted in her and I felt like the first rescuer at the scene of some large-scale tragedy, faced with the sole survivor blinking in disbelief. A tiny smile must've spasmed across my mouth, a tic of generosity. My niece was coming over with Bradley in the morning, but they wouldn't be too early. It'd be fine. This woman seemed harmless and lonely. That whole big house and just her; there was a story there.

"Sure," I'd said to her. "Why not."

Three little words, and you've never seen a person's face light up so bright.

Christ. The claims centre. I'm with Southern Insurance myself; they've got my employment history, my personal details, everything. She'd have known I was close to what went on at the station; she'd have known I was a way to see inside the investigation. Someone open to new company. Someone nobody would think twice about. I was just the right person.

No wonder she can't say Sheena's name aloud.

I take a breath and let my hands go loose around the piece of glass. I need to stay focused; it won't do me any good to lose my wits. Jesus, if I'd kept my head straight I could have seen it earlier. And Justin might still be here.

Above me, the window lets in the thinnest flicker of light. Right on cue, I hear boots scuffing through the grass; the jangle of keys. I sit up on the fertiliser bags, my shoulder ringing out like an angry bell. I go to stand but there's no time; instead, I tuck the glass inside my fleece, there for me to reach with my good arm. The door opens out, and the dark square becomes thin silver.

"Morning."

He's carrying something in each hand this time. Another basket with a tea towel on top and a fresh bucket of water. He sets them both by the door and resumes his perch on the oil drum, giving me a proprietary look.

"Sleep okay?"

I stare into his face and try to see what Patty must see, arranging his features into familiarity, into belonging. It's impossible; all I see is a hawk lingering in the currents, watching for movement below.

"Fine."

"Not too cold, I hope?" He nods to the empty sacks strewn across the makeshift bed. "Gets a bit of chill in the air, even at this time of year. It's been hard on the tomatoes, you know. The berries, too. Bradley's been helping me lay some netting for it. He loves a project, that kid."

He gives a small smile, encouraging me to do the same. I try to make the shape with my mouth—lulling, safe—but I can't. I cannot smile at this man. I feel the glass tucked against my side, and I imagine pushing it into him.

"That's what this all is, really," he says. "A project. Or the start of one, anyway." He scratches at an elbow. "I know you won't see it that way, but that's what it is."

"You're right," I say. "I don't."

He doesn't seem fazed. "If I told you how many kids came through my classroom wearing shoes two sizes too small, their toes crunched up, the same set of clothes every day for weeks at a time. No one turning up to the parent interviews, except sometimes the grandmothers. A sachet of Raro for lunch. You wouldn't believe how often I've seen that. A dry packet of instant noodles if they're lucky." He shakes his head. "How the hell can a person see that every day, year after year, and not want to do something?"

"So put on a lunch. Sign up for those school breakfasts. Jesus, open a few scholarships." I lean forward. "You don't have to rip the bloody families apart."

"Charity is just welfare that feels better. A Band-Aid, that's all." He points a finger sharply through the air. "You know it as well as I do, Lorraine. Welfare has completely stuffed this country. It wasn't enough to step in and take all the best bits for ourselves. We had to put everyone on the teat as well. Just enough money to keep them from helping themselves out, not enough to give them a proper leg up. And the pay goes up with every kid you push out. How's that for an incentive? How the hell's anyone supposed to get on their feet with a deck stacked like that?" He looks me in the face. "This is the only way there is to really change things. I know you see it. I know you do."

I watch his eyes as he speaks, the glint of conviction in them. He's been waiting for a moment like this. Christ, he's probably written this all down somewhere. If I can just keep him talking, he might give me an opening.

"Why Precious?" I hold a hand to my collarbone. "Why start with her?"

A proud smile. "She's gifted, that girl. Sharp with numbers, picks things up nice and quick. And she thinks with systems. She doesn't just learn things one at a time—she's figuring out how it all fits together. But that wasn't it, really. It was her parents. That dropkick dad always hanging around those patched guys, and the mum—out of it in the supermarket, dead behind the eyes." He's quiet for a long moment. "You know she came to school with bruises, right? The arms and the wrists. The neck too, once or twice."

"You could've called someone."

"Right." He smiles sarcastically. "And what happens then, eh? They move schools. I've seen it before, you know. Child, Youth and Family hardly lift a bloody finger. No, she was too smart for that. Too smart to be moved. I knew if I could just protect her, keep her somewhere away from all the crap, the useless wasters at home, her other mates, then she'd have a chance. They all would."

My throat feels parched. I nod to the bucket of water, and he carries it over to me, setting it down beside the empty one. As he bends down, he shows his neck to me, the tanned stretch of skin and sinew waiting for the glass.

It's so close. My hands itch.

No. I exhale slowly. I've seen enough animals stuck with knives to know how uncertain it can be. Get it wrong and I might just force him to kill me. Then Bradley and the other kids will never get away.

I take the cup of water.

Calm. If I can keep him nice and calm, I can make it through the day. The night will be its own opportunity.

I raise the mug and drink, watching him. "What about Pākehā kids then, eh? They don't need your help?"

"Oh sure, sure." He nods vigorously. "Some might. But

pick any metric you like, and the picture's clear. Educational achievement, overcrowding, whatever. Those three kids are the best place I could possibly start. For the future? I wouldn't rule anything out."

There's something of the preacher about him when he speaks: the world already sorted, all questions answered in advance.

"The way I see things, Lorraine, there are two ways for us to go here." He speaks slow and clear, like he's explaining something to a child. "We haven't had the best start. I know that. But if you could only see how well these kids are doing here, you might just change your mind." He leans forward, his eyes clear and sincere. "You could help me, Lorraine. You could help me with them. I know you see what I see. There are plenty of others out there. We're only just scratching the surface."

I stare back at him, doing my best to keep a straight face. And Patty, I think. What about her? How would he expect me to cope with that grenade of information?

"And the second way?" I ask.

He shakes his head. "I can't let anything happen to these kids. Not anymore." His voice is grave, every letter etched in stone. "If you can't see your way to letting it go, then I'll have to do something I don't want to do."

The words hang between us, heavy in the air. He reaches down for the basket of food and sets it on the sack next to me, then gathers the empty one from the wall.

"Wait," I say. "What . . . what about when they get older? What then?"

He gives a self-assured smile. "Kids can forget almost any-thing if they're stimulated. And we've got enough distractions out here to keep us going a long, long time. After that, who knows. Whatever happens to me, it will have been worth it." He nods his head pensively. The easy martyr. "Think about it. I'll be back in the morning."

The door swings shut, and the padlocks click back into place. I feel tears roll down across my cheeks. I close my eyes, and all the weight of exhaustion falls over me. His footsteps shush back across the field, away into the dawn creeping over the land.

"Bradley," I whisper.

It's down to you now, kiddo. All of it.

BETWEEN RATIONING THE basket of food and cutting one of the fertiliser sacks into a sling for my bad arm, I make the hours pass. I'm listening, despite myself, for sirens in the driveway, the chief's booming macho voice cutting this situation open. After a time I tell myself to stop. Not every kind of hope is useful.

I tie the sling tight against me, trying to keep the fracture as still as I can. It's awkward but it helps take some of the weight at least. As the sun falls through the afternoon, I listen for changes outside, keeping my time at the window to a minimum. There's nothing much to see, anyway; Prendergast knows better than to let the kids into view with me still in here, waiting. I close my eyes.

I'll have to do something I don't want to do.

No reason not to believe him. It wouldn't be easy, I'm sure, but he'd do it. His eyes told me he would: their surfaces hard and bright with conviction. It'd be just like with Justin, only I'd know it was coming. At least for him it was over quickly. He never had to sit in a shed for days, sweating into his clothes and knowing those children were so close.

As the afternoon ebbs away, I think back to his hotel room. The way he'd looked at me: really looked. There's anger in me too; all it takes is to think of Patty in my lounge, leaning back in Frank's old chair, and my heart starts thrashing. I lie still and try to rest, my brain shifting between those two speeds of memory.

Whatever happens next, I'll need the energy.

Bradley comes earlier than I expected. The night has only just thickened to black, the window letting in the last embers of daylight before the moon takes over. My morepork companion is calling out from the trees, closer to me, as if he's perched on my shoulder, speaking into my ear.

There's the soft scratch of footsteps outside, slower and more careful than last time. I sit upright and tuck my arm into my side. Everything inside me is rushing.

"Aunty?" He's behind the door, whispering. "I got them. I got the keys. They were in his jacket, like you said."

I swallow a sob of relief. The open air, the movement. But most of all, seeing this boy, and holding him. He's so close.

"How many are there, kiddo?"

A quiet clinking of metal. "There's . . . there's heaps. Ten, maybe. I can't . . ."

"Try the little ones first." I speak through the gap in the frame, watching his shadow. "The littlest ones should be for the padlocks."

"Okay." It's his concentrating voice. His Lego voice, and his Saturday-morning Batman voice, a bowl of cereal on the carpet, eyes fixed to the screen while his favourite hero leaps and punches, always slipping out of danger at the last second. There's more clinking, then a metal snap from the padlock up top. "I got one!"

"Good kid!"

I crouch down and wait for him. My body is calling out to me in all its shades of hurt: the hip and the shoulder, the bruised ribs. Right now, I can't feel any of it. There's more of the low jangle, and then a sweeter sound than I'll ever hear: the click of the second padlock coming open, and the sliding of the bolts. The door swings slowly outwards, and he's there in front of me, staring inside with slices of moon in his eyes.

"Come here, my love." I'm crying, my words thick and wet. His arms come up and around me, slowly. "Gently, now. Gently."

He settles his head on my good side, and I press my face to him. He's taller, I'm sure of it. His chest seems thicker too, his belly rounder than before. He holds on to me, quiet and still.

"Are you okay, Aunty?"

I wipe at my nose. "I am now, baby. You don't know how much we've missed you." He's close enough for me to see his expression; there's a spark of shock in his eyes. "I must look a real fright."

"You smell like egg sandwiches," he says. "Just a bit."

I can't help but chuckle. "It's the fertiliser, look. I've been sleeping on it." He pokes his head inside. "How's that foot of yours?"

"It's okay," he says. "I just scratched it under my big toe. What happened to your arm?"

"Don't worry about that." I squeeze his arm. "Can you still run?"

He nods, looking serious. "Yep. I can run."

We step out into the field, held in the thin silver coming through the clouds. There's a touch of wind, and the smell of rain on the way. Bradley guides me in a wide circle around the glass; I'm shaky on my feet but after a few steps the rhythm comes back to me. We reach the fence and follow it, heading to the gate under the pines. It's almost too much, being in the open again. There's so much dark, so many angles and shadows that could be hiding him. I keep a hand on Bradley's shoulder, reassuring myself that I'm not alone.

Such a miraculous thing. How long have I spent wondering about this boy, and hoping? And here he is. He looks up at me, focused. Even in the dark, I can make out a version of Keith's serious expression hiding in him.

"The car's in the hayshed," he whispers. "There's a lock on that door, too."

"Here." I motion for the keys. "You'd better give me those."

He hands them over. There's a car key, and what feels like a few more padlock keys. I tuck them into the pocket inside my fleece, next to the piece of glass.

"Where does he keep the rifle?"

"It's in the hayshed, in a locker." He points through the row of trees to a darker lump of shadow: the wooden shed with the wide doors. "He takes us to shoot rabbits, sometimes. Behind the woolshed, next to the potatoes."

We come to the gate, and Bradley swings it open with a slow squeak. It's hard to make anything out under the pines, though there are still marks on the ground where the horse went down. To the side, there are divots from a tractor, and a wide patch of flattened needles. He must have dug a hole somewhere nearby.

Maybe that's where Justin is, too.

"Are you okay?" Bradley stands in place, watching me.

"Come on." I wipe at my nose; it won't do any good for him to see me upset. Not when we have a job to do. We move across the paddock and through another gate. "Where are the other kids?"

"We all sleep upstairs," says Bradley. "They didn't see me, I don't think. Hēmi talks in his sleep sometimes, but he doesn't wake up. Most of the time Precious just throws a pillow at him."

Our feet meet the gravel; we need to walk softly now. There: that's where we parked the car, the friendly sun coming down, the horses trotting over to see us. Over there is the spot Justin was standing. An electric tremble runs through me, the same old feeling of spiders over my shoulders. There's no time to dwell. We come to the hayshed, to the thick wooden gates on their steel rollers. My hands feel for the padlock at the edge of the door, and I try the keys one by one until the clasp pops open. I lift a hand to slide the doors across, but Bradley grabs my arm.

"Not yet," he whispers. "It's noisy."

I nod. "Show me the locker."

Around the side of the shed, we step through a door streaked with gravel dust. There's the cooing of pigeons high in the ceiling, and the waft of oil in my nose. It's dark in here; Bradley has to lead me forward by memory, placing his feet carefully over the concrete floor. I reach out, and my good hand knocks against metal. It must be Prendergast's car, the station wagon. I can't see the colour but I have a feeling it's apple-red.

"Over here," says Bradley.

He guides my hand through the dark to a thin metal safe, a padlock over the latch in the middle. It's hard going by feeling alone; it takes me a minute to find the right key. Then, the door swings open, and I reach inside. My hands register the wooden shape of the stock, the cool metal of the barrel.

Keith's hand tight on my arm. Justin coming up from the track below, the light shining, and the waves murmuring in the distance. How am I supposed to tell this kid about his dad? Assuming Prendergast hasn't already broken the news, somehow. There's so much to get across, and no time.

"He keeps the bolt up there," says Bradley. "On the shelf."

My eyes are adjusting now; I feel for that strange piece of metal, a smooth cylinder with a hook on the side like a stuck-out thumb.

"There are bullets in the magazine," says Bradley. "He keeps them ready, for the rabbits. You just click that bit backwards, and then . . . here, I'll show you."

He lifts the rifle from my hands, and we step out through the door into the moonlight. Crouching down, he slips the bolt inside the end of the barrel just under the scope, clicking it forward with a comfortable snick.

Prendergast is right. The boy does love a project.

"There's one in the chamber now." He hands the rifle up to me, and I take it with my good hand, resting the stock against my sling. "The safety's off. You just need to push the bolt bit down against the side. That's all."

"All right, Rambo." We turn towards the farmhouse, the two storeys looming through the dark. "Where does he sleep?"

There's a long pause. "What are you going to do, Aunty?"

"Nothing, kiddo." I bend down to him, close enough for him to see me. "You go upstairs and get the others, quiet as you can. I'll stay outside his room in case he wakes up. Then, once we're all outside in the car, we can open those big doors, okay? We'll be gone before he knows what's happening."

He looks at the rifle. "That's all?"

"That's all."

"Okay," he whispers.

On soft feet, we move across the gravel and around the side of the farmhouse and past the vegetable patch. There are no lights on anywhere; the whole house is shrouded and silent. My heart is lurching in my chest; I'm acutely aware of every complaint in my body, the shoulder like bone gravel, the ribs aching with every step. And yet, I'm focused.

Three kids. Three kids, and I can leave this place. I'll get to the nearest phone and call Ambrose. Then it'll be over.

"Wait."

We come to the verandah, and Bradley holds his hand up for me to stop. He takes the wooden steps one by one, pointing out the squeaky spots. In a slow zigzag across the boards, we come to the back door. He eases it open, making room for me to step inside. There's a narrow hallway and a doorway into the kitchen. Moonlight is pooling in the sink, but besides that it's pitch black. The smell of soap lifts into my nose; beneath that, the faint tang of wood lacquer.

Bradley creeps past the edge of the table, ducking into the hall and motioning me to follow. There are patches of less solid dark here, the shadow gauzy and thin in places: open doors, maybe, leading into other rooms. At the bottom of a wide set of stairs, Bradley moves closer to me, making a two with his fingers and pointing up the landing. Then, he points to a closed door just past the edge of the stairs, with a single finger held up. Prendergast. I nod, and he creeps up the stairs, one at a time.

Breathe.

There's sweat running down my back; I clutch the rifle tight in my good hand and edge towards the door, holding it at the ready just in case. My eyes adjust, and a wooden cross comes into view, hung just to the side of the doorway, watching over the hall.

It's quiet enough to hear my heart in my ears. Then there's a soft squeak from one of the stairs, and a tiny cracking through the hallway ceiling as the house shifts. A breeze, maybe; it was picking up outside as we came in. Even in here, I can taste the rain on my tongue, an easterly wind carrying it up over the hills from the ocean.

There. A footstep upstairs, clear and distinct. A shiver runs across my shoulders; I listen for movement behind Prendergast's door but there's nothing. I look up the stairs, waiting for Bradley to appear. What if they're not coming? What if Prendergast is up there already, waiting with them?

Breathe. That's all you have to do.

I pull air through my lips and try to hold myself still. In a few moments, I hear steps coming back down the stairs, careful and light, and a tide of relief washes through me. I turn and see the faint outlines of a familiar face. Hēmi Larkin, watching me as he moves downstairs. He reaches the bottom and moves behind the banister, staring at me like I'm a monster from another dimension. I want to whisper to him. I can't risk it.

"It's okay," I mouth. "It's okay."

We stand there, each watching each other, and waiting. The dark passage hangs above us. They should really be down by now, those two. Bradley and Precious. I'm hot, suddenly. I'd wipe my forehead but just the sound of my fingers on my skin is loud enough to be heard. Then, a second shape emerges from the dark, taller than the boys. I see her hair around her shoulders, and the outlines of her eyes watching me, scrutinising. It's Precious. The three children, all walking and breathing, all within arm's reach.

Sheena, Queenie, Cath. There will be tears, joy and relief. A treasure returned. A state of belonging.

Bradley stands behind Precious, his hands urging her forward. She won't move.

"Who are you?" she whispers. "What are you doing?"

"Shh!" I jerk my head towards the kitchen, mouthing the words. "Go!"

In the dark, I see her look to the rifle, then back to me. There's a moment of calculation, the wheels turning in her head. I try to decide whether to just grab her; I can't hold the rifle with my bad arm.

"I don't want to." Her voice is rising. "Mr. P won't . . ."

"Shut up!"

Bradley shoves her down another step, raising a clatter of feet. There's a murmur from behind the closed door, and the sound of steps across the floorboards. I feel blood rush into my face.

I turn to the children. "Get behind me."

Dragging Precious down the last steps, Bradley stands to the side of the banister with Hēmi. She tries to smack his hand away but he holds on tight. She's bigger, stronger; he's determined. The edges of the door start to glow, then it swings open. Prendergast appears, holding a lamp. The light is soft but, after such thick dark, almost blinding. There's a flicker of disbelief in his face, before he looks past me to the children.

"Don't you fucking move." I point the barrel at his chest,

my voice as steady as I can manage. "The car, Bradley. Get everyone in the car."

"Mr. P," Precious calls past me. "I'm scared."

"It's okay," says Prendergast. "Kids, this is Lorraine. She's Bradley's aunty." The lamp flickers slightly, making his features tremble. "Lorraine's going to be staying with us, here. We've been talking. She's decided to help us with our projects."

"Shut up." I stand in place. "Get everyone outside, Bradley."

"No," Precious whines. "I don't want to. Tell her, Mr. P. Tell her I don't have to go."

"Listen to me, now." I'm speaking over my shoulder, my eyes still fixed ahead. "I went to see your mum, Precious. She's worried sick, you know that? Your dad too. They just want you back home. Don't you want to go home?"

"This is their place now," says Prendergast. "Isn't that right, kids?"

I reach forward and slide the bolt down with a click. The stock is unsteady against my bad arm but I manage it. "I'm taking them. It's done."

His eyes are twin pools of shining black. "Why don't you put that down, and we'll figure this out, eh?" He nods past me. "They don't need to see this sort of carry-on. We can just . . ."

"Where did you put him?" My voice is thick. "Where did you put Justin?"

A silence hangs between us. The walls seem closer now, pressing in tight.

"Who's Justin?" asks Precious.

"The man," says Bradley. "The one lying down in the driveway. I told you."

"It's not important, kids." Prendergast keeps moving closer. "Aunty Lo's going to put the rifle down, and we're all going to go into the kitchen to talk. Okay?"

My hands are shaking. "Stay there. I mean it."

In the light, I can see the bristles on his chin, the dark shoots peering through his skin. Outside, the first drops of rain clatter against the awning.

"Whose idea was it?" I take a step forward. "Was she in the driver's seat? Or did she just go along?"

"Who?"

There's a blockage in my throat; I can barely say her name. "Patty."

"Ah. I was wondering." A terrible flicker shifts inside his eyes. "You have her to thank, actually. I was ready to sort things out two days ago but she thought you might hear us out." He shifts his body, placing his weight on his back foot. "It's really something, how close you two have become."

My finger pulls tighter against the trigger. Bradley's voice lifts into my ear, urgent and strained. "Aunty."

Everything happens in a rush. Prendergast reaches for the lamp, darting towards me just as he turns the hallway black. There's a scream from the kids. I pull at the trigger, and the rifle jumps with a loud crack, a white flash flaring through the dark. A heavy thud, and a man's voice screaming, then he's on me, hands reaching for my throat, the fingers strong, yet slick with something. The rifle crashes to the floor; the hallway fills with yelling. All I can see is the outline of his shape, heavy, the fingers pressing into my throat, wrenching my collarbone and pressing the loose jagged pieces against each other. My vision flickers with pain, a white and blinding flash.

"You won't take them!"

I'm pushing at him but he's too heavy. Smaller footsteps come closer. I hear Bradley's voice in my ear, before Prendergast reaches out and throws him aside with a crash. A gap opens up between our bodies, small but enough. My fingers reach inside my fleece, clutching at the keys, then the shard of glass, the nylon sacking ragged and frayed around the sharp edge. Then, he's back on me, both hands at my neck, pinching my throat closed. It's like I'm underwater.

A tray of pork and cabbage. Gin and lemon. Patty, watching me from her chair.

I point the glass upwards into his belly and push against it with all the weight I have. There's some resistance, before the soft layers of him yield: his shirt, then his skin. The edges of the glass slice against my fingers, but I keep pushing until I can be sure more of it is inside him than outside. His hands go slack, and ragged breath fills my lungs.

"What . . ." Disbelief, and shock. "What did you . . ."

I turn away under his body, scrambling to my knees. He falls away.

"Bradley." I can barely hear myself.

"My head, Aunty." He sounds muffled and distant. "It hurts."

I can see their outlines in the hallway now. Bradley is sitting against the wall, his hands to his forehead. At his side is Hēmi, still hidden beside the banister. I feel a presence beside me—it's Precious, holding the rifle, the metal shape shaky in her hands, the barrel pointed at my chest. With my good hand, I reach out and grab it, wrenching it off her and nearly lifting her body from the floor. On my feet, the whole dark channel is spinning. My bad arm has come out of its sling; I swing it through the air, the palm of my hand connecting to her cheek with a sharp slap. It hurts me more than it does her, but it's enough to show how serious I am.

"You silly girl!" I grab her by the shoulder, hard, and pull her towards the kitchen, sniffing and moaning. "Bradley, can you walk?"

He climbs unsteadily to his feet. "I think so."

"Hēmi, come and help him."

I bundle Precious through the doorway with the two boys in tow. There are scuffling noises against the floorboards, and a scrabbling, gasping sound.

"Wait!" Prendergast yells out. "Stop!"

We stumble into the kitchen, and my hip cracks against the edge of the table. There's moonlight in here; I can see the dark patches on my front.

"Ow!" Precious wriggles inside my hands. "Let go!"

I grit my teeth and shove us through the back door, hearing the boys close behind. The air is cool against me; we step out from the verandah, and I feel rain on my face.

"Here." I hand Bradley the rifle, then feel inside my pocket for the keys. "Hēmi, you slide the door open."

"How do I do that?" His voice is small and scared.

"I'll show you," says Bradley.

The boys run out ahead, their bare feet going quickly across the gravel. I duck through the hayshed door with Precious still snivelling, my fingers tight around her. I fumble around, looking for the driver's door. It's on the wrong side; he's reversed into the shed, ready for a quick departure. So much the better. Slowly, the front of the hayshed door slides open on its tracks, both boys pushing as hard as they can, the runners giving off a shrill squeak. The shed floods with milky moonlight, showing me the station wagon.

Apple-red. In the moonlight it looks like dried blood.

I pull the door open and push Precious inside. There's a thud as she knocks against the seat; there's no time to be gentle.

"Don't you dare bloody move."

I hold the keys up in front of me, pushing the longest one home into the ignition. With a deep breath, I turn it over. The headlights come to life, knifing through the dark in bright columns. Then the car lurches forward and sputters to a stop. The clutch. It's been years.

"*Fuck.*" I lean forward in the seat, my hand reaching for the gearstick. The back doors open, and Hēmi and Bradley slide in, the rifle glinting in the light of the dash.

"Lock those doors," I bark. "And you two, hold on to her."

The boys do as they're told. My fingers fumble around at my side. It takes an age but eventually I manage to slide the seat forward, and my foot finds the clutch. I push it down and turn the engine over, my fingers wet and trembling. The engine catches. It's a more welcome noise than I can ever remember.

I keep my foot hard against the accelerator until the whole frame of the car hums with the vibrations. I set my good hand to the wheel, my shoulder screaming as I reach for the gearstick. I think it's in first; I try to remember Frank's hands over mine, guiding me in the old Morris, shuttling from our place to Debbie and Billy's, all the neighbours watching from their porches, raising mugs of tea to salute my slow progress. I take a long breath and let the clutch out, moving forward and away.

"Stop!" Precious cries.

From the edge of the open hayshed door, Prendergast lurches in front of the car, falling to his knees. A hand reaches up onto the bonnet—in the headlights, the blood covering his fingers shines in a bright ribbon—and he pushes himself higher, until he's leaning down against the car, his mouth open, long strands hanging from his lip. One of his arms is bleeding near the shoulder. There's a wide dark patch in his shirt across the belly, and a glint where the stub of the window shard is poking out.

"It's okay, kids." His eyes are wide and unfocused. "It's all okay. You can get out now. I'm going to talk to Lorraine. That's all."

Precious reaches a hand to the door.

"Don't you fucking dare!"

The boys hold her tighter as she struggles. I stare ahead through the glass, my eyes tight to Prendergast's.

"It's not about us." He lifts himself up straighter, wincing.

"It's for them. All of it." A grin moves at the edge of his mouth. "I know you understand."

I feel my eyes narrow. Behind him, the headlights illuminate the spot where Justin lay kicking in the gravel. My thoughts run together in a boiling mess of images and impulses. The furred black ball held so tight in Patch's mouth, the tūī chick's useless little movements, the teeth around its neck so sharp and sure.

"I do," I whisper. "I do understand."

I let the clutch out and keep the accelerator steady. The car rushes sharply forward, and Prendergast falls back. Screaming fills my ears. There's disbelief in his eyes as his feet give way, a half-second of realisation as the metal shape comes across his chest, the blinding lights pressing down. The wheels move across him with a sound like stones rubbing. Then, with a last jump of the wheels, we're gone.

I turn the car hard through the gravel, aiming away to the road. In the rear-view mirror, the taillights cast a red glow over his prone body, the arms outstretched, his cheek pressed into the gravel as if he's trying to look through it.

Dots of rain lick at the windscreen, a sanction and a blessing. I shift gears, and the engine leaps as we approach the cattlestop. Bradley's hand is on my shoulder, the good side, squeezing me in reassurance. In the seat next to me, Precious is a whimpering ball. I see Hēmi in the rear-view mirror, face pale with fright. I aim the car through the channel, and the metal slats of the cattlestop send a loud vibration up through the car and into our bodies.

"It's okay, kids." My hands are unsteady. "Everything is okay."

Eyes wet, I drive. My fingers move against my throat, feeling the bruises already coming. I open my mouth and draw in a long breath. The night is a full and deep shape, the sky letting down friendly water to meet us. The road rolls out under the car, every corner taking us further away.

TO FEATHERSTON SHOULD be an hour, tops. With my rusty one-handed driving and these winding roads, I make it in closer to two. It doesn't much matter, though. Not now.

When we pull into those quiet and empty streets, the storm is starting in. The tentative early rain has thickened into a screen of static; Bradley leans forward and helps me fiddle with the wipers just so I can stay on the road. I turn right past the train tracks, thinking of Justin making the same turn, his sinewy hands gripping the wheel, the hard sunlight flooding the car. I can hear the low creaking of his voice, like worn leather.

It's with me still. I hope it stays.

In the rain, the Kīngi house looks even more desolate than before. I pull slowly into the narrow driveway and the head-lights shine out across the rusting carcasses of the trucks and cars. It's too dark to see the ranges lifting beyond, but they're there, those thick green shapes. They're always there.

"We're here, girl." I put a hand on Precious's shoulder. "We're home, look."

She pulls her knees tighter to her chest. Silence.

I pull to a stop by the house, and a dim light comes on at the porch. There's a man staring out through the rain from the open door, thick in the shoulders, stout trees for arms. Bruce Kīngi. He moves to the edge of the deck, staring down at us like an angry crab.

"Who the fuck are you?"

I wind the window down, letting him see me, and his anger turns to confusion. He looks past me into the passenger's seat, to the dark-haired girl tucked into the corner, and a bolt of tenderness shoots through his eyes. With his mouth hanging open, he leaps down into the gravel and across the car, throwing open the door and setting his arms under her. He lifts her up into his chest, his eyes closed, his hands moving again and again through her hair. The rain is drenching them both.

"Who . . . how did you . . ."

There's a squeal from the front door, joy fighting disbelief. Another shape appears, tall, a baggy set of trackpants beneath a long grey T-shirt, hair wild above thin shoulders. Cath steps to the edge of the deck, staring from her daughter to me. I cut the engine, and there's only the sound of the rain drumming against metal.

"Lorraine?" Her eyes are wide saucers.

I reach for the door, my fingers cracked and stinging. "I need your phone."

Bruce gets the fire going while Cath fusses in the bedroom. It's not cold enough, not even close to it, but he seems to need a job to do: the jug boiled, sugary coffee for me, Milo for the boys, the teaspoon so tiny in his huge hands. As grim as the kitchen might be, it's a welcome sight after the farm.

"Have some bikkies, eh boys?" Bruce pulls open the cupboards, rustling around inside with his mitts. "Gingernuts, eh?" He rips the packet open at one end and sets it down on the tabletop. The boys reach ahead, Bradley first, then Hēmi. The biscuit is halfway to Hēmi's mouth when he pauses and offers it to me. It looks huge in his hand.

"I'm fine, lovey." I take another sip of the coffee, sweet and milky, the granules still collecting at the bottom. There are fresh tears in my eyes. "You go ahead."

Bruce stomps himself down in the seat next to mine, making it groan beneath his weight. "This Prendergast prick, the teacher. He's out past Martinborough, you said?"

I nod, feeling a sharp twinge through my shoulder. The rain rolls against the roof, louder now, as if it means to get inside. A Panadol would go a long way right now. A Panadol and a stiff gin.

"Whereabouts? What's the address?"

There's a rising spark in his eye, and a sheen of something ready to break apart. "You don't have to worry about that, mate." I don't want to get into too much detail; these boys have seen enough tonight without reliving it. "Just bring me that phone. A towel, too, if you don't mind. This sling's poked."

He holds my eyes for a long moment, deciding. Then something shifts and he does as he's told. The phone clangs down in front of me, and he disappears into the hallway, muttering.

"What about your fingers, Aunty?" Bradley looks across the table. "They're bleeding."

"Don't worry about that, kiddo. I'll be fine." Truth is, they're stinging to buggery; my pinkie is damn near cut to the bone on the middle joint. I flex them carefully, picturing the edge of the glass, the curve and the hook. "You all right there, Hēmi?"

He stares up at me, his Milo clutched like a shield. I want to reach out to him, the comfort of warm skin, but I can't risk the movement on my bad side.

"Yep."

I smile at him. A real talkative fellow, he is. My hand goes to the phone, and I dial the after-hours staff number for the station. After a dozen rings, someone picks up.

"Yep?" I hear a baby fussing in the background.

"You on call tonight, eh Dion?"

There's a stunned gap in his voice. "Lorraine? Is that . . . where the bloody hell have you been? Hayes is missing, and nobody's heard anything about . . ."

"I've got them," I say. "I've got the kids."

More silence. I can practically hear the words register one by one. "What?"

"Get Ambrose and meet me at my niece's. Just you two, all right? We don't need a big palaver."

"The kids, you said?"

"That's right." I look from Bradley to Hēmi, smiling. "All three."

"What about Justin?"

I close my eyes. Feel the tears cross my cheeks. "I'll fill you in."

I set the phone against the cradle and bring my good hand to my face, my eyes closed tight. Then, I feel arms around me, gentle and sure. Bradley sets his head on my good side, squeezing me just so. I lift my hand to his back, filling my nose with his smell.

"We'll go back for Patch." My hand moves in slow circles. "We'll find her."

"She'll be fine, Aunty. She's grown now."

Cath appears in the doorway, flushed in the face. She's carrying an old sheet.

"How's that girl of yours?" I ask.

"Bruce is getting her settled." She steps closer and takes the seat next to mine, then rips the bedsheet into a long strip, her strong hands shaking. "She said you ran him over with a car. Is that true?" I nod, looking to the boys. "That fucking prick." She shakes her head and leans closer, tying the sling much too tight.

"Easy," I say. "I'm all knocked about."

"Sorry." She lifts her hands from my shoulder, then ties the sling behind my neck. "That okay?"

I let it take the weight. "Much better. Thanks."

"You'll struggle to drive, I think." She lights a cigarette from the pack on the table. "I could come with you, if you need?"

"These fellas can shift the gears." I nod to the boys. "It'll be an adventure."

Bradley gives me a wide grin, and Hēmi looks less sheepish for a moment. I finish my coffee and stare at the phone. "Do me a favour?"

"Sure." Cath blows smoke across the table. "Anything."

"Would you take these two into the lounge for a second?"

She looks at the boys, then back at me. "Let's go see what's on the telly, eh?"

They file into the hall, and I stare at the phone. I can hear my heart under the steady drum of rain on the roof. After a long breath, I pick it up and dial for the Wikaira place. The phone rings and rings, the tone rhythmic in my ear. I wait as long as I can before I hang up. A cold feeling settles across my back.

Of course. Where else would she be?

I dial my own number. In three rings, Patty answers, breathless from the walk to the kitchen.

"Hello?"

Her voice in my ear is a tree falling, a huge and improbable shape crashing to earth. I close my eyes; it's too much, knowing she's there, on my couch with Tilly and the kittens.

"Lorraine?"

I hear doubt turning to certainty in her voice. She knows

who it is. My whole body is shaking. I lift the phone away from my ear and set it back in its cradle, holding my good hand over my face.

"You all right there, love?"

I jump in my chair. For such a big guy, Bruce has some real stealth. "I'm okay."

He sets himself down next to me, his arm laid out against the table like an arrow nocked, the fist clenched tight and ready. "Anything you lot need, anything I can do, you just say so." The slate in his eyes is layered with feeling. "I can't tell you what it is for us, having that girl back."

At the top of his singlet, a web of tattoos runs out across his skin, a thicket of darker colour. I know what he could do with this body. But that's not the way I want it to go. I missed the signs; it's me who needs to put the puzzle back in the box.

Wiping at my nose, I nod through the rain-streaked window to Prendergast's station wagon. "Help me reverse that bloody thing, would you?"

BRADLEY AND HĒMI huddle tight in the front seat, one seatbelt slung across them both, taking turns to slot the gears in place. The music warbles inside the rain's steady patter: Tom Petty singing about wings and flying, the bright jangle of guitar, the drums with their quiet punch, and our ragged group bound together inside the radio's neon glow. The rifle is laid out on the floor in the back seat, tucked into shadow.

"All right, fellas." We come to the end of the long straight past the timber mill, then over the bridge where the tractor dealerships begin. "Down to fourth."

"Your turn," says Bradley.

I press the clutch in, and Hēmi clicks the gearstick gently home. He smiles up at me, teeth shining, pleased to have a job to do.

"Good kid."

I steer us through the long corner, seeing the lights of the petrol stations up ahead, everything shuttered for the night. The hotel looms through the dark on our left: the reception and the complimentary biscuits, the walk to Justin's room, and the steady thwack of the tennis balls outside. I can't wipe at my eyes without taking my good hand from the wheel, so I let the feeling come. The boys can't hear me crying over the music anyway.

We pull through the centre of town, Bradley shifting gears once more, the streets filing past in damp rows, the streetlights arranged in struggling vigil. I make the turn onto Colombo, Hēmi's street, and I feel the boy stiffen in his seat. I catch Bradley's eye.

"One more shift." He doesn't hear me. "Hēmi?"

"Huh? Oh." I press the clutch in for him, and he shoves the gearstick forward with shaking hands. There's a crunching sound, before Bradley helps him out. It's all this rain, maybe; it's just like the eel night. It's only natural, him being edgy.

We come to the end of the street, and the gardens start to get bushier and more unkempt, the cars older, rustier. There: the Larkin house is smothered by the rain, the leaning awning and the gap-toothed fence like an apparition through the water. I pull to a stop at the kerb, and Bradley reaches across Hēmi to unclick the seatbelt. There's a glow through the lounge room windows, the television's wash of blue and green lapping against the thin curtains. Hēmi sits still, staring through the falling water.

"You okay, boyo?"

He looks up to me with unsure eyes. I reach across my body with my good arm and put a hand on his chest. "Go on, now. Go in to your mum."

He climbs over Bradley and out into the rain, leaving the door hanging open behind him. We watch as he steps through the garden gate, walking slowly, as if he means to get himself soaked. Then, he ducks under the awning by the front door. I'd get out to make sure he's okay but I need to keep this shoulder still. And anyway, Queenie will be there for him. There's a last lingering stare, eyes peering out beneath the fringe stuck against his forehead. He's asking us for something, maybe. The door swings slowly closed. I imagine the sounds of reunion inside: the squeals and the yelps, the crying.

The rain is too loud. It's no matter; we won't be too far away. I can come back and check on him any time.

Once the job's done, of course.

"All right, kid." I look to Bradley. "Home time."

I push the clutch down, and he clicks the gear into place, his hands deft and sure. The car swings into the road, the wheels slick under us. There's no one else out driving. The streets hold only rain, rushing through the gutters like something set free.

"She's missed you so much, your mum." I try to picture Sheena's face when we pull up: her puffy cheeks flaring with colour, the slack mouth animated again. "She's hardly slept a wink these last weeks."

"I've missed her too," says Bradley. "Heaps. And Dad."

I keep my eyes ahead. Keith. We're still a few minutes away; it'd be enough time to tell him about the night in the pines, about the shack and the logging path. A shiver runs across my shoulders. I take a breath and gather myself.

"He might not be there, kiddo." Careful now. "Not right away."

He looks up at me inside the car, this precious boy, and he smiles. "I know, Aunty. It's okay. He goes away sometimes."

Such trust. Even now, after everything. We've shown him all that people can do to each other, and it's still there within him.

I look away through the window, not bothering to wipe my cheeks. I've done my fair share; not every problem is mine to solve.

I see them as soon as we turn the corner: the lights from the patrol cars sweeping over the houses in watchful arcs, the row of faces illuminated in their bright orbit. The neighbours are all on their porches, peering out into the warm screen of rain. As we get closer, I see my niece coming fast across the lawn, her eyes fixed on us. Bradley sits high in his seat, breathing hard. I pull up behind the patrol cars.

"Away you go, boyo."

He pushes the door open as Sheena reaches us, and she wraps him up tight against her, sobbing. He's swallowed in her loose hair, the boy disappeared in their frantic reunion. Then, she looks through the open door to me, and a golden thread of recognition spins out between us, wrapping us tight. There's nothing to say. It's all there in her expression. Uncomplicated; the last flecks of resentment swept away.

My hands click the engine off. Ambrose is coming through

the rain with Dion close behind, his eyes hard and searching. I feel heavy, weighted with every one of my movements and decisions, my footsteps and my words, my thoughts, my dreams, all the known world falling on me at the same moment. I close my eyes and set my head back against the seat. The door opens. Raindrops dot my bare arm, the wet breeze licking across my skin. When I open my eyes, Ambrose is staring down at me, eyes white with surprise.

"Jesus, Lorraine." He looks at my arm in the sling, at my hands cracked with blood, and my eggplant cheeks. I must be a little on the ripe side; it's been days since I washed. "What the hell happened?"

"I . . ."

There's a rising hollow in my chest, a hot void pressing into my throat. He kneels and takes my good hand, squeezing it. When I look at him again, he's looking past me into the passenger's seat, then into the back.

"Hayes?"

I shake my head. My mouth opens but no sound emerges. He leans me forward into his shoulder and takes my weight. With his hands steady against my back, his voice slides into my ear, telling me everything is okay.

It's not. And yet I let everything go, and I let myself be carried.

SHEENA'S LOUNGE HAS never seemed so small. She's tidied up since my last visit, at least: there are no more sleeping bags and no pools of ambiguous liquid creeping from under the fridge; the old musty smell is gone for the most part.

I hold a second cup of coffee in my hands, nibbling at jam toast cut by Dion into toddler squares. Thoughtful. Ambrose sits across the table, watching while Dion does what he can with my shoulder. There's a voice recorder set out between us, its red light shining. On the couch, Sheena has Bradley tucked tight in her arms in fresh pyjamas, wrapped in a blanket, dozing. Moko leans against the doorway, fingers toying with the gold disc at his neck.

The whole chorus, and everyone listening to the tale.

"Ow," I say. "Jesus."

Dion lifts his hands from my collarbone. "You've got a nasty break there. Through the skin, almost."

"No shit." I meet his eye. "Just tie it. I'll deal with it later."

"So. Hayes had you in on the files, did he?" Ambrose crosses his arms. "Even after our meeting?"

I nod. "He knew I could help." I take a long breath. "And I did. I did help."

He meets my eye, and his body shifts. There's a moment of calibration in him: frustration and relief, fear and calm.

"I still don't get it." He taps his notepad, his forehead furrowed. "We interviewed all the teachers, right?"

"Prendergast had retired," I say. "He wasn't listed as Precious's teacher. She had some new woman. Irvine or something."

"Irving," says Dion. "I think it was Irving."

"Still." Ambrose shakes his head. "We should have brought him in."

"Well," I say. "You didn't."

"Aunty." Sheena looks across from the couch, her eyes huge and shining. She pats a spot on the couch, the other side of Bradley. Moko helps me up from the chair, drawing glances from Ambrose and Dion.

"One last thing." The chief leans forward, then looks over to where Bradley is sleeping, lowering his voice. "What do you think he did with Hayes?"

"I don't know." There's a sting in my eyes, sharp and salty. "I asked but he wouldn't say."

"And the rifle? Where's that?"

I watch Bradley's face, the mouth slightly open, those dear eyes shut tight.

"I don't know," I say. "Still in the hayshed, probably."

With Moko propping me up, I move across the room to the couch and lean gently against the cushions. Sheena sets her head on my good shoulder, whispering low.

"Thanks, Aunty." She sniffs. "You did it. You and that man. You did all of it."

"It's okay, girl. You just rest, now."

She shakes her head. "All I ever did was get septic. With you, and with the others. Jesus, the things I said."

I lean across and kiss her forehead, moving as slowly as I can. These two loves of mine: the boy bundled tight; the girl, the woman, gathering his little body to hers. Whatever else happens, they're here.

"That'll do us for now." Ambrose reaches over and clicks the recorder off. "Some blokes from head office are on their way, heading over the hill. I'll meet them in Martinborough and we'll head out to that farm." His eyes are hard, his movements pointed ahead into the future: all loose ends tied, these fuzzy impressions turned into clear and clean lines for the papers, for the morning bulletin. "Dion, you get Lorraine to the hospital, and take a full statement while you're there. I want to make sure we get every possible detail. We'll get to the Larkins and the Kīngis afterwards."

"Righto."

"We'll talk later, Lorraine." The chief stands in the centre of the room, hands on hips, watching me. Eventually, he clears his throat. "Great job."

There's a nod from him, and a look in his eyes I've not seen before. Not for me, anyway. Real admiration, or at least the younger sibling of respect. Then he's gone. The house is quiet, even restful. Dion sits at the table looking over his notes, and Moko busies himself in the kitchen, washing our plates. I tuck Sheena in closer to me, leaning down into her ear.

"There's something else," I whisper. "I need you to hear me without reacting."

She lifts her head closer. "What, Aunty?"

My eyes press shut; my heart is pushing against my ribs, a balloon blown too tight. With a long breath, I tell her. There's disbelief, first, before her shoulders stiffen. She looks at me with a hard boil of menace. What's in her eyes could shatter glass.

"She was helping him." I lean closer, whispering into her ear. "She used me, Sheen. For information."

"That fucking . . ."

Dion lifts his head from the table to us. "Everything all right?"

"We're fine." I nod, and he turns back to his notes. With a long breath, I lean back against Sheena.

"I need you to do something for me." I swallow hard in my throat, leaning into her ear again. "Take Bradley into the bedroom and call Dion. Tell him you've just remembered something, about the birthday party, or Mataikona, or whatever. You figure it out. Just . . . keep him there, for as long as you can."

A moment passes between us. I hold her eye, letting her see what's on my mind.

"I should come." Her gaze narrows. "I should be there."

"No, darling." I kiss her neck. "It has to be me."

She lingers in place, but eventually she seems to understand. Turning away, she lifts Bradley up from the couch and into her arms. They disappear into the hall, their footsteps hushed inside the thrum of rain, and I try to gather myself.

"You two holding up all right, with that boy of yours?" My voice is dusty. "Getting enough sleep?"

Dion looks up from the table. "We're doing just fine. Better than most." He smiles wide, fishing in a pocket for his keys.

"Officer?" Sheena calls from the hallway. "Could you come here a second?"

He sighs, tucking his notepad into his shirt pocket. "I'll just be a tick."

"Righto."

I close my eyes and take a long breath. Truthfully, I could sleep right here, even with my shoulder a bag of broken plates, and my hip giving me arseholes. It's quiet, and the cushions are the softest cradle I could ever imagine.

"Need anything, Aunty?" Moko leans against the table, dishcloth over his shoulder. His eyes are warm. I measure the breadth of his shoulders, the strength held in them. But like I said, it has to be me.

"Help me up, would you?"

He offers a hand. I move quietly down the hall, my feet shaky under me. At the door, he says nothing; his face tells me what I need to know. Whatever happens, he'll be here, with my niece, and with Bradley. Wherever I end up, I can count on that. The door swings softly shut, and his footsteps recede into the house.

Outside, the rain comes down over me, every drop mixing with the swirling currents inside my heart. I pull the back door of Prendergast's car open and reach down inside, taking the rifle by the stock. It's heavy in my hands. I turn for home, my feet knowing every step in advance.

From the neighbour's porch, a face watches me. A woman, someone I've met at Sheena's; some party or other, some evening with too much noise and drink. She meets my eye, then registers the object clutched in my hand. A quick look, but it's enough. Her eyes fall back into shadow, a book sliding closed, my secret carried with her. I walk onwards. A new wind comes down from the sky, cradling my body and urging me forward.

RICKETT'S CIRCLE. THE mossy gutters, the houses with their curtains like hooded eyes. There's one with lights still burning: a square of brightness held inside the dark trembles.

I balance the rifle against my sling.

You just need to push the bolt bit down against the side.

Yes, kiddo. I slide the metal back towards me, and a finger of gold leaps out from the chamber and into the gutter, swept along in the rushing water, through the mouth of the storm drain and away. Then forward, the bolt clicking into place, and a new round waiting.

I keep expecting lights to shine on me from behind, Dion's patrol car sliding to a stop next to me, his voice coming through the murmur of the water. It'd take things out of my hands, I suppose.

Maybe that's what I want. Maybe that's all anyone wants.

Oblivion and rest, the passive innocence of the child, all decisions someone else's to make.

But the road stays empty. There's only me and my work.

I move from the footpath up my driveway, feet waterlogged inside my shoes, past my kitchen window to my front door. Even in the dark, I can feel the lushness of the garden: all the leaves open to receive this rich moisture like a visit from an unexpected friend. My hand pushes at the door. It swings open, unlocked.

No answer from inside. Still, there's the flickering light.

She's here. I can feel it.

I kick my shoes off by the door, my socks sopping against the linoleum. The kitchen is tidy: a few dishes stacked to dry on the bench, some flowers in a vase on the windowsill, posies from the Wikaira place and a fresh stick of white delphiniums. Everything smells of dish soap.

There's a light shining in the lounge, a golden brightness reaching across the floor and over my swollen feet. I move forward into the hall, past the garage door propped open. Inside, I make out the shapes of the young cats in their box, long limbs arranged in a haphazard sleeping pile.

In the lounge, Patty's in her usual seat, body held calm and still, watching the doorway. Her eyes meet mine, shining in the firelight. She sees the rifle cradled in my good hand, but nothing in her expression changes.

I ease myself down into the couch, my usual spot, next to a sleeping Tilly, a mottled crescent of whiskers and fur. I lean the rifle against the armrest, ready. In the fireplace a few sticks of pine crackle against each other, throwing sparks out against the guard in tiny explosions.

"Warm in here."

She doesn't respond right away. "Thought you might need to dry off."

I reach across with my good hand to Tilly, my fingers moving behind her ears, and she looks up at me, blinking slow. A long pink yawn before she settles back into herself.

"I've been feeding them, the kittens and all. They've been quite happy, I think." There's a new waver in Patty's voice. "The garden, too. I took care of the weeding down the back . . . trimmed the agapanthus."

"He's dead, Patty." I hold her in my regard, watching as the information hits. "I shot him in the shoulder and stuck a piece of broken glass in him, right through the belly." I point to my stomach, then hold up my hand to show her the cuts. "He was choking me. See?" My fingers go to my throat. "He meant to do it. Your husband."

She shakes her head. "Lorraine, you don't have to . . ."

"Then, he came outside when we were in the car, and I ran him over. Outside the hayshed, in the gravel. Ran the bastard right over with his own car, with those kids inside, too. Hadn't been behind the wheel since Sheena was a girl, but I managed it. Made a hell of a loud scrape."

She holds my eye for a long moment, then stares away into the fire. Her eyes hold the flickering glow, twin orbs of suspended flame. She's weeping.

"I tried . . ." She coughs into her hand. "I tried to convince him, after everything with that detective, that he should give it up. It was . . ."

"After he shot Justin and left him to die, you mean?"

It's quiet between us now. My hand itches for the rifle, to hold its weight and feel its cold, simple shape, the wood and the steel, the leather strap.

"I never meant for any of that," she mumbles. "It wasn't what we talked about."

"Speak up, for God's sake." I turn my head to the side.

"It was just supposed to be the girl." She wipes at her cheeks. "The Kīngi girl. They were so close in class, and she . . . she loved him. She really loved him, Lorraine. They had such a connection. She needed us, both of us. To take her away from that horrible place, and to show her something else. How things could be if she only had the right chances. The right support."

I think back to Precious holding the rifle, the barrel pointing through that dim shadowed hallway, the confusion in her face, the hesitation. Yes: the love.

"You saw her house," says Patty. "That horrid mother of hers, and the father out doing who knows what. They weren't fit for it, Lorraine. Anyone could see it."

"Patty." My volume surprises her. "He killed Justin. He tried to kill me. And you let him." There's a tide rising inside me, tossing and churning. The smudge of lantern light across the field, and the Fiesta's familiar rattle through the dark. "You knew I was there, in that poxy fucking shed. And you left me. You left me there."

She folds her hands in her lap. "It didn't have to be like this." Her voice is hushed. "All he wanted . . . all we both wanted, was to help some of those kids. God knows they needed it."

"Bradley too, you mean?" I'm clenching my teeth. "Everything you put my niece through, all those nights she lay awake, pulling her hair out while she waited for news?" I sit up straighter, all of the aches inside me gathering into a single throbbing ball. "And Keith? Did he deserve what happened to him?"

She meets my eye for a long moment. There's a stubbornness in her, a conviction that still won't break apart. She looks to her glass on the low table between us, a murky liquid still and waiting.

"I've crushed up some pills," she says. "It'll be enough."

"What?"

A long sob comes through her teeth. "I know what I've done, Lorraine. So, I'll do it. For you, and for those kids. And for him. For the detective." New moisture runs out across her cheeks. "I'll take my penance, and I'll answer for my sins."

"Oh, fuck off, Pat." Spittle flies from my mouth. "It's always the holiest thing with you, isn't it?"

She looks to the floor. "If it's what you want, I'll do it."

The fire cracks again. My hands are shaking with fury; everything I've had to do to get those kids back: the days in that shed, the sling and the glass, staring on tiptoes through that broken window, and Prendergast flat in the gravel. And still, she won't even take this job off my hands. It's mine alone.

"Was any of this real?" I nod through the window to old Mrs. Wikaira's house. "You tell me, now. You and me, here, together." My voice thickens. "All that time. The gin and the roasts. You've been closer to me than anyone."

"Of course it was real." Her face shifts; I want to believe her. "You don't know what it's been like for me, Lorraine. You don't know the things he made me do. Creeping around for him, lying to you, and knowing that boy of yours was safe the whole time. Better than safe, even. He was thriving, they all were."

"Don't." My voice goes taut. "Don't you dare."

"Look me in the eye and tell me otherwise." She's leaning forward now, one hand pressed to her chest, her eyes leaping with colour. "I know you love your niece, but you can't tell me you wouldn't have done the same. That boy needed good people in his life. Steady people. They all did." She pats at her heart. "That's all we did, Lorraine. We gave them that. Just like you gave your niece when she needed it."

I shake my head, watching her. What a thing it is, being in the same room as someone capable of such a thing. To have to see her, to share the same warmth. How can a person breathe the same air, knowing what she's let happen?

Bradley. Hēmi. Precious.

The most precious thing. Our most precious thing.

"Sheena's my family, Patty. You didn't give anybody anything. You took. It's all you did. And now two people are in the ground. Keith and Justin." Tears turn the room to a single long smudge. "Wherever that bastard put him."

She looks away, chastened. "He dug a hole under the pines, the far edge of the shelter belt, by the old fence. It was all done by the time I got out there."

Under the pines. It's something, at least. To know.

I watch her face and feel everything fold together, the room collapsing into nothing. All our evenings and afternoons, our words together. Everything, and yet, nothing. A tree rotted all the way through; a smaller animal stalked by a larger one. I reach down and take the rifle in my hands. There's a rushing in my ears.

"Pick up that phone." I nod to the bookshelf. "I need you to decide."

She looks up at me. Her face pales, all colour washing away, her cheeks turned to chalky circles. "I can't do it," she mouths. "Lorraine. I can't."

"You have to."

I rest the rifle in my lap, my fingers calm, all the weight and certainty of the wood and steel held inside these hands, and I watch her. The tracks on her cheeks catch the firelight in tiny flaring stars. She shakes her head, and they run down and away, and over her shoulder the window holds back the night, the wide sky so tilted and unbalanced, the animal world held at bay for this moment and no more.

We pulled up in Mr. P's car outside my house. It was raining real hard and Bradley's aunty patted me on the chest with her hand with all the cuts on it. Go on, now. Her fingers had red bits like Mr. P's at the edges but worse. They looked sore. Go in to your mum she said. She was smiling but her eyes had tears in them. My feet got wet in the gutter outside and the garden gate was hung all the way open. Dad hates that. I closed it but it wasn't clicking right so I left it a little bit open.

I didn't know how to go inside. It felt weird like some place I'd never been before. I knew Mum and Dad would ask what happened. I'd have to say about the eels and getting in the car and all that. Dad would be angry. He always said about cars and what to do if someone new starts talking to you and you don't know them first. A stranger. But Mr. P wasn't a stranger once he started talking. By then we were already being friendly and he had the radio on with the lollies and all that. But then he went under the car with a big noise like crunching cereal and we left him there in the gravel.

The front door was left open a bit so I didn't have to look for the key under the special brick or go through the garage window. Bradley and his aunty were still parked in Mr. P's car with the lights on. I couldn't see inside but they must have been waiting to make sure I was okay. I didn't know if I should wave or something. Then they left and the car went away real slow in the road probably because Bradley was changing the stick. I watched until the lights went away.

Everything smelled the same inside. There was the salty ground smell of Dad's work boots and Mum all in the air through the whole house like always. Her soapy smell and the other smells like clothes drying and that. Manaia's nappies too from the bucket in the laundry. Kellen used to pinch his nose at the nappy smell when he came around but then Dad told him one day to pull his head in and after that he only did it at school for the others.

The TV was on in the lounge and Mum was on the couch all curled up like a little possum. That's what she would call me sometimes when I fell asleep on the couch like that. My little possum. Dad's chair was empty so I knew he must be out somewhere. Mum had a blanket over her though all nicely tucked like Dad taught me to do with

Manaia so he could breathe and he wouldn't roll over and get himself into any trouble. There were bottles and stuff on the floor and some bits of the glass too. They were all grubby and smelled like that old smell from before.

I knew Mum wouldn't wake all the way up. Not right away. I put my hand on her shoulder and said to her Mum. Mum it's me. She moved around a bit and she was smiling a sleepy smile and then she tried to say some words but her voice sounded croaky. Her face looked different from before. Her cheeks were all puffy and her eyes had dark bits under.

I sat on the floor with my head touching her legs. There was a cartoon on the TV it was weird seeing it again. A cat was chasing a mouse around a table and there were too many colours and everything was too fast for my eyes. I watched the cat chase the mouse for a bit. I knew he'd never get him. The cartoon would have to stop if he did because he'd bite the mouse in the neck and the mouse wouldn't be running around the table anymore or playing funny tricks. They couldn't make a thing like that for kids to watch. It would be inappropriate. Mr. P said that a lot. Inappropriate.

The rain got real loud then on the roof and I felt Mum move around behind me on the couch trying to get comfy and I felt a bit funny inside. I thought I might be hungry so I went to the cupboard for some cereal. There were onions in there growing green bits and a little bag of flour I remembered from before and some ready salted chips but those would be too loud and anyway they made me think even more of Mr. P. The fridge had some bread still. I didn't know if I was hungry or if it was just the way I was feeling from being at home again.

Baby. Baby is that you. Mum was sitting straight up then with her hair everywhere. She was rubbing at her eyes but she was awake this time. Mum I said I'm back. I could see her in the light from the fridge. She was smiling but she still looked a bit scared like maybe she didn't believe me. Then she came over and bent down and held me real tight until I couldn't breathe. We stayed like that for a bit with her just saying baby baby over and over in my ear and squeezing me and her hands moving all over my back like she was looking for something.

Baby.

She moved back a bit and shifted her hair away and her fingers were shaking a lot. She said what happened. I wanted to start from the eel night but it was too hard to say about any of that. A lady drove me here with Bradley I said. What lady. Bradley's aunty she's got grey hair and she walks funny. Aunty Lo she said. The whole time we were talking the fridge door was open. That's even worse than the garden gate but Dad wasn't around to say anything and Mum didn't notice. I said she came to the house with a man and Bradley saw him in the gravel and then she was at the bottom of the stairs in the middle of the night and Precious wouldn't go. Then Mr. P went under the car. Wait Mum said. Just wait. I'll make us some Milo and then you can tell me proper. I said there's no milk Mum. I haven't been to the shop my love. I've been looking for you we all have.

Then she squeezed me again and I closed my eyes. First I just smelled the glassy smell but then I could smell the old Mum smell like after we used to come out of the bath together and she would put the same towel around us both and hop down the hallway playing bunnies on the way to my room. Baby she said. You don't know how much we've missed you me and your dad. I said where is he where's Dad. She looked at his chair. He's out. He's looking for you. But I'm here though. I'll call him okay. She wiped at her eyes and her fingers were still shaky. I'll call him and he'll come. You just stay here. She smiled at me and I felt warm. You just stay here my baby.

She stood up maybe too quick because then she had to put her hands out against the bench and breathe in and out for a bit like Bradley's dad shows us at rugby practice if we get dizzy. One and two in and out. Then she went into the hallway where her phone charger is. I could hear Manaia in his room. I went and stood in the doorway so he could see me. He was standing up in his crib holding on to the little wooden slats looking out. Dad calls it his little prison it's funny when he says that. Manaia was crying a little bit but when he saw me he stopped. Mum was talking in the hallway saying come home now don't worry about any of that shit it doesn't matter anymore come home he's here.

I went over to Manaia and he just looked up at me the way he does sometimes. Not making any noise only looking. I picked him up and checked his nappy then carried him into my room. He likes it in there. I sat down on my bed with him like I used to making sure he was sitting up nice and straight between some pillows. My bed felt real soft after the room upstairs next to the trick door. My racing car blanket was still there and my old pillow with the dried peanut butter on the corner.

You're big now I said to Manaia. You're grown. Look. I held him under the arms and tried to show him. He felt more heavy in my arms than I remembered. Mum was still talking in the hallway and crying a bit. It doesn't bloody matter love she kept saying. Just come home. He's here we're all here.

Manaia was watching me while I was talking with his little legs going up and down against my knees. Then he put his hand out and touched my mouth and made a nice noise. I started talking and I told him about the rain and the car and Mr. P with the sour worms and the vanilla Coke and then the long drive and the house and Precious and the lady coming out there sometimes and crying in the gravel outside the house. The gun and the yummy soup and the rabbits with the blood and Mr. P's lessons about the forge and the big fires for making the steel. The carbon and the smelter and the ore. All the things Mr. P's people did to my people. Your people too I told Manaia. The things everyone did to each other. All that stuff.

He listened to me talking and his mouth was moving like he was trying to copy me. Then his eyes got sleepy so I put him down next to me and put my hand on his tummy because he likes that. Mum was walking up and down the hallway still talking on the phone so I made some shushes. I kept saying things to him and he started making his wriggles. His legs were moving all on their own running the hundred metres in his dreams like Dad says. I was talking and saying I've been away Manaia but I'm back now and I won't go away again.

His breathing started to get nice and slow then. The rain came down against the roof like someone whispering. I put my arm around him and moved closer so I could smell the special smell of his hair and I could feel his heart going through my clothes.

ACKNOWLEDGMENTS

Sincere thanks to: Steven Thomas, Liz Owen, Patrick Whatman, Emma Scott, and Kate Stone for your notes and feedback on draft versions of this novel; Michael Heyward, Mandy Brett, and the entire Text Publishing team for your faith, support, and telepathy; Caitlin Landuyt at Anchor and Jade Chandler at Baskerville for taking Lorraine to new places; Michelle Rahurahu rāua ko Alex Lodge mō tō pononga me tō manaakitanga; Dragan Todorovic, Amy Sackville, and Yelena Moskovich for taking this story seriously; and William Brandt, Tim Clarke, Chris Luman, and Peter Bayliss for your early encouragement. To my enormous family, I miss you all. To Sarah Vallance, Harry Baragwanath, Andrew Vallance, and Bridget Clark, thanks for indulging my reading habits. To Ali and Sri Utari Wahyudhi, thank you for helping me find time to write in France. To Mary Baragwanath and Pamela Warner, thank you for your countless gifts. Dianny Wahyudhi, you make my life real nice. If you've made it this far, then congratulations.

Tom Baragwanath is originally from Masterton, New Zealand, and now lives in Paris. His short fiction has been widely published. Between pastries, he's working on his next novel.